Leigh Ann's Civil War

OTHER NOVELS BY ANN RINALDI

My Vicksburg

The Letter Writer

Juliet's Moon

The Ever-After Bird

Come Juneteenth

An Unlikely Friendship

Brooklyn Rose

Or Give Me Death

The Staircase

The Coffin Quilt

Cast Two Shadows

An Acquaintance with Darkness

Hang a Thousand Trees with Ribbons

Keep Smiling Through

The Secret of Sarah Revere

Finishing Becca

The Fifth of March

A Break with Charity

A Ride into Morning

Leigh Ann's Civil War

A Novel by

ANN RINALDI

Harcourt

Houghton Mifflin Harcourt

BOSTON   NEW YORK   2009

Harcourt is an imprint of Houghton Mifflin Harcourt Publishing Company.

www.hmhbooks.com

Text set in Adobe Garamond.

Library of Congress Cataloging-in-Publication Data
Rinaldi, Ann.
Leigh Ann's Civil War / Ann Rinaldi.
p. cm.
Summary: Recounts the experiences of a spunky young girl, just eleven when the Civil War breaks out, as she watches her brothers go to war, helps care for her mentally ill father, and falls in love with a boy determined to be a soldier. Includes historical notes. Includes bibliographical references.
ISBN 978-0-15-206513-3 (hardcover : alk. paper)
1. United States—History—Civil War, 1861–1865—Juvenile fiction. [1. United States—History—Civil War, 1861–1865—Fiction. 2. Brothers and sisters—Fiction. 3. Family life—Georgia—Fiction.] I. Title.
PZ7.R459Ldm 2009   [Fic]—dc22   2009019520

Printed in the United States of America
MP 10 9 8 7 6 5 4 3 2 1

In memory of my sister Ruth

PROLOGUE

Summer 1864
Marietta, Georgia

I T WAS the dog who did it.

If I had shot the dog with the Enfield rifle Sergeant Mulholland had given me, everything would have been agreeable to him. But I could not bring myself to shoot it.

All six were dead in the pen near him. Flies buzzed around them in the July heat. The one I was supposed to shoot sat there, eyes fixed on me, just as Cicero, our dog at home, would do.

How could I shoot it? How could I ever face Cicero again, if I did?

There was nothing else to steal at the ransacked plantation, anyway. So the Yankees were down to killing the animals. They had already shot the last three remaining cows. I think the mistress had sent away the horses. At least I hoped she had. I could not bring myself to shoot a horse. I'd die first.

The mistress, a frightened young woman who did not look old enough to have two children, had tearfully told me that we were the fourth group of bummers to come this day.

"The others already took everything," she cried.

Mulholland had sent me to the house to see if there was anything left worth taking. "Any corn or foodstuffs in the larder," he directed. "Any flour or sorghum, hominy or pea-meal. Eggs. Some of these people keep chickens in the cellar and hide eggs.

"Get anything you can, Conners, and if I find you left her with anything I'll beat your Southern behind worse than I did last time."

I did find some flour and eggs. I begged her to hide them under her bed upstairs. After all, she had children. Then I heard a low moan from below.

She had a cow in the cellar!

"Keep it quiet," I told her. "We're leaving now, anyway."

I stood, Enfield rifle in hand, in front of the dog, praying Mulholland and the two other boys, Ressen and Parker, would soon come. They had finished at the house and were down at the stream taking a quick wash.

The dog whined like he knew I was suffering. Dogs always do know when we're suffering. *So,* I thought, *I'm not a good bummer after all, am I?*

What was a bummer?

Well, another name for them is wastrels. You see, the Yankee general William T. Sherman's soldiers were made to leave their food supplies behind when they started on their grand march to destroy the South. So they had to live off the land as they went along. And somebody had to get the food for them.

They called it foraging. And the young boys who did it were called bummers.

It wasn't my idea to be one. When the Yankees came to our town of Roswell on the fifth of July, General Kenner Garrard, who led the invasion, arrested me, along with hundreds of other women and children, black and white, who had to do with the Roswell cotton mill.

Garrard placed me under arrest because of my connection with the mill.

And so here I am, serving under snake-in-the-grass Mulholland.

He does not know I am a girl. My boys' clothes have served me well.

He has already smacked me around twice. He has whipped me once with his hard Yankee belt so that my bottom hurt. No one except Mother has ever whipped me, and she just that once.

My brother Teddy, who raised me up, never laid a hand on me.

The fault is mine, of course, that Mulholland mistreated me. I never showed him the protection notice that the Yankee major J. C. McCoy gave me before I left Roswell. It says, in an official way, on official paper, that the person it is presented to is not to beat me or starve me or they will answer to him and he will see to it they receive severe disciplinary punishment.

I was saving it for a crucial moment.

I may have to use it soon.

The dog was still looking at me.

"Don't worry," I told him. "I'm not going to shoot you. I'm going to stand up to Mulholland. Even if I have to use my protection notice here and now."

The dog lay down, crossed his paws, put his head on them, and waited.

Mulholland was coming back with the other boys, laboriously scaling the hill from the creek, his ample body breathing heavily. "Didn't you shoot that damned dog yet, Conners?" he yelled out as he came toward me.

He grabbed my Enfield. "What kind of a bummer do you think you are?"

At this the dog got up and growled at him, just as Cicero would do.

Mulholland readied his aim. "No!" I shouted, and at the same time pushed the rifle so when it went off it missed the dog.

"Damn you little . . ." Then he used a cuss word I'd never even heard my brothers say, and they could cuss beautifully when the occasion warranted it. Mulholland came at me as if to give me a blow at the side of my head.

Oh, I wanted to pull the protection notice out of my trouser pocket. But somehow I knew that I had to save it for a better reason.

I stepped back to avoid his blow. He grabbed at my shirt and there was a ripping sound.

My shirt tore away in front. I screamed and put my hands up to cover myself, but it was too late.

He saw my bosoms. The other two boys did, too.

"Holy God," Ressen said. "He's a *girl!*"

Parker just whistled and stared.

I gathered the remnants of my shirt and held them to me. Tears came down my face.

The unexpectedness of it put Mulholland in a daze. "They giving me women now? Well, I'm going to report this to headquarters. My brother is in charge of these shenanigans, remember. I want no more to do with you. I'll have him ship you back tonight."

Still clutching my shirt in front, I grabbed his arm. "Sergeant Mulholland, sir?"

He pulled his arm away. "Now what? Don't think I won't beat the pants off you even if you are a girl."

"Would you have my sister-in-law Carol and my sister, Viola, shipped back, too?"

He scowled. "Now why should I do a thing like that for a brat like you? Wait a minute. You say your name is Conners? Why does that name sound familiar to me?"

I drew myself up proudly, in spite of my dusty trousers, dirty face, and torn shirt. "My pa is Hunter Conners, sir. He built and owned the mill in Roswell that you all burned."

"They say he's crazier than a bedbug."

"And you were always hovering around my sister-in-law Carol Conners, sir, on the way here, if I may be so bold as to say."

"You may not be! I've got a right to. She's the spoils of war. And so are you. So watch yourself. And here, cover yourself up."

He grabbed an extra shirt from his haversack and threw it at me. It smelled, but I put it on.

"Your sister-in-law, eh? Which one of your brothers is she married to?"

"My brother Teddy."

He laughed. His laugh was evil, nothing less. "The mill may be burned, but that's some fine plantation he's got there. And rumor has it that before he went crazy your pa put all his Confederate money into Northern script. Secretary Chase's greenbacks, you people call 'em. Maybe your brother even has some gold coin. All you plantation folk are worth a lot of money."

More laughter now. This time, calculating. "That Carol of his is some looker. No doubt he misses her sorely. Am I right?"

I decided not to answer. And I would never admit to him that she was pregnant.

He grinned, showing three gold teeth. "I was planning on taking her north and making her my woman. Where is she now?"

"Working in the field hospital. Major General Grenville Dodge got her and Viola jobs as nurses there," I said importantly.

"Well, as I said, my brother is in charge of this whole Marietta operation. All I gotta say is I want Carol and I'll get her. Not for my own. But to send back where I can get a handsome price for her from your brother. Hell, you people buy and sell slaves all the time. And my brother likes money as much as any man."

My mind was working fast. I felt loath to say anything to this despicable man.

Should I show him the protection notice I had from Major McCoy? No, I decided. He had his plans all set. He might rip it up and pretend it never existed, especially since he had already mistreated me.

I would give it to his brother. I would use it to get Viola released along with me and Carol, and for protection for all of us on the way home.

"All right," he said. "Come on, we're going back to camp to have a talk with my brother."

As the four of us made our way back to the camp, nobody said anything about the dog who trailed along next to me.

❧

MAJOR THOMAS MULHOLLAND and the Army of the Cumberland were headquartered at the Georgia Military Institute on the hill. The lovely, rolling grounds were spotted now with things that should make them quarantined. Yankee tents and horses, and all the cooking and military gear soldiers need to convince themselves that what they were doing was not a crime but brave. That it was all right to trample flower beds, once so lovingly cared for, and pee in the hedges and strip bare the fruit trees and mangle neat fences.

At the moment, the institute also housed mill workers waiting to be taken by rail to Nashville, but Major

Mulholland's headquarters were in a separate part of the building.

His brother left the other two bummers outside and took me right to him. The dog went with me.

"He can't come in here," Sergeant Mulholland said outside his brother's office.

"He goes where I go," I said firmly. "I leave him outside and they'll shoot him. He stays outside and I'll tell your brother you beat me."

It was chancy, but it worked. He nodded. The guard opened the door of the office and announced us, and in a moment we were ushered in.

It must have once been the office of the commander-in-chief of the military academy, or whatever fancy name they called him. For it was very commodious, with shelves full of books that told young boys how to make war, paneled walls, oaken floors covered with Persian carpets, and velvet drapes on the windows.

Major Mulholland was not a bad-looking man for a Northerner, if I, at fourteen, am a judge at all of men. And having grown up around my brothers, I think I am.

For one thing he was physically in better condition than his brother the sergeant. And although he wore a beard, it was kept in tow and not allowed to grow wild, all over the place. His fingernails were clean; I could see that right from the get-go. Both my brothers were fastidious about their fingernails. I fancied that taken out of that Yankee uniform and put in some human clothes he could be downright passable.

"What's this, Sergeant?" he asked his brother. "You know I don't meet with any of the mill workers. And what is that dog doing in here?"

"She isn't a mill worker," Mulholland answered. "She was passed off to me as a bummer. And I can explain about the dog."

So he did, in crisp, careful words, with no cussing. It was clear that he respected his brother. It was also clear that he knew how to get around him.

The major listened carefully, nodding and thinking. "So she's been arrested by Garrard. What gives us the right to go against his orders and send her back?"

"She's trouble, Tom. Talks to birds. Knows all that negro hoodoo crap."

"So, we'll ship her off to Nashville with the rest of them."

"We could. But I have another plan."

"*You* have a plan. Excuse me, Russ, but we're not kids at home anymore planning to raid the pantry. I've got a good record in this man's army and I'm not about to ruin it."

Sergeant Mulholland stepped closer to his brother's desk and, lowering his tone, imparted his plan to his brother.

The major listened again.

I watched his face.

He raised his eyebrows, looked over at me, bit his bottom lip, looked over at me again, shook his head no, and this time took my measure from head to toe and nodded yes.

Then he opened a drawer of his desk, took out a bottle of whiskey and two glasses, and offered one to his brother. They both drank the amber-colored liquid down quickly, because obviously Russ's plan necessitated it.

"Tell me why," he asked me, "should I let you and the Viola girl go and not just this Carol we're to negotiate for?"

It was time.

I reached into my pocket, took out the protection notice, walked over to his desk, and gave it to him.

He read it and his face went white. "Major McCoy, eh?" he said. "A high-ranking Yankee official."

"Yes, sir," I answered.

"It doesn't say we have to let you go."

"No, it doesn't, sir. But your brother here beat me and smacked me around. He tore my shirt in front and exposed me. I can report that to Major McCoy."

He thought for a moment. "Did you show this notice to my brother?"

I felt a cloud of dread. "No, sir. I was saving it for the right moment."

He laughed. "Then you have no complaint against him. You gave him no warning." He laughed again. "I always did say you Southerners were dense. Did you know that we caught the person sent here from Philadelphia to spirit you and your sisters away? Could have arrested him. Sent him back." He was gloating.

I thought quickly. "Either we all go home, sir," I told him, "or none of us goes."

"What's that you say?"

"I'm just telling you what my sister-in-law Carol will tell you. What she will say. Carol won't go without me and Viola. She wouldn't let us come on this trip alone and she won't let us continue alone. I just thought you ought to know."

"Damned stubborn Southerners."

"Yessir."

"Why are you so polite?"

"I was raised that way, sir."

"Who raised you? They say your pa's crazy and your ma's a slut."

"My brothers, sir. Louis and Teddy. They are both Southern gentlemen."

He humphed. "Manners are all they got left. All right, all right. We'll use this protection notice for all three of you to be sent back under the guidance of my brother here. And for God's sake, Russ, no more beating her or smacking her around, you hear?"

"Yeah, I hear."

"And get her some decent clothing."

"How am I gonna do that?"

"Excuse me, sir," I said, "but I'd just as lief stay in my boys' clothes. I can get another shirt. And if I can take the dog with me."

"The *dog*? Are you sure there isn't anything else you want?"

"Yessir. I'd like my protection notice returned, if you please."

He leaned back in his chair, smiling. "Russ, secure a horse for each of them. And five days' worth of rations for each. And the dog. As for the protection notice, little girl . . ." He held it in his hands, looking at it. "You've used it up. It's like Yankee script. Once you've used it, it's spent. Did your brothers teach you nothing about money?"

I stared at him in disbelief. "This isn't *money*, sir. It's an official notice, from a major in your own army!"

"Good man he is, too. One of the best. Well, of course if you insist upon looking at it that way, I can always tell him you lost it. That I never saw it. That you claimed you had it and went reaching in your pocket and couldn't find it, but out of the goodness of my heart I let the three of you go anyway. Couldn't I?"

This man was beyond the pale. He might as well have foam dribbling out of his mouth. I felt as if I were drowning, standing there. I felt out of breath of a sudden, as if I'd been running and had come to a skidding stop.

I had best get out of here, I thought, *while I still can. I had best quit talking while I still have the promise of Carol and Viola and my own way home.*

While I still have three horses and five days' rations for each of us and the dog.

"Thank you, sir," I said. When what I wanted to say was, *You are the slut. You are the crazy man. You are the one who is dense. And I hope someday your house comes crashing down on you. No, I hope someday your world comes crashing down on you, so there.*

"Come on, dog," I said. And we left.

CHAPTER ONE

Spring 1861
Roswell, Georgia

I WAS ELEVEN when the war started. I didn't understand enough to worry, but I did understand it when Miss Finch, my teacher, said that since Georgia had been out of the Union since January we weren't going to be called Abigail Adams Academy for Young Ladies anymore but must find a new name. And Georgia might as well be cut off from the rest of the country.

As my brothers got ready to leave for the fighting, there was muster on the town square every day. Cicero and I went each morning to watch. So did Primus, our negro overseer, when he could get away.

When Louis caught me crying one morning after drilling was over and asked me why, I said, "Miss Finch said Georgia is no more part of the country."

"Miss Finch is an idiot," he said. "She speaks in idle fabrications. If I had my way, I'd take you out of that ridiculous school run by that raving maniac and have you tutored at home."

"Can't you tell Pa that?"

"You know Pa hasn't been himself these days, sweetie. Teddy makes such decisions. And Teddy has too many other things on his mind. So for now at least, we'll leave things as they are."

Pa's mind was already starting to turn because he had money worries, Louis had told me, because his Northern customers wanted him to continue shipping goods and he wouldn't.

But I had other worries. "Who will take care of me when you and Teddy go away?"

Louis knelt before me so that his fine sword scraped on the cobblestone walk. "First, we won't be gone long. We'll have this thing with the Yankees over with by Christmas. Teddy and I are going to have a meeting about the care of our women tonight. Likely it will be Viola and Carol. Do you think you can mind them?"

"Viola and I are friends. Carol never liked me. She's been acting strange lately. She and Teddy fuss a lot."

"That's their business, Leigh Ann."

"I know why," I persisted. "Viola told me. It's because she hasn't been able to give him a baby in the year they've been married."

He scowled. "What do you know about women giving men babies?"

"Everything. Viola told me."

More scowling. "I don't know whether to be angry or not. On one hand, Viola has saved Teddy and me a lot of trouble. On the other hand, she's done it too soon."

"Don't be angry with Viola. I asked her. But that's not the only reason Carol and Teddy fuss. He wants her to stop teaching at the school for mill children. He says it wears her down. She won't. And she's jealous of the time Teddy gives me. The other day she slapped me for being impertinent to her."

"Were you impertinent?"

"I suppose so. But she didn't have to slap me. You and Teddy never slap me."

"Does Teddy know she slapped you?"

"No. I didn't tell him."

"Good girl."

"Or, she might want to be in charge because she's always wanted permission from Teddy to paddle me. He won't give it. If he's not here, no one can stop her. Please, Louis, you mustn't let Teddy leave her in charge."

"Well, Teddy and I will discuss all this and likely leave it to Viola to care for you. She has sense. I'll suggest that if things get bad Viola write to Grandmother Johanna in Philadelphia for someone to come and take you all on up there until things settle down."

"Why is Grandmother Johanna so nice when Mother is so bad?"

"It just happens that way sometimes, sweetie."

"Mother whipped you once with a riding crop, didn't she?"

"We don't want to talk about that now."

"And you were twenty years old! Viola said you were in your cups, and you laughed and came out of the barn and said you didn't feel a thing, then fell down and fainted. Teddy had to carry you in the house."

"Leigh Ann . . ." It was said with icy admonishment. So I kept a still tongue in my head.

And so he explained the war in fine fashion. I thought he looked so handsome in his captain's uniform. I was puzzled as to who was more handsome, he or Teddy. And

I teased them both about it that afternoon in Louis's bed-room, until Louis came at me playfully and I ran down-stairs, just in time to see Pa coming up.

He went into Louis's room and began to take on about his boys leaving to fight the battle of some "no-count, money-hungry bankers and grubbing land-stealers up north." All relatives of his wife.

"They want the Southern lands," he shouted. "First the Indians wanted it and now the Northerners. I'd rather give it all back to the Indians, though they didn't have the cour-age to fight for it but let the white man take it from them!"

He bellowed. The walls shook. At that last remark about the Indians, Louis came tearing out of the room, his cheekbones high with color, his boots stamping on the stairs as he passed me.

"Louis!" I cried.

"Out of the way," he said gruffly. "Before I knock you over."

I'd seen him this way only once before, when Pa had accused him of "doing a bit of thrumming" with one of the women negroes.

That's when he had run away for two days and Teddy had to go and search for him and fetch him home. Louis had come home leaning over his horse, which was led by Teddy, and Louis had been so full of a cheap excuse for mint juleps that Mother had ordered him to the barn. The servants had to hold Teddy back, Viola told me. Mother had another servant tie Louis's hands to a wooden rail and asked Primus to whip him, or be whipped himself.

Primus said no. So Mother did it. And she is strong. And Primus *was* whipped later. And the bond between Louis and Primus became so strong, nobody could break it.

I asked Teddy what "thrumming" was. He wouldn't tell me.

So I asked Viola and she told me. Viola, at fifteen, knew everything. So it led to my asking her how women gave men babies. And she told me that, too.

From the hall steps I immediately burst into tears as I watched Louis go into Pa's library and slam the door. Pa came down and saw me and picked me up, sat down on the bottom step, and held me on his lap.

"Don't worry your pretty little head about Louis," he soothed. "He acts like that because he's part Indian."

I just stared up at Pa's face. Was this part of his "madness" coming on?

"He most positively is," he assured me. "Can't you see his dark hair? And eyes? And how he'd rather ride with no saddle? And his high cheekbones? And how good he is working with silver?"

I only saw one thing. That if Louis was part Indian, he was not my brother. Mother's hair was fair. Pa's was white. Viola's and mine was light brown and sun-streaked. Teddy's hair was the same as ours.

I leaped off Pa's lap and ran through the front door, off the front verandah, and around the side of it, where I hid under the sweet gum trees and cried my heart out until Louis himself came to find me.

CHAPTER TWO

"Come on, Leigh Ann, before I come over there and scalp you."

"Is that before or after you knock me over?"

He'd taken off his sword and unbuttoned his gray jacket and shirt underneath. I could see some dark hair on his chest.

"You're getting a little cheeky there, aren't you?"

In school we'd studied about Indians. They didn't have hair on their chests, did they? Teddy and Louis did. I'd seen them tear off their shirts several times when brushing down the horses or jumping into the stream in their small clothes.

"I don't care. You had no call to say such to me. You're supposed to have manliness and courage and honor. That's what Miss Finch said all our Southern men from eminent families have."

He tried to hide a smile. "I try, Leigh Ann, I try terrible hard, but it's downright difficult sometimes. What else did she say we're supposed to have?"

"She said they're supposed to defend their mothers' and sisters' honor to the death if they have to."

"Well, if the day comes when I have to, I'll gladly do it, Leigh Ann. Now why do you think I've come out here?

There are different ways of defending one's little sister's honor. There are different kinds of honor. You've been told by Pa that I'm an Indian. Am I correct?"

I said nothing. I looked at the ground.

"And you've been shocked and hurt and you likely have come to the ugly conclusion that I'm not your brother. Am I right, sweetie?"

I looked at him. "What did you study at college? Hoodoo?"

He and Teddy had gone to the University of Virginia in Charlottesville, Thomas Jefferson's university. Louis, older by two years, had graduated. Teddy had left at the end of his second year to join the army.

Now Louis laughed. "I have the gift of hoodoo because I am half Indian. Do you want to know about it?"

"Yes, but first I want to know what you've got in that box you just set down." It was considerable large, that box, bigger than any of Mother's hatboxes by half.

"Then come out of there and I'll show you. And I'll tell you the secret we've all been hiding from you. Let's take a nice walk down to the stream. But you must remember that I speak the truth, and it's a good truth. And it's your truth, too."

I just stared at him. "Are we going to bury it?"

"You can never bury the truth, Leigh Ann. It always comes to the surface when you least expect it to."

"I mean the box. You've got a shovel." It was lying on the ground next to the box. He just kept smiling and I could not fight that smile. I stood and went to him and he brushed me off.

"Yes, we're going to bury the box. And I'm going to ask you a very respectable favor this day and hope you will do it for me."

I'd once told him I'd do just about anything for him and he'd admonished me never to say that to anybody. Not even to him. Or Teddy. I was puzzled, but made no further inquiry because he'd used what I'd come to know as his "We don't want to speak of that now" voice.

We walked in the direction of the stream that ran beyond the cows' meadow. There stood a line of dogwood growing a little distance in front of a complete grove of pine trees. We sat down in back of the dogwood, cut off from the rest of the world.

"This is a good place to tell you," he said.

I sat across from him with my skirts billowing about me. In the distance I could see two fat deer, with their beautiful antlers etched against the sky, running through the rows of Indian corn. I felt a sense of peace settle over me such as I'd never felt before.

It radiated from Louis's smile. I often found that peace radiated from Louis's smile.

"Pa is a full-blooded Indian," he said quietly.

I just looked at him. But the smile never wavered. It remained the same.

"A Cherokee," he elaborated, just in case I needed to know.

My eyes were wide now. I don't know why I didn't cry, or say, "No, it isn't so," or get up and run away. I knew I couldn't do that to Louis.

Were the deer real, running through the Indian corn? Or were they sent to prepare me? My friend Careen believes in such signs. She also believes in spirits, can read signals in clouds, visits the plantation graveyard and talks to the dead, and is very otherworldly.

"Are you all right, Leigh Ann?" he inquired gently.

That grave concern of his brought me back on track. What would he do if I wasn't? Take it all back? Say he was only teasing? I had to be all right. He was counting on me. I nodded my head yes.

"It'll take time," he said, "for it to sink in. But not long. There's nothing to be ashamed of."

My first thought was, *Do I look Indian?* My hand flew to my face.

"No, you don't," Louis said, reading my thoughts. "You don't look Indian at all."

He could do that sometimes.

"Does Teddy know you're telling me this?"

"Yes. We were going to wait until you were older, but then Pa went and spilled the beans. And Teddy said I'd best tell you. Did you learn about the Cherokees in that ridiculous school?"

"Yes, we learned this was their land, here on the northern banks of the Chattahoochee River."

He nodded his head in silent approval. My spirits were roused.

"What did the Cherokees call this place?" he asked.

"Enchanted Land. And they said the white people were forbidden to be on it. But they came anyway."

"You should know the Cherokees were the first American Indians to have an alphabet and written language. One of their chiefs, Sequoyah, was a talented silversmith. They had the first American Indian newspaper. They tried to get along with the white people. They had their own shops and businesses."

"Where does Pa come in?"

"He was one of the Cherokees who was living with the white men. He worked for one named Hunter Conners, who had no children and who gave him a fine piece of land and, in the end, his name. Then gold was discovered and hundreds of settlers came and the government took the land back from the Cherokees."

"Did Pa have gold?"

"No, he was growing tobacco. He made eight thousand dollars on two trips to Baltimore selling tobacco. That's where he met Mother. She was visiting her uncle, who purchased the tobacco. Pa had men working for him. Slaves. He made trips to Baltimore every year."

"What did he do with the money?"

"Well, he always thought that this area, with its big forests and its powerful waters, would be a good place for a mill. So the money, back in 1838, was enough to start building a mill."

"Oh, that's a good story."

"Do you know what else happened in 1838?"

"They got all the Cherokees together and marched them out of here, and everyone calls it the Trail of Tears."

"You don't know how lucky you are that you are aware of that. If you weren't, it would grieve me beyond belief."

I looked into his dark eyes. He was not teasing. This Indian inheritance must go deep with Louis. I threw myself into his arms and he held me close. "I never would do anything to grieve you," I said. "I promise."

Then he told me how Mother and Pa had wed soon after they met, and how successful the mill had been. And no, he didn't know why Viola and Teddy and I didn't have dark hair or eyes, but I must promise him never to be ashamed of the part of me that was Cherokee.

I promised. Then he said, "Now let's pay mind to the box."

He was about to move. I pulled away from him. "Not before you tell me why Pa is getting so strange in his mind."

He shook his head sadly. He shrugged. "Of course it's the money he's losing on the mill. He's paid more tariffs to the North than he can afford. But I think it started when he found out that Mother is a secret Yankee. To get back at her he changed his will and had her name taken off as inheritor of everything. We children are slated to inherit. Which is probably why she hates us so. And why Mother and Pa have been holding their own war since."

"And she's been running around with other men since, hasn't she?"

He scowled. "I won't have you talking that way about our mother, Leigh Ann," he said severely.

"That's what Viola says about her."

"I'm not concerned with Viola at this moment. I'm concerned with you. No matter what she does, she's still our mother. Do you hear me?"

"Yes, Louis."

"All right, sweetie. Now come along. We're going to bury the box under that pine tree right over there."

CHAPTER THREE

H E TOOK OFF his uniform coat, rolled up his shirt sleeves, picked up the shovel, and started digging.

"Why didn't you bring along Primus to dig for you?" I asked. I knew he and Primus had a special bond. Most of the negroes had feelings for him that went beyond common charity — Bench and Tumble, Cyrus and July, to name just a few. And Cannice, the "best cook this side of the Mississippi," as Teddy called her, mothered the boys by giving them special late-night treats in the kitchen, by overseeing the perfect laundering of their shirts, by listening when they wanted to talk.

"I didn't tell Primus," he said.

You didn't even confide in Primus? This must be important. But I knew better than to say anything.

I did ask, "Can I know what's in the box?"

He stopped digging. He'd already dug a respectable hole. He took out his handkerchief, wiped his brow, knelt down, and pried the box open.

Inside was a heap of silver. It glistened in the sun. It was made into necklaces and bracelets, rings and armbands, all hammered with intricate designs.

I'd never paid mind to the silver shop Louis had set up in a simply built little cottage he and Primus had made in the line of outbuildings in the quarters a distance behind the house. He spent hours there sometimes. Pa had said, "Leave him be. He needs time alone to practice his hobby. Viola likes to paint, doesn't she? And doesn't Teddy like to hunt with a bow and arrow? And what do you like to do, Leigh Ann?"

"Read," I'd answered, "and gather sweetheart leaves to perfume the lye soap. Sometimes the servants let me mix them in. Teddy is teaching me to use the bow and arrow. And to swim in the stream."

He frowned. "I hope you wear clothes."

I laughed. Pa had taken a fancy, recently, to swimming naked in the stream. Teddy had caught him at it a couple of times and scolded him severely and made him put on some small clothes.

"I wear my chemise and pantalets. Viola says that's sufficient."

So I'd never bothered Louis when he worked on his silver. And, this, *this* is what he'd been about all that time. Like Sequoyah, the Indian chief.

I stared at him across the box of silver. "Can I touch it?"

"Go right ahead. It won't melt."

I did so. Gently, respectfully.

"Would you like a sample? A gift? On the occasion of my going off to fight for the independence of Georgia?"

"Not if you're giving it to me in case you don't come back," I told him.

He bit his bottom lip, trying to hide his feelings. "I'm coming back, sweetie. I promise you. Now go ahead, pick out a piece of jewelry."

"You pick one out for me. Was there any piece that, when you were making it, made you think of me?"

He started moving the jewelry around. "Matter of fact, there was." He drew out a medallion on a silver cord. The head of Sequoyah was in the middle. "I thought of you with this, yes."

Tears came to my eyes as he draped it over my neck.

"Can I wear it in front of the others?"

"I'd like to see anybody try to take it away from you. I've got these special Indian powers, remember. I can do some bad things with smoke and prayers."

He smiled innocently. *I think he is one of God's angels,* I told myself. Never mind the Indian business.

"Now we've got to bury the box." He stood up. "Can't waste any more time. The family will be wondering where we are. I've got a confab with Teddy tonight. We leave tomorrow."

"Why are we burying it?"

He talked while he worked. "It's worth lots of money, Leigh Ann. And we're going away, Teddy and I. And so, here's the favor I need from you. I want you to remember where it is and use it if it is needed in an emergency to help the family. Only you know it's here. You mustn't tell anyone. *No matter what happens.* Do you hear me?"

"Not even Teddy?"

He hesitated a moment. He rubbed his nose. "Only if things get real bad do you tell Teddy. If he's here. If things are bad and Teddy isn't here, get Primus to dig it up for you. And then use it. To save the family."

I didn't like all this desperate talk. It bespoke matters I could not contend with.

"And if I'm still . . . well . . . write to me. You understand?"

"Yes, Louis. But why didn't you ask Viola to do all this?"

He stamped the earth down over the hole with his boot, not looking at me. He put the turf back down and stamped it, too. "Viola is sweet, and smart, and I love her dearly, but she talks too much." He put his jacket on, brushed his hands together, and picked up the shovel.

"I have one more question."

"Have at it."

"If you're the oldest, why don't you want to be in charge of things? Why do you leave it to Teddy?"

He just smiled. "I guess I thought Teddy would do a better job of it than I would. It's a terrible responsibility. Ties a man down. I'd take *you* if he'd let me. But he won't. Said I'd spoil you. Said I'd likely take you west and let you ride bareback and learn the Cherokee alphabet. Besides which, I'm not up to the fight that's coming with Mother for ownership of everything. Teddy's not going to get off scot-free, you know. But he can outwit her. Does that answer satisfy you?"

"Yes, Louis. But you wouldn't spoil me."

He shrugged. "I can't stand to see you cry. Teddy can."

He leaned over and kissed me. "I love you," he said.

"I love you more."

"I knew you'd say that."

We walked back to the house, singing the country song: *"We are going down to Georgia, boys, To see the pretty girls, boys, We'll give 'em a pint of brandy, boys, And a hearty kiss besides, boys."*

The sky was clouding overhead. Tears were coming down my face. Louis and Teddy were leaving tomorrow.

He never looked down at me, but before we went up the verandah steps Louis leaned over and wiped my tears away. "Remember, I can't stand to see you cry," he said.

CHAPTER 4

THANKS TO LOUIS, I went back into the house dry-eyed. He went straight upstairs to dress for supper because, he said, "There's going to be a feast this night so Teddy and I will never be hungry in the army."

I went in to change, too. Teddy was waiting for me in the doorway of his room. He motioned me in. Carol was in her private room in front of her dressing table, making last-minute touches to her beautiful straw-colored hair. Carol looked like all those pictures of princesses in my books. And she acted like one. Never did she lose her poise.

She was from the Balls, one of Roswell's first families.

Teddy sat down and drew me to stand in front of him. "Louis told you?"

"Yes?"

"You all right?"

"Louis made it all right. All's I got is a headache coming on." I was prone to headaches, and this one promised to outdo all my others.

"Louis is a fine fellow. He has a benevolence of spirit, a great driving force, and he is gifted with moments of quiet. And patience. You still have the headache after supper, I'll give you a powder. It's something new, down from the North, Dr. Widmar says. It's what Abraham Lincoln takes for his headaches."

"Oh, for heaven's sake, Teddy," Carol's voice floated out. "It's one thing to have her emulate Louis, but do we have to hold up Abraham Lincoln as a model, too? You're confusing the child."

Teddy had a square jaw, a straight nose, heavy brows, and eyes that bore into you. You didn't fool around with a face like that. "I would hope that on our last evening together before I go off to war, you would desist with this bickering, Carol," he said.

She picked up a silken shawl and breezed on past us. "You'd best cut your Sermon on the Mount short. You're not dressed yet and neither is she." She went out and closed the door.

Teddy ran his hand across his face for a moment. "Look," he said, "just because we're half Indian, you're not to confuse us with wild Indians out west. Even Pa's generation removed themselves from that culture."

"I know. Louis told me."

"Good. Did he tell you that Chattahoochee is an Indian name meaning 'flowered stones'? For the colored stones on the bottom of the river?"

"No."

"Then I'm telling you. And when I come home, I will dive to the bottom of the river and fetch you some of those colored stones. Would you like that?"

I hugged him. "I love you, Teddy." I said.

"Love you too, sweetie. Now we'd both best get dressed for supper."

❧

As I walked into the dining room and saw the food being set down on the table, I whispered aloud, "This is better than the marriage feast of Cana in the Bible."

Teddy frowned. Louis gripped my shoulder as he pulled out my chair. "Don't be blasphemous," he chided.

The supper was like Mother used to have when she had special guests. She was not here, although her place was set, as always, at the opposite end of the table from Pa's.

But this evening there was a card on her fancy gold and pink plate. Teddy nodded ever so slightly at Louis, who said to me, "Fetch that card for me, will you, Leigh Ann?"

I lifted it off the plate and gave it to Louis, who read it. His face blanched and he handed it over to Teddy.

"It's an apology," Louis said. "A friend of hers is sick. She can't come."

"Damned liar," Pa grumbled.

"Pa," Teddy admonished.

Teddy read the card, too. And his eyes were absolutely sodden, like somebody had died. He set it behind him on the buffet and we commenced to eat.

Cannice had outdone herself. We dined on drum fish and prawns, stuffed peppers, steak and onions, roast turkey and jellied sliced chicken bits, tender glazed ham, mashed potatoes, pâté de foie gras, Hamilton green peas in creamed sauce, carrots in browned sugar, and Cannice's special light-baked buns. For dessert there was vanilla-frosted pound cake and Georgia peaches in cream. And in the middle of the table there was a pyramid made out of jellied candies.

The men, of course, had their share of Madeira and their other favorite wines.

As we enjoyed dessert, a silence fell. We were starting to digest the real reason for the supper along with our food. Of a sudden no one knew what to say.

Louis spoke. "If someone could coin a good way to say goodbye, he'd end up richer than the men who found gold here in Roswell," he said quietly.

Teddy nodded. Carol reached her hand out on the table and Teddy covered it with his own. Viola's eyes filled with tears.

"None of that," Louis told her severely. "We'll have none of that, now."

I just sat wide-eyed. My head was throbbing. My family never failed to fascinate me. They were better than a good book. One never knew what would happen next.

Louis spoke again. "America is a myth," he said in soft, measured tones. "The sooner we get to learn that, the better off we'll all be. The sooner we'll stop breaking our hearts over her."

Everyone sat respectfully, listening. Cicero, the dog, who always sat next to Teddy at meals, thumped his tail on the hardwood floor approvingly.

"And now," Louis went on, "we're either going off to kill that myth, or to save it, and the only problem I have is . . . Not going off to fight. No true Southern male minds that. The only problem I have is that I don't know which I'm going off to do — kill it or save it. And that's what troubles me."

Silence. Everyone was moved.

Cicero inched closer to Teddy, sensing uneasiness. Teddy reached down and rubbed one of the dog's long reddish-brown ears. Cicero settled down.

Then Teddy spoke in a mild voice. "Well, I can't let my big brother outdo me. I've something to say, too, though it can't come up to what Louis said. What I'm about to tell you all is simple, and I'd like you all to keep it in mind in the days ahead. It's this: *This place where we all live is not a plantation. It's a homestead.*"

The force of it hit us in the face, in the stomach, and everywhere else you can be hit by words. After that, nobody knew what to do. Viola must have thought the same thing, too, because at that moment she got up, tears streaming down her face, and she hugged Teddy.

I got up, too. So did Carol and Louis. The only one who remained seated was Pa.

We all started hugging one another and saying wonderful things and making promises and giving one another advice to be followed until we were reunited with the boys again.

Surprisingly, Viola, who loved reading stories about knights and warriors, whose idol was Joan of Arc, said to

Louis, "Don't be a hero, Louis" and then, "Teddy, you either, we'd rather have you back. We need you," and then, in turn, my brothers mouthed endearing things to us.

Then, gradually, we dispersed. Teddy and Louis still had to have their meeting this night. And Viola's beau, young Johnnie Cummack, who was also leaving tomorrow, was coming to call.

"Will you be all right on your own?" Viola asked me. "I'm going on the verandah to wait for Johnnie."

I said yes, though my headache was getting the upper hand.

"We have to retire to the library," Louis said. But before he and Teddy left the room, both turned to look at Viola.

"Remember," Teddy cautioned, "you bring him to the front parlor. And the door stays ajar."

Viola stamped a satin slipper on the floor. Louis smiled. "Sorry, sweetie. We know he's leaving tomorrow. But that's just *why* we want the door ajar."

Louis kissed her forehead and went out of the room with Teddy. Carol went into the back parlor to play the piano. Viola went out to the verandah, where enough torchlights were lighted to make even an innocent kiss county business.

I was the last to leave the dining room. And what I did, stealthily, was look at the card from Mother that Teddy had put on the buffet.

It was an insult of the highest order.

There was no sick friend. There was no goodbye to the boys.

It was a *carte de visite,* a calling card such as the one used when one came to call and, finding no one home, left the card announcing they had been there. There was nothing at all personal about it.

And likely Mother had had someone deliver it for her.

It was an insult to the occasion, and my brothers knew it.

❧

BECAUSE I WAS feeling so terrible, because my head felt squeezed in a lead hat, I went directly to my room, closed the door, and sat on my bed. The lace summer spread had been folded back, and my dolls — Miranda, Suzy, Baby Cassie, Judy, the cornstalk doll that Viola had made for me, and Jemima, the pioneer doll — all sat on a pine chest. The windows were open and organdy curtains fluttered in the late-dusk breeze. The mosquito netting around the bed was arranged just right.

Night was coming. I heard the hoot of an owl, the last going-to-sleep sound of some birds, the barking of Teddy and Louis's hound dogs in the pen. Then the hoofbeats of a horse rapidly making its way down the tree-lined approach to the house. Viola's Johnnie.

I took off my shoes and my silken hose, my dress and petticoats. Standing in my chemise and pantalets, I looked in the standing mirror. I would *never* get bosoms like Viola. Once I had stuffed the top of my chemise with cotton and it had done the job perfectly, but then old Teddy had looked at me crossed-eyed and whispered something to Viola and she'd taken me upstairs, where she removed the cotton and scolded me.

Oh, I was miserable. I took off my underclothes. I should wash myself good, all over. Viola had taught me that if I felt too sick or tired, I at least *must* wash my face and hands, my neck, under my arms, and between my legs. I commenced to do so. There was a basin of warm water. I dipped the soft flannel cloth in, lathered it with scented soap, and honored Viola's instructions, then dried with the even softer towel, put on my cotton, lace-trimmed nightgown, got into bed, and secured the mosquito netting. But I could not sleep.

I dozed once, and all I saw were men marching and aiming guns, as I'd seen them doing in practice. I *heard* the guns. I saw men falling. My dreams came in jerky fragments of fear. I awoke with a start. Sweat covered my brow and my nightgown was drenched with it. I sat up shaking with cold. The lead hat on my head was even heavier now. But the terror I felt was worse. I knew better, but it seized me and shook me the way Cicero shakes an old towel in a game of tug-of-war.

Teddy had promised me a powder like Abraham Lincoln used. He must have forgotten. The house was dark. I tiptoed out of my room and made my way shakily down the stairs. I could see light from under the door of Pa's library.

My head resounded at every chime of the grandfather clock. The door of the front parlor was ajar, as Teddy had instructed. The soft, romantic glow of candlelight flickered from within. I wanted Viola. But I would never forgive myself for barging in on her last night with Johnnie. So what to do?

Carol was out of the question. That would be like going over to the Yankees.

I felt myself drawn to the door of the library. From within I heard muted male voices. I lifted my hand to knock, could not, and pivoted away. Dizzily, I fell. Stupid me. What was I doing on the floor? Quickly, in a move that I supposed was ageless, I reached and pulled my nightgown down to my ankles.

Two things happened at once. From one direction I heard Viola's voice. "What is that?" and "What happened?" from directly behind me, that being Louis.

"Leigh Ann!" He helped me up. Then, "Teddy, this child looks like yesterday's grits!"

In a bunny-hopping minute everybody was there and I was so embarrassed, I wished I could slither away like a garter snake. Teddy was saying, "My God, I forgot the powder." Viola was crying that she just knew she should have put me to bed and it was all her fault.

Teddy said, "Quiet, Viola, it isn't. Go back to the parlor with Johnnie," and "Take her up to bed, Louis — I'll get the powder," and "Her nightgown is damp with sweat." Then he looked apologetically at Viola. "Sorry, honey, you'll have to change her."

Viola told Johnnie she'd be down in a minute. Louis carried me upstairs and both of them waited outside my room while Viola changed my nightgown, powdered me down, and assured me that yes, I *would* someday have bosoms.

I told her to go downstairs, that this was a good time to kiss Johnnie. And she flew out of the room.

Louis put me to bed. Teddy came with the powder and some water. I lay there propped up on pillows while the two of them paced, continuing their meeting.

I heard words like "crop yield" and "still good local demand for the cloth," and "Jon Bench's salary for looking after Pa."

Teddy had a pencil and pad, and they were going over items already written down, it seemed. I was getting sleepier and sleepier, but I hung on to consciousness until I heard the words I was waiting for.

Viola to be given full authority, in lieu of ours, to be in charge of Leigh Ann until we return.

I fell asleep.

CHAPTER FIVE

T HE NEXT MORNING the sun was a written red promise in the east, my headache was gone, and I was about starved. The grandfather clock struck six. I grabbed my robe and slippers and ran downstairs.

My family was in the dining room at breakfast. Eggs, ham, fish, fruit, biscuits, grits, and coffee were set out on the table, as if nobody had eaten last evening. Pa was being handed a dish of food by a striking young man with a face like a god and one arm that hung limp. He smiled at me. There was a certain amount of boldness in the smile. I didn't like him.

"Leigh Ann! You all right?" they asked in unison.

I pronounced I was.

"She looks as good as Cinderella," Louis said.

"I think Cinderella was written by a crazy person," I put forth. "Who else would write a story for children about a man marrying a girl just because her shoe fit right?"

Louis choked on his coffee. "Where does she get these ideas?" he asked.

"Living with all of us," Teddy said, "and listening when she isn't supposed to."

I noticed that the boys were dressed in jodhpurs and regular shirts. "We were up at four," Louis boasted. "Took our horses on a last ride. Saw first light. God, this homestead is beautiful."

Viola fixed me a plate of food and tea. From across the table her eyes twinkled at me and I knew she had gotten her share of kissing Johnnie last evening.

"Jon," Teddy said, "this is our little sister, Leigh Ann. You've been told about her. She's of no concern to you."

"Yes, sir."

"Leigh Ann," Teddy told me, "Jon is in our employ to care for Pa's every need, to keep him company. You are not to bother him, tease him, or hover around him. Understand?"

"Yes, sir," I mimicked Jon.

Teddy dismissed him and frowned at me. "You don't give me much assurance of behavior when I'm leaving," he said sadly.

I went around the table and hugged him. "I'm sorry," I whispered.

He kissed the top of my head. "I know you are. Now go eat."

THERE WASN'T much time now. Teddy stood up, reached into his jodhpur pocket, and drew out three gold double-eagle pieces of coin. He gave two to Viola and one to me.

"They're Yankee," he told us. "Coveted around here. They're worth twenty-five dollars each. Hide them."

Now Louis winked at me. And the burying of his silver that we'd done only yesterday seemed like ten years ago.

"Now I think we ought to change into our uniforms, Louis. We're due for muster at nine and I've still got to see the mayor."

"Yes, sir!" Louis stood up and saluted.

We laughed as we were meant to. "Why do you have to see the mayor?" Viola asked.

Teddy put his arm around her shoulder. "That paper I left with you? I'm registering a copy of it with the mayor's office. I'm having it notorized."

"Oooh." Viola was taken aback. "Thank you, Teddy."

"It'll strengthen your claim," he said.

❧

OF COURSE, we were going to the square to see them off. Viola and I, Cannice and Careen, Primus and a few of the other favorite servants, even Cicero. All but Carol. She could not bear public scenes, she told Teddy. So she went with him to their room to help him dress, but they were in there a long time. Teddy came downstairs, still buttoning his shirt, his jacket not yet on. We waited for him in the center hall. Louis gave him a sly look.

"We were saying goodbye," Teddy apologized.

"Well, maybe you've finally found the right words," Louis said as he helped his brother button his jacket. "You'll have to tell me what they are sometime."

THE ROSWELL GUARDS would assemble to listen to some orders and instructions, so we still had time. Viola came to my room to inspect my toilette. Careen had been helping me dress.

Viola did a muster of her own. Was my hair fixed right? Were my pantalets white enough, my hoop skirt manageable, my shoes spotless? How many petticoats was I wearing?

I think she felt, at fifteen, the drawing away of her mother's love and wanted to make sure I didn't miss the care at least. Her fussing over me was the sweetest deed imaginable.

"Where is your sash? I told you, a pink sash goes with that dress."

"It makes me look like a little girl."

"Well, I haven't discovered you to be anything else. Careen, get the pink sash."

It was fetched and she slipped it on, turned me around, and made a solemn business about making me a splendid bow.

"I want to be grown up like you," I mumbled.

She turned me around. "Mother of God, not *this* again! I told you, you soon will be. What's the big rush?"

"You have beaus. And if you don't have one to escort you to dances, either Louis or Teddy or sometimes *both* take you."

She sighed and drew me to her. "We won't be having that anymore, Leigh Ann, with the war and all. Lots of things will change. I won't have any beaus. They've all gone for soldiers. I'll likely be an old maid."

"Louis said it will all be over by Christmas."

"That's not what Johnnie said. And his father is a high mucky-muck officer. Now, speaking of Louis, tell me, did he give you that silver pendant you were wearing last night at dinner? And that you've got hidden under your dress this very moment?"

She was like Teddy. I could not run rings around her. She ordered me, in a voice too much like Teddy's, to unbutton the top of my dress and take the pendant out.

I did so.

She took the pendant in her hand. "It's beautiful," she said reverently. "Louis didn't give me one."

"I don't think he has any more," I lied.

"Why did you hide it today? Did Louis tell you to?"

"No. He said if anyone took it away from me, he would do some bad things to that person with Indian prayers and smoke."

"Ohhhh." Careen raised her hands above her head and turned around and around, chanting, "That Louis has powers, he do!"

"Hush, Careen," Viola scolded. But she believed it without question. "So he told you the family secret. Well, it's about time. They both threatened to disown me if I told you. Now, you wear the pendant outside the dress, like you're supposed to. And listen: I have something important to tell you."

I knew what was coming, but I let her have her say.

"Teddy and Louis have left me in charge of you. Which means you are to mind me. Do you think you can do that?"

I said yes, I could. "We've always been friends, haven't we?"

"But that's just it. It has to be different now. Sometimes you'll have to forget that I'm your friend. Sometimes I'll have to forget. Like with you and Teddy."

I made a pouting face. "You won't spank me, will you?"

"Of course not. Teddy doesn't, does he? It's why he left me in charge and not Carol. A copy of the paper saying I'm in charge is being registered with the mayor's office. Now come on. Let's go see the boys off."

CHAPTER SIX

The Roswell Guards had gone through inspection, heard the orders of the day, and were now released to say final goodbyes. The town square was filled with families, children and dogs running about, and sutlers selling coffee and hot buns.

In an instant both Viola and I spotted the new Confederate flag fluttering in the morning air. "Oh," Viola gushed. "Look, Leigh Ann. We've never seen one before!"

I was used to seeing the Stars and Stripes. This one had stars and bars and, oh, it was beautiful! And then Viola nudged me again. "Look!"

Louis! Across the square he was headed toward a brown-haired, slim woman in periwinkle blue. She looked to be about nineteen. The word "pretty" did her an injustice. With her was a girl about Viola's age in pink, just as lovely. They were sharing the weight of a blue silk flag decorated with large white satin letters — RG. It had eleven satin stars and blue tassels.

They handed the flag to Louis, who in turn handed it to his commander. The band was playing "Soldier's Joy," an old country tune. It was a perfect moment.

Viola and I *ooh*ed and *aah*ed as Louis took the girl by the shoulders and kissed her politely on the cheek. Everybody clapped — for the flag or for the kiss, they did not know.

But I knew. It was for Louis, who wanted to kiss her on the mouth, like a lover, but was too honorable to do such in public. Louis, who was nothing if not honorable.

"Who is that?" I asked Viola. She did not answer.

Teddy came over, grinning. "You girls think Louis is a monk? That's his lady love, Camille Smith. The family is important but lives simply in a spacious farmhouse north of town. He's been wooing her these last six months."

"Why didn't he tell us?" Viola said with a pout.

"You all know Louis is closed-mouthed. With the war coming, I suppose he didn't want to make any carved-in-stone announcements."

"I wish we had made the flag," Viola said enviously. "And I'll wager she took those tassels from her cape."

"Now, now, there's plenty of work to be done," Teddy told her, "and the women will soon be organized to do it. You'll have your share."

"I see Johnnie," Viola announced. "I'm going to join him."

"Go ahead," Teddy said. He smiled at me. "You got any beaus waiting, sweetie?"

I hugged him. "I can knit. I'm going to make you a pair of socks."

He picked me up and kissed me. "Sweetheart, I'm going to miss you terribly." There were tears in his eyes. "Now why don't you go and say goodbye to Louis while there is still time."

Now the band was playing "Barbara Allen." I made my way through the crowd and came up behind Louis and listened before he knew I was there.

"Why is the band playing old mountain songs?" Camille was asking him. "Before they played a song from when we belonged to the Union. Why don't they play 'Dixie'?"

"The bigwigs don't want it as our official theme song because they think it lacks dignity," Louis told her, "but our band will play it. You'll see. We have no other war songs of our own yet. Our music is going to have to be written from loneliness and sorrow, fear and the strange geography of war. Out of tears, not ink. All we have in our heads now is dancing times and feasting times. Times of hunting and family and times with beautiful girls like you. Only the backcountry folk know how to write soulful music."

"You're so right, Louis," she said fervently, "and you always know how to put things into words when no one else does."

Then she saw me. "Yes, little girl, may we help you? Are you looking for someone?"

Louis turned, saw me, and grinned. "Camille, this is my little sister, Leigh Ann." He drew me toward him, and then like Teddy he picked me up.

"Well, I've heard so much about you," Camille offered.

She was a lot like Louis. Her eyes gave off that special kindness in a warmth that reached out to you. She was not like Carol. Not one bit.

"I understand you give your brothers quite a time of it," she teased.

I blushed. I did not know what to say.

"Listen," she whispered, leaning toward me, "Louis loves you very much. And so, I understand, does Teddy. You're a lucky little girl." She kissed me on the cheek.

Tears came into my eyes. I reached out my arms and hugged her, breathing in the scent of lavender. Then I hugged Louis, burying my face in his neck.

He patted my back. I whispered to him that I was going to leave him now so he would have time with his lady love. He kissed me and set me down. And I ran, not looking back.

The band played "Hail Columbia."

Too soon sharp orders rang through the soft Georgia morning air, where sharp orders did not belong. Soft breezes belonged, as Louis would say, and peach trees in blossom in the middle of February, and the neighing of sleek horses in the meadow, the low, heart-rending songs of the negroes at sunset.

Commands rent the air, and the men complied like toy soldiers, rifles already a part of them, gray uniforms already etched in our memories.

The band played "Dixie." It was rousing. People cheered.

And then we stood, stunned, watching our loved ones go.

Tears fell on every female face in the crowd. Sentimental tears. Bitter tears.

We stood staring until the last dust raised by the men had settled and the town was quiet. Until the men were gone.

Gone where? I could not accept this word *gone*. Viola was crying, and she held my hand and I was gulping tears, too. I turned around and saw Camille and her sister going in the opposite direction. Camille waved at me and I waved back.

She left a warm place inside me, Camille did.

WE WENT BACK to the homestead. Pa was settled in his rocker on the verandah, the boy named Jon giving him a second, or third, cup of coffee.

"Well, did they march off like the toy soldiers they are?" Pa asked.

Viola burst into deeper crying and ran into the house. I stood there. "Yes, sir," I answered, "they're gone." I could see he was very much himself this morning.

"Did your mother go to see them off?"

"No, sir," I said.

He answered with a word I would spend two hours in a chair in the library for using.

"Come here and give me a kiss," he said.

I did so. He was cleanly shaved and wore a crisp white shirt and trousers. He smelled of tobacco and mild soap. Jon was doing his job, but I wished he wouldn't linger and watch us. Pa hugged me strong. "I'm here to take care of you," he said. Then he released me.

The empty house was not to be borne at first.

I expected to see Teddy come out of Pa's library and demand, *Well, where have you been? You missed breakfast, and you know I won't tolerate that. Where have you been?* I couldn't tell him, of course. Because I'd been down to the stream with Careen, and with some lighted torches, we'd smoked some snakes out of a pile of rocks. Teddy would have a hissy fit if he found out. Anyway, he would set me down in a chair in the library and pick up a book and I'd have to sit there for an hour until he thought I'd been sufficiently punished. No matter that I was about starved or that I had to pee. Neither request would move him.

I would give anything to have that hour in that chair in that room with him now.

I stood in the wide center hall, looking at the Persian runner, the Duncan Phyfe table, the gas lamp, the hunt scenes on the walls, as if I'd never seen them before. How many times had my brothers clambered down those wide, carpeted stairs?

The emptiness of the rooms mocked me. Normally I wouldn't even bother with my brothers, or them with me, if they were home. My chief goal would be to avoid them so that I could go about the business of my day, which would consist of mischief. Unless Teddy offered to teach me to bow-and-arrow hunt. Or swim in the stream. Or

Louis suggested we ride into town and "see what all was going on."

I wished I could do something for them now. Maybe I could make some cookies and send them.

"What are you doing?" Careen sauntered toward me.

"Just wishing I could do something for my brothers."

She smiled. "You can. I can show you what you can do."

"What?"

"I can show you how to do a spell and tell if'n your brothers will be safe."

I gasped. "Let's do it," I agreed. Surely this wouldn't be naughty. Surely, this is what we all needed right now, wasn't it?

CHAPTER SEVEN

"WE GOTS to have a fire," Careen said.
"In here?" I asked. "In this heat?"
"Jus' a little fire," she coaxed.

The fireplace in the front parlor had been scrupulously cleaned for the spring. Boughs of ivy had been expertly arranged inside over a few cords of beech wood.

"I gots matches," Careen said. "An' salt. Take away that ivy. We needs some paper to light the beech wood."

"We'll dirty the fireplace," I told her. And "What if we get caught?"

"You such a scaredy-cat. Massa Teddy ain't here to punish you. Anyway, anybody else catches us, all we say is we's doin' it for the boys. C'mon now, do as I say. Git some paper."

I ran across the hall to Pa's library, found an old newspaper, and brought it to Careen. She soon had a rosy glow going in the hearth.

"Now all's I gotta do is throw some bits of salt on the fire, an' in the sparks that flame up I'll see the messages we want. You gotta be still, though, and quiet. And think on your brothers. And chase out all other thoughts and noises."

I nodded. I trusted in her powers.

If her mother caught her she would be punished. She didn't care.

She looked at me now. "Take off the hoops," she said, "so's you kin get closer to me."

I stood up and did as she said, leaving my hoops on the floor. Now I was able to snuggle more comfortably near her. She reached into the pocket of her apron and threw a pinch of salt on the fire. It crackled and flamed up and made sparks. I jumped back.

"There, there!" she said in a loud whisper. "There I see Massa Teddy. He firin' a gun."

"Is he all right?"

"Yes." Another sprinkle of salt. More crackling flames. "He stopped firin'. He crawlin' on the ground to somebody. Crawlin' an' crawlin' to help somebody."

"Who?"

More salt. More flames. From out on the verandah I heard people arguing. I heard Cicero barking. The voices were loud and nasty. They sounded like Mother and Pa used to sound before Mother left home. I was hearing things, like forces were trying to distract me. Oh, I mustn't let them distract me. Careen had said I must block out all else if this spell was to work.

"Who is he trying to help?" I asked.

"What is going on in here? What are you two terrible children doing, playing with fire? Do you want to set the house in flames?"

Mother! She came up behind us out of nowhere. Mother? It couldn't be! She never came home! Was this part of the spell? Was I being dragged into some netherworld?

"Careen! Tell me, who is Teddy trying to help?"

I saw Careen being seized by the arm in brutal fashion, dragged to her feet, and slapped back and forth on the face by Mother. "You fiend, teaching my daughter your negro trash."

I don't think Careen even felt the slaps. It was as if she were somewhere else, in the world she had created, where she had seen Massa Teddy firing his gun and crawling to help someone. As Mother hurled her out of the room, she turned and yelled, "Louis. He been hurt. But it be aright. It be aright."

The words echoed through the house as Mother came at me like the wicked witch in all the fairy tales.

She picked up her riding crop, which she always carried with her. It was both her talisman, Teddy had said, and her weapon.

"She come through the keyhole. She come through the *keyhole*," I heard Careen screaming, "like a slip-skin hag that goes out to make trouble after dark."

Then Mother grabbed me and held me face-down across her middle and whipped me.

I fought her, but I couldn't get free. No one had ever whipped me. I could not believe the pain. I screamed and screamed, "Help, help, Teddy, Teddy!" I lost my voice. I gulped tears. Everybody came running. Even Carol, who made no move to stop Mother. Viola came into the room and fought to wrest the crop from her, until Pa lunged in and pulled it out of Mother's hands and shoved her away and down onto the couch.

"You ever lay a hand on this child again and I'll kill you," he said.

"That's what she needs," Mother said. "I've heard from her teacher what an uncontrollable brat she's become. I'll not have my daughter growing up with the reputation of an unruly child in this town."

I was sobbing so that I couldn't catch my breath. Cannice was there in an instant with a cold rag on my face. Viola clasped me to her. She was trembling.

"I want you out of this house," Pa told Mother. "You have ten minutes to get out."

"I've come for some of my things," she told him.

"Ten minutes," he repeated. He was breathing heavily.

Jon had come in. "Come on, Mr. Conners. This is no good for you. What say you take a nice soothing dip in the stream?"

Pa went with Jon to take a nice soothing dip in the stream. Cannice left the room. Carol gave me a superior look and left, too. There were only me and Viola and Mother left. All was silent for a moment, and then Viola said, "Go and get your things."

"You're telling me what to do?"

"I'm in charge of Leigh Ann while the boys are away."

Mother laughed. "Go and tell that to the cypress trees. You? You haven't got the sense God gave a raccoon." She drew herself up. "I'm taking her with me for a few days. My driver is waiting outside. Come along, Leigh Ann."

I heard Viola's intake of breath. "You don't *dare*."

"Oh, don't I? We'll just see."

"I have a paper to prove I'm in charge." Viola released me and stood straight. "Teddy and Louis drew it up and had it notarized and registered at the mayor's office. I have a copy. I can show it to you."

"Darling, Teddy and Louis are gone. Going north to fight my people. Who knows if they will come back?"

"So that's what's put you into this rage," Viola said, "that your boys have gone away to fight your people. I thought *we* were your people. *Your children.*"

"Nobody understands," Mother told her in a gravelly voice. "I was never meant to be a mother. Some women are just not molded for it."

"Then why are you taking Leigh Ann?"

"Because I have a reputation to keep. Now get out of the way — I'm taking her. Just for a few days, to teach her some manners and discipline."

"To turn her against us, you mean."

"I can use this riding crop on you, you know," Mother threatened. "I used it on Louis when he was twenty."

"We all know the story," Viola said wearily. She was losing her fight and she knew it. "Mother, don't, please!"

But Mother pulled me by the arm, and when I refused to follow, she picked me up and carried me out through the hall and verandah to her waiting carriage. I kicked and yelled. "Viola, don't let her take me!"

Now on the verandah, Viola was sobbing. Cannice wrapped her arm around my sister's shoulder. Other household negroes came out and begged Mother not to take their little lamb.

"Massa Teddy ain't gonna like it," Cannice told Mother. "Massa Teddy gonna be right angry."

But the negroes knew they were helpless in their fussing with Mother. So they started to sing one of their spirituals, low and heart-rending.

And Pa was taking a nice soothing dip in the stream.

Before I knew it, I was shoved into the fancy black and gold carriage and the door was closed. Inside, my hands were tied with silken cords and I was pulled into the netherworld that had all started with some salt sprinkled on a fire.

The driver clicked at the sleek thoroughbred horses and we started to move.

The negroes were singing something about Paul and Silas being bound in jail as we drove away.

CHAPTER EIGHT

I T SEEMED as if we rode and rode, on and on, forever. I was still gulping tears and my breath was coming in short spurts. My ear and my bottom hurt. I was indignant at this unspeakable treatment. Cannice had told God's truth when she had said, "Massa Teddy will be right angry when he finds out."

As soon as God permitted it, I would write to Teddy and tell him. He would do something, I was sure of it. Even from far away, he would do something.

She had told Viola that she was not meant to be a mother. Well, about this one thing she was right.

She lectured me in a steady, grating tone all the way to her place. She told me that I never had known what proper behavior was, that my brothers had spoiled me so that I was like a rotten Georgia peach. And now that they'd had their sport with me, they had left me to break into fragments in the glare of everyone's disdain.

She said she knew of a very strict girls' boarding school in New York: "All that will be taken out of you there. And you will have some true Yankee values instilled in you." The words tore at my soul. I had no tears left in me to cry.

"If your brothers live through the war, they will never find you," she said.

My head swam with the fear of it all. My mind was in some dark place, full of vines that snagged me as I tried to escape. I was frozen silent.

We rode through town. I saw people I knew out the carriage windows, people who were friends of Louis's and Teddy's, who respected and honored them. People who would help me in an instant if they realized I was in trouble. But I could do nothing. We passed the town square, where just two hours ago I had said goodbye to my brothers. Then, too soon, we went by the town hall, Hoover's Confectionery, where Louis had so often taken me for treats, a dram shop, where my brothers went to drink and meet friends, the post office, a dressmaker's, all these at the end of town, and then we were on a dusty road north trimmed with fences and trees.

Her place of residence was about a mile north of town. By the time we got there I decided that if she sent me to that boarding school in New York I would run away. I would go to Grandmother Johanna's in Philadelphia, and from there write home.

The carriage passed a three-story colonial home constructed of bricks made of red clay from a nearby stream. I recognized it as the handsome house belonging to Reverend Nathaniel Pratt, pastor of the First Presbyterian Church, our church. Down a short road to the side of the house was a smaller version of it, also owned by the reverend. He rented it out.

Here the carriage drew in the drive. A very fat negro woman waited on the porch. Our driver leaped down and opened the door.

"Amber, come see what I've got," Mother yelled to the negro woman, like I was a bushel of peas.

Amber helped Mother out and stood, hands on hips, staring at me still with my hands tied.

"Well, where'd you git her? And what she for? To help me with the housework? She indentured?"

Mother gave a rich laugh. "You never cease to say the right thing, Amber. Indentured, indeed. It would do her good, a little housework. But no, she's my youngest, Leigh Ann."

"Why you bring her here? And why her hands be tied?"

"Because she's become a hopeless brat, Amber. My sons spoiled her. And I've taken her for a few days to tame her a bit. Get her down, will you?"

Amber let go a deep, throaty sound as if she didn't approve, but she did as she was told, then carried me into the house, which was smaller than ours by half, but perfectly appointed.

Mother closed and locked the front door. She started to untie my hands, then decided against it. "No, I think I'll leave you bound up until I see how you behave. And if you're thinking about running off and appealing to Reverend Pratt, think again. It'll only earn you another whipping."

"I have to pee," I told her. "How can I with my hands tied?"

"A lady does not use that word."

"It's what I tell Teddy when he makes me sit in a chair for an hour for being naughty."

"So that's how you are punished? It's no wonder you've become so unmanageable. Amber will take you to your room and help you use the chamber pot. And Amber is to be obeyed. Go along with her now, and no tricks."

I got the feeling that Amber did not like any of this, that she was longing to say something comforting to me but her fear of Mother held her back. So I did as I was told and didn't make any trouble for her. She was firm with me, but kind.

My "room" was prepared for me, for a little girl. It was what I supposed was Yankee plain. The bedspread was of sturdy cotton with a wide blue hem. In the middle was stitched an American flag. A Betsy Ross doll was propped against the pillows. A small cherry bookcase held schoolbooks. One large one was *The Constitution of the United States*. There was a child's desk, all fit out for study. On the wall hung a pencil sketch of General George Washington kneeling and praying in the snow at Valley Forge. There was no mirror in the room.

It all frightened me. Mother had been planning this for a long time. She had been waiting for the day Teddy and Louis left to come and get me. And she had not waited beyond an hour or so after they had gone.

For my noontime meal my hands were still tied. I was seated at her dining room table and served jellied cornmeal mush and water. She ate ham glazed with brown sugar, hominy grits, creamed corn, and fresh tomatoes. She drank sherry wine and followed it with peach upside-down cake and fragrant coffee with cream, with shaved chocolate sprinkled on top.

I thought about my family. Were they going to come and get me? They wouldn't just leave me here, would they? And then it came to me.

None of us, not even Teddy or Louis, has ever known where Mother lived. None of us has bothered to find out. We thought she flitted about from place to place, staying with women friends, or worse yet, men. And of course, Reverend Pratt, being a minister, could not tell. He was sworn to secrecy.

All this thinking I was doing while my tied hands sat in my lap. Amber fed me the jellied cornmeal mush, spoonful by spoonful, like I was a baby. Quiet tears rolled down my face and Amber wiped them away. Mother sat enjoying her food, sipping her sherry, and smiling at me wickedly.

After my noonday meal she had Amber change my dress. I was brought upstairs and my hands were untied briefly while the beautiful, but now mussed, white organdy with the pink sash was taken off and thrown aside. Then the petticoats were removed and a plain blue and white checkered dress with a slim skirt was slipped over my head. It had long sleeves with white cuffs and a round white collar.

"Right down from Vermont," Mother said delightedly.

She sat me at the desk and set a Bible in front of me, then rifled through the pages until she found what she wanted.

I was to memorize Psalm 51, begging the Lord to wash me thoroughly from my wickedness and cleanse me from my sins. I was to acknowledge that my sins were forever before me.

The part about my mother having conceived me in wickedness was crossed out.

She left me there, warning me to memorize it all. All right, I would. And I did so, including the part that was crossed out. I would recite it to her that way. It was the word of the Lord, I would tell her.

Likely she would whip me again, but I did not care. I knew, as sure as if Louis and Teddy were standing in the room with me, that I must have the mettle to stand up to her. I must show her I had values, that she could not make me cower, *that my brothers had done right by me.*

I went over the words again and again in my mind. The windows were open and the warm wind blew in along with the drowsy sound of afternoon birdcalls and katydids. My eyes went heavy. What was I supposed to be saying? Something about my sins, and my mother having conceived me in wickedness. Slowly, I put my arms down on the desk and my head down on them and dozed.

I did not hear the approaching footsteps on the stairs, or the door opening.

"So, that's how you study, eh? Get up, you lazy girl!"

I stumbled to my feet, dragging myself awake. Where was I? Oh, yes. The Betsy Ross doll on the bed grinned, reminding me.

"Well? Have you memorized the psalm?"

"Yes, ma'am."

She pounded the end of her riding crop on the floor. "Recite," she ordered.

So I did, clearly and precisely. All of it. Including the line about her having conceived me in wickedness. I gave special emphasis to that part.

"Stop!" she shouted, and slammed the riding crop on the floor again. *What was that you just said?*

"It was a line from the psalm."

"I know what it was. It was crossed out, wasn't it? Don't you know what that means? Are you stupid as well as disobedient and unruly?"

I stood straight and tall. "It is the word of the Lord," I told her.

"I'll *tell* you what the word of the Lord is. How dare you interpret it on your own!" She reached to grab me, but I backed away, just far enough to the window to see a carriage pulling up in front.

Our carriage!

And people getting out!

My people. Viola. And Cannice. And the dog Cicero. And the mayor. And Pa, with a gun.

She grabbed me and threw me face-down on the bed and raised the riding crop, but I rolled and jumped up and away from her. "Pa's here and he's got a gun," I told her, "and you know what he told you. That he'd kill you if you ever hit me again. And Pa's just crazy enough to do it."

"You lie," she growled. "You lie."

I ran out of the room, down the stairs, and through the hall. They were just bursting in the door. Amber was there to greet them.

"These are my people, Amber," I told her. "They've come to rescue me." And I threw myself into Viola's arms. "Oh, am I glad to see you all." Then I hugged Pa, who hugged me back. He did not have his rifle. Mayor Hanley must have made him leave it in the carriage. Cannice grabbed me in an embrace and called me her lamb. Cicero jumped up and licked my face.

Mayor Hanley held a paper in his hand. I curtsied to him.

"Where is she?" Pa boomed. "Where is the woman who kidnapped my daughter?" He started to advance toward Mother menacingly, but Mayor Hanley held out a restraining arm.

"Let me handle this, Hunter."

But Pa saw the riding crop in Mother's hand. "Did you hit her again?" he demanded. He looked at me. "Well, did she?"

For a minute they all looked at me. Even Cicero, who sat expectantly, waiting. I felt a darkness pass over us, like when there is an eclipse of the sun. *She was about to,* I could say. But then, sure as God made eight-foot alligators, Pa would head outside to fetch his rifle and, no matter what Mayor Hanley said, come back in and shoot Mother dead.

Then he'd be sent to jail, maybe hanged. I couldn't let that happen to Pa, to us. So I stood there and said, "No, she never hit me, Pa. She never even hinted at it."

Pa nodded and settled himself. I saw Viola and the others sigh in relief, saw Cicero wag his tail. Mayor Hanley officially presented Mother with the paper Teddy had left in his care, saying that Viola was in charge of me. "It's been notarized, Mrs. Conners," he told her. "I'm afraid you'll have to give the child up."

Mother was trembling. In the twisted disorder of her mind she was already planning something.

"He's never officially been named her guardian."

"But he's been responsible for her for how long now? Since before he went to college, Viola told me, which puts her at about three or four. And while away at college. Viola showed me letters from him, with directives from there. And when he wasn't around, Louis was responsible. And her father, until he took sick. You left the family, Mrs. Conners. Everybody knows that. You abandoned your child."

The air went out of Mother. She seemed to diminish in size.

"Come now, let's be on our way," the mayor said. "Get your things, child."

"Where did you get that horrible dress?" Viola asked. "Where is your other one?"

"Upstairs in my room."

We both looked at the mayor, who nodded his permission, and I took Viola upstairs, where she went white in the face as she looked about the room. She said not a thing. Just scooped up the dress and petticoats. I grabbed the pink sash and we went back downstairs. The others had gone out to the carriage. Only the mayor waited with Mother in the hallway.

"Goodbye, ma'am," the mayor bade her.

We said not a word to Mother, nor she to us, as we went out.

⚜

"WHICH PUTS HER at about three or four," the mayor had told Mother.

I was four when it happened.

And I remember the why and the how of it like it was yesterday, only nobody, not even Teddy, knows I remember.

It stands out in my mind like a painting, like the one we have in the hall of the Dutch girl with the pearl earring by Vermeer.

Sometimes I think only Teddy and I know about it. But then sometimes I think that, as close as he is to Louis, he must have told him about it. They share everything.

What I know is that Teddy carries the burden around with him. Blames himself for the whole untidiness of it, the breakup of our parents' marriage. And that is why he is so moody sometimes, so strict with me and Viola.

He does not want us to turn out like Mother.

So there I was, four. And Teddy was sixteen. And Mother was still living at home and we were, on the surface at least, still one normal family living happily ever after. Then one day this man named Nicholas Waters comes along, this very rich man from Sweetwater Creek, thirty miles away, who owned the Sweetwater Factory, a textile mill much like ours.

Apparently Mr. Waters needed to meet with Pa about some mill business, so he stayed in Roswell at the home of a Mr. Angus Brumby, whom he knew and who was away at the time.

Somehow, Mother and Mr. Waters "had something going" as Teddy would say. And she made arrangements to meet with him at Angus Brumby's house.

This was, I learned later in life, not Mother's first act of unfaithfulness to Pa.

She had been "having something going" with various men ever since I was born.

This particular afternoon, Cannice had taken Viola to town. I was down sick with a fever and in the way of Mother's plans, so she solved the problem by taking me with her.

Teddy, who always suspected her of carrying on, now knew for certain she was. Unable to locate me about the house, he was told by Primus that she'd taken me off in the fancy carriage. So he rode to the house of Angus Brumby.

What I remember is sitting in the parlor of Mr. Brumby's house, propped up on the couch and covered with blankets, both shivering cold and hot at the same time, and playing with my doll.

I knew Mother had gone into the bedchamber with Mr. Waters to take a nap. Times when Pa came home afternoons, she often took naps with him and I was told not to disturb them. So I did not disturb her with Mr. Waters. Although I wanted, more than I wanted some taffy right then, a drink of cool water. But there was no one to get it for me.

Suddenly I heard the sound of a horse outside. *Oh good,* I thought, *Pa's come to get me. Now I can have my water. And maybe some taffy, too.*

The front door crashed open and my brother Teddy, already a man at sixteen, came into the hall. He saw me on the couch in the parlor, looked around, and said, "Where's Ma?"

"She's taking a nap with Mr. Waters," I said. "I'm not to disturb them. And I haven't. I've been good, Teddy."

He looked at me and felt my face with his hand. "You're burning up," he said. He looked around and asked me which room. I pointed toward it. "Stay here," he said. "Don't move, no matter what. I'm coming right back to take you home."

Then he crashed right through the door of the room I'd pointed to and it made a powerful bad noise and my head hurt. I heard yelling and screaming from inside and knew Mother was giving him what-for because he'd woken them up.

Next thing I knew they were out in the hall, he and Mother, and she was in her wrapper. They were saying terrible things to each other.

"How dare you come here?" Mother was saying.

"How dare I not? You bring Leigh Ann? And leave her sitting there with a fever? What are you teaching the child?"

"She's *my* child!" Mother told him. "I'll do what I want with her."

"Not while I live and breathe," Teddy snapped back. "If it's not this Waters popinjay, it's somebody else. Any judge or lawyer would take her away from you."

"Oh, and who would tell them?" Mother challenged.

"Me," Teddy told her. "I would."

"And who would be responsible for her then? Your father? He's never around. He practically lives at the mill. Sometimes he doesn't even come home at night."

"I'll be responsible for her," Teddy vowed. "For her and Viola, too. 'S'matter of fact, I heard Pa say if you did this sort of thing again, he didn't want you home anymore, that you could just pack your things and get out."

"And how will he know?" Mother pushed.

"Because I'm going to tell him," Teddy said.

"You wouldn't," she challenged. "You haven't the mettle. And again I ask *who would be responsible for her?* And Viola? You?" And she laughed in his face.

Teddy was not laughing. "You've been neglecting both of them since Leigh Ann was born. If it weren't for Cannice, God knows what would have happened to them.

"Last week when Cannice was down with a stomach ailment and Viola was at a party, Louis found Leigh Ann by the stream, muddy as hell. Never mind that she could have *drowned!* He brought her home, and because all the servants were busy he had to bathe and change her. You didn't know that, did you? Well, I'm telling you now. I'm telling Pa tonight what's going on here. And as sure as God made eight-foot alligators, Pa's going to put you out. If he doesn't end up shooting Waters and you first."

With that, Teddy came over, picked me up, and took me outside, where he sat me in front of him on his horse to take me home.

I don't remember the rest of it, but after that Mother *did* move out. Actually she'd been moving out little by little all along, coming home less and less, only for the sake of appearances. Like the time she came home for two days when Louis got drunk and she whipped him.

There were rules in the house, set down by Pa. When she came home, for one or two days, we did not have to obey her but we had to respect her.

But from that afternoon on there was a line drawn. Teddy was in charge. So was Louis. Pa said so. Viola and I had to listen to them.

❧

"WHICH PUTS HER at about three or four," the mayor had said.

Four, mayor. I distinctly remember it.

Teddy doesn't know I remember it. He doesn't know that I know he has dark moments when he blames himself for the breakup in our parents' marriage. When he wonders if he is being punished for it when he and Carol do not get on.

Times there are when I want to say something to him, when I want to tell him he did the right thing, not to blame himself. And the right thing is not always the easy thing.

How many times have you told me that, Teddy?

But I dare not say anything at all.

CHAPTER NINE

Things went on sadly at home after the boys left to go fighting. Everyone tried to fall into a routine to keep from thinking of them. I saw them at every turn in the house. Viola kept me busy, playing. She took me riding and swimming. We baked cookies for the boys and Johnnie. She took me to sewing bees and bandage-rolling get-togethers. Carol went home to stay with her parents. Every day Viola and I went into town for whatever newspapers we could get.

Our president, Jeff Davis, and Abraham Lincoln were both being pressured by public opinion, she told me. Which meant that the public wanted the armies to fight.

The Roswell Guards were camped in Centerville, Virginia, and we had not heard from Louis or Teddy because all letters were being intercepted.

And we soon learned that the *Baltimore American* was a Yankee paper and we couldn't believe a word it said.

I started having nightmares. I saw terrible scenes of men firing their guns, of bullets hitting soldiers between the eyes and blood spurting out, of heads being blown off, of horses rearing and screaming, fire exploding out of their mouths, of cannon roaring, of men flying through the air.

I screamed out. Viola came running. "Leigh Ann, Leigh Ann, you've got to stop this."

"Teddy's been hurt. Teddy's dead."

"He's not dead. We would have heard."

"Louis, then."

"Oh, sweetie." She used the endearment the boys called me. She held me until I stopped trembling. She stayed until I fell asleep. When I woke in the morning, I found her nestled beside me in the bed.

❧

AFTER A LOT of fussing on the part of both armies, they finally clashed in Manassas on the twenty-first of July, a Sunday. Probably because it was the first battle of the war and they wanted to be reverent about the killing.

The North wanted to be festive, we found out later. Women came in droves, in carriages trimmed with ribbons, bearing picnic baskets, to watch. These were the Yankees my mother wanted me to be like?

On the Thursday morning before that Sunday, Pa, Viola, and I were at breakfast when we heard Cannice arguing with someone at the back door. Viola and I got up to see what was going on.

A negro woman of about sixty, wearing a faded dress, a neckerchief, and a bandanna around her head, was standing in the doorway. She was carrying a basket full of fresh vegetables. We watched, open-mouthed, as she slithered into the kitchen. Not even Cicero's barking discouraged her.

"What is this?" Viola demanded.

"She just worked her way in, Miss Viola," Cannice said.

"What do you want?" Viola asked.

"Ise gots some fine vegetables heah," the woman said, "the best in the county."

"We don't need any," Viola told her.

Jon, who had been in and out of the dining room, attending Pa, came in. "Do you need any help, Miss Viola?"

"No," she said sharply. She was getting impatient with Jon. It seemed he was always around, in her way, never giving her any peace. "I can handle this myself. Go back and see to Pa."

Jon bowed and left. I still didn't like him.

The woman held up some carrots. "You wanna jus' try these?"

Viola frowned. She was growing suspicious. "I said no!"

Then the woman did a funny thing. She winked at Viola and gestured with her head that they should go upstairs. *Upstairs?* I saw the question on Viola's face.

The woman nodded yes, then did another funny thing. She mimicked, with her moving lips, the reading of something. It was just our good fortune that Cannice had turned back to her work.

"Why, yes," Viola said, "perhaps it would be a good idea to let Pa take a look at the vegetables." And without further ado she led the woman into the hall and up the stairs and into her bedroom.

I followed. By now, of course, I expected that the whole world had gone mad. And I accepted anything.

In her bedroom Viola closed the door and said firmly, "This had better be for a good reason, or I'll have you thrown out of the house lickety-split."

Without a word the woman set her basket down, removed her neckerchief, and reached inside the top of her stays. She drew out a letter and handed it to Viola, who grabbed it and gave a low cry and clutched it to her bosom.

"Oh, thank you, *thank you!* But who are you? Is this what you do?"

The woman wagged her finger and shook her head no. No questions. "We gots a way," she said. "Negro womens in South to negro womens in North. If'n you gots a need to send a letter, put a quilt over the fence in front. You gots a quilt?"

The woman left, refusing one of the gold double-eagle pieces of coin from Viola, mumbling, "Cain't have no Yankee money on me." So Viola gave her Confederate script.

The letter was from Teddy and Louis.

Dear Viola and Leigh Ann:

I'm afraid we've come here with romantic ideas of patriotism and war. The enemy, from what we can see of them, looks formidable in force. Up to now we have spent hours waiting around in boredom. It is difficult adjusting to the food and, of course, at night, with some men playing harmonicas and singing, thoughts of home grab at the heartstrings through the firelight. What have we gotten ourselves into? What is it all for? In spite of such considerations, we have met some fine fellows from other regiments. We are forming lasting friendships with men from the 8th Georgia Infantry, the 7th Georgia, and the 17th Virginia. Louis has even met an old college buddy. They say we will soon go to battle. Pray for us, and if anything befalls us, remember that we love you all beyond words to tell.

We trust everything is fine, that you girls are helping to hold home and hearth together, and abiding by everything we taught you. Viola, we realize we have left a lot on your shoulders, but know you are equal to the task. Leigh Ann, we also trust, sweetie, that you are doing your best. Don't disappoint us. Give our best to Pa, and, Viola, Johnnie is fine and sends his utmost sentiments. He will be writing to you soon. Don't write until this battle is over and we know where we will be. We send our love and prayers, Teddy, Louis, and Johnnie.

ON FRIDAY MORNING Pa received a note from a man named Olney Eldredge. Jon gave it to Viola. It said that Mr. Eldredge would consider it a pleasure to see Pa this day.

"Your pa's not himself," Jon said. "He wants you to take care of it."

Viola was almost paralyzed with dread. "Olney Eldredge is the new superintendent of the mill that Teddy hired before he left," she told me. "Oh, I don't know tiddlywinks about mill business, but we must invite him to dinner just to be courteous."

He came to dinner that very night, a middle-aged man with downward-slanted eyes, large lips and jowls, and a worried look on his face.

"I am a native of Massachusetts," he told Viola as she offered him a glass of sherry in the front parlor. He wanted her to know it upon meeting him. In case she felt it necessary to throw him out of the house, I guessed.

"But I've heard you've been here awhile now." Viola had done her homework. She had searched Teddy's desk for the folder on Eldredge and read his background.

"You've been in Georgia since 1846," she told him.

Oh, Viola was smart! I was so proud of her. She knew his wife had died and that he had three children, and at the dinner table she asked about them with real interest.

"Because the mill lost clients in Baltimore, Philadelphia, and Newark early this year, it had to lay off thirty people," Eldredge told Viola. "Now we have lost at least ten male workers to the army. And we are getting large military contracts from the Confederacy. I would have liked your father's permission to hire more hands."

"He isn't well," Viola said. She did not elaborate.

"I would write to your brother Theodore, then. Is it possible to get mail through?"

Viola and I looked at each other. We were both thinking the same thing. The lady with the basket full of vegetables.

"First, Mr. Eldredge," Viola told him kindly, "I am sure that when my brother hired you he gave you full authority to hire people when they are needed. That is why he made you superintendent, is it not?"

He swallowed deeply and took a sip of wine. "Yes, I suppose you are right, Miss Viola. I am, you see, not as confident as I used to be. Not since my wife died."

Viola nodded. "So why don't you just go ahead and hire them?" she suggested. "And then write to Teddy and tell him about it? If you leave the letter with me, yes, I have ways of getting the mail through. But not until the battle they're about to fight is over. Not until then, Mr. Eldredge . . ."

Her voice trailed off. We all fell silent. The grandfather clock in the hall struck seven.

CHAPTER TEN

WITHIN A WEEK or two of Manassas, which was what we called that first battle, we got the telegraph in Roswell. But even without it, we knew the next day from couriers arriving on horseback from Marietta that the South had won.

To say there was rejoicing in Roswell makes words cheap. The dram shops were overflowing. The women opened their houses and had high teas. The band played in the town square all day. People had picnics on their front lawns. They put up colorful ribbons on their front porches. The churches held special services for the wounded.

That afternoon more couriers arrived with handbills saying that the Confederate Congress in Richmond called for a day of thanksgiving. They also said that our army had 387 killed, 1,587 wounded, and 13 missing. The Federals had 460 killed, 1,124 wounded, and 1,312 missing.

We sobered when we heard that. Viola hosted a high tea and invited Camille Smith, her sister, Emily, her younger brother, David, her parents, Archibald and Anne Smith, as well as the Reverend and Mrs. Pratt. Now she looked first at me, then at Camille, who had another brother off fighting.

"How will we know who was killed or wounded?" Viola asked.

"We'll hear soon," Reverend Pratt promised. "Another courier will come."

The tea soon ended. Camille and her parents hugged us as they left. Viola and I sat by candlelight at dusk, staring at the remains of the rum nut pudding cake, petits fours, the pudding pecan pie, the sparkling punch bowl, and the brandied cherry ring.

From the distance we heard faint shouts of celebration and band music. Viola had a glass of sherry in her hand. *When did she start drinking sherry?*

I said nothing. Jon stood in the doorway. "Is there anything I can do, Miss Viola?"

She did not even turn to look at him. "No."

"I know you are worried. I never told you all, but I feel guilty because I can't go and fight. I should have been at Manassas. Your pa's asleep. Now why don't you let me take you for a little walk outside in the garden. It will do you good."

Now she did look at him. "Because it isn't your job to take me for a little walk in the garden, that's why."

"You are a beautiful young woman, Miss Viola. And your sister soon will be. But I have no untoward motives. I feel protective toward you and your little sister is all."

"My brother Teddy told you we were not your concern. And my brother does not take easily anyone who goes against his wishes."

"No man can tell another what his concerns should be, Miss Viola."

My sister had confided to me that she thought Jon wanted to "take liberties" with her, and told me never to be alone with him. "And if he starts anything with you, scream, kick him, bite him." And she told me a few other secrets girls have to protect themselves.

Now her suspicions about Jon were confirmed. "You will please leave us now, Jon," she said sternly.

He hesitated for a moment. "I wonder if your brother would take easily the information that in his absence you are drinking sherry."

Viola slammed her fist down on the table. "Get out!"

He left.

We sat until the grandfather clock chimed ten, while Careen and Cannice cleared the table, and Cannice finally came over and pulled out my chair and said, "Time for my lamb to go to bed."

Viola had forgotten it was past my bedtime. She jumped up. "I'll do it," she told Cannice. "I just wanted her company. After all, it is a special day."

And then, just as she was about to lead me up the stairs, Cannice came to us. "Miss Viola, that vegetable lady, she be here again."

Viola fled through the kitchen to the back door. "Come along, chile," Cannice said to me. "I put you to bed."

All I could think of was that the vegetable lady had a letter! I broke away from Cannice and fled to the kitchen to be with Viola. A letter meant news. Either both Teddy and Louis were dead or wounded. Or one of them was. I had to know.

Cannice was right behind me. Viola did not order her away. The vegetable lady stood in silence until Viola told her it was all right, that Cannice could be trusted, and then she took off her neckerchief and drew out the letter.

Viola snatched it, tore it open, and read it in silence. Her hand flew to her mouth. "What?" I demanded. "Tell us!"

"Louis has been shot. In the ankle." She spoke in a low, shaky voice. "Teddy pulled him off the field and while doing so was shot in the arm. They were both sent to a hospital in Richmond for medical care."

I burst into tears. "No," she said, "no. It's all right. They will both be all right. They will soon be home to recuperate." She held me.

"And Johnnie?" I asked.

"Teddy wrote that Johnnie was unhurt. He remains with the Roswell Guards. And he will go on with them to wherever they go to fight next. He will write to me soon."

"Soon's here." The vegetable lady drew another letter out of her bosom and gave it to Viola, who grabbed it and kissed it.

Coffee was heated up for the vegetable lady. And she was given some pudding pecan pie. "I knows," she told us, "that you all's got the telegraph. I done saw the poles on my way here. But I knows, too, that both armies ain't gonna let those lines be gettin' messages through wiffout bein' cut. Those lines jus' beggin' to be cut. So I still be sellin' my vegetables, thank you all."

Viola nodded and said, "Oh, Cannice, please put your lamb to bed."

She was clutching the letter from Johnnie to her breast as she said it.

❧

THE BOYS came home two weeks later.

Carol came back to us a good week before and insisted on being the only one to ready things for Teddy. This was the first time I saw the other side of Carol, the side that truly loved him. Now Viola and I stepped aside and let her have her own way in preparing for his homecoming.

We got things ready for Louis. We were going to fix up the back parlor for him, deciding he wouldn't be able to make it upstairs. Then Camille dropped by.

"Louis being Louis," the girl said, "he'll make it upstairs if it kills him. He'll be uncomfortable sleeping downstairs."

She was right. And Viola asked her to help us prepare his room, and she did.

They came by train to Marietta, thirteen miles north of us, and then by stage to Roswell. Viola and I went with Primus and Carol and Camille to meet them in town.

Viola held me back as they got out of the stage so Carol and Camille could greet them, could hug them and receive their kisses and return tears and whispered endearments. We busied ourselves paying the stage driver.

Out of the corner of my eye I could see that Teddy was wan and his arm was bound up. Louis was on crutches and he looked thinner. Both wore their uniforms, a little worse for wear.

Then Teddy looked at us, not quite knowing what to say. He'd never been anything but strong, capable, and well, and now he looked as if he wanted to apologize for his imperfection. Instead, he grinned. "The stage ride was as bad as the battle." He winked at me and it near tore my heart out. He held his good arm toward me and I hesitated, not wanting to hurt him. "Come on," he said. "They haven't broken me, not yet."

I hugged him.

"Have you been good?" he asked.

"Yes." I would never tell him about Mother whipping me. *Never.*

Louis was next. He smiled his wonderful Louis smile. *Oh, thank you, God,* I said to myself. *They didn't take that from him.* I hugged and kissed him. "I'm glad you're home. I missed you."

"Wouldn't be here if Teddy didn't pull me off the field," he said. "I missed you, too, sweetie."

We got into our carriage. It took a while because Louis had some difficulty. Then Primus drove us home, where Cannice had waiting a wonderful supper that, she promised, would include ice cream.

I got out of the carriage first because I had to hold Cicero back from jumping all over the boys.

CHAPTER ELEVEN

THE ANNOUNCEMENT in the *Richmond Enquirer* read:

The Conners brothers of the Roswell Guards distinguished themselves in Manassas, 21 July 1861. Ordered up to support General Bernard Bee, the Roswell Guards found Bee's Brigade routed and took the lead. In four hours of desperate fighting, Captain Louis Conners was in front of the line, encouraging the troops, when he was shot and his ankle shattered. Lieutenant Theodore Conners took his place, leading the Guards in the bullet-laden air, shouting, "Forward, boys" until the Guard completed a gallant charge, which contributed to the victory of the day. Lieutenant Theodore Conners then rescued his brother from the field.

Pa was not himself. He greeted the boys as if they had been away to the horseraces in Savannah.

"You fell off a horse, eh?" Pa scolded Louis. "Told you that bareback riding would cripple you someday."

Everything was the same, yet everything was different. My brothers were heroes and people came to call and made a fuss over them, but a somberness was in the visits. At least seven other Roswell men had been badly wounded. And four others were killed.

Louis made his way up and down those stairs once a day. He always came to the table for meals. Sometimes in the mornings he set himself up on the verandah in the shade. I stayed with him there. I kept him supplied with fresh cups of coffee and he told me of things he and Teddy had done as little boys. He confided in me that he was in pain. I asked him why he didn't take the laudanum that Dr. Widmar had given him.

"It puts me in another world," he said, "and I like this one too much."

Then he asked me, "Would you get me some of that medicine that Cannice used to make and give us for pain?"

In the afternoons Camille came. They'd hole up in the back parlor, which the shade favored in the afternoon. She played the piano for him, or read Tennyson or Longfellow. He loved Tennyson and Longfellow. She was there, as well as Teddy, the day Dr. Widmar came and examined Louis's ankle. I sat on the couch and held his hand. Camille sat on the other side and held his arm. Dr. Widmar told him it would take a year to heal, at least.

Teddy sent me from the room at that pronouncement and then he left, too, with Dr. Widmar. "He's planning to rejoin the army," Teddy told the doctor. "So am I."

"He may never be able to walk right again," the doctor told Teddy. "You'll be all right in a month or so. But not Louis. And I think he knows it. He's right smart."

EVERYTHING WAS DIFFERENT. I had knitted socks for both Teddy and Louis and they were home before I could send them. I gave Teddy his, but I did not know what to do with Louis's.

"Give them to him," Teddy advised. "He still has to wear socks."

"He wears *bandages!*" I flung back at him. "I heard the doctor say he'll likely never walk right again."

Teddy scowled. "If you give him the socks, you'll give him some hope."

I threw the socks on the floor. Teddy told me to pick them up. I did not. I stomped out of the room. At no other time would he have allowed this, but I suppose he knew my bones were bruised and my innards twisted by what had happened to Louis.

Yet everything was the same. Their concern for the mill was the same, and although Louis could not go along to inspect things there with Teddy as he usually did, Teddy went every day. One quiet afternoon Camille came and she was so tired that she promptly fell asleep on one of the sofas in the back parlor. Louis left her there and was practicing walking around the house on his crutches. I was in the front parlor, reading *The Confessions of a Pretty Woman* by someone named Pardoe. I'd gotten it from Viola's room. It was what I supposed a French novel was like.

I was so taken with it, I scarce heard Teddy approach.

He came around to read the title and took the book from me. "Where did you get this?"

I sighed. There went some good confessions. "I found it around the house."

"Well, you're not reading it." He snapped it shut.

"So, what do you want me to read? *The Three Little Kittens?*"

I don't know who was more shocked, he or I. His shock passed across his face as hurt, not anger. I'd never spoken to him like that before. My shock came across me in waves.

Just at that moment I saw Louis standing in the doorway and I thought, *Oh, no — I've hurt and shocked him, too.* I looked from one brother to the other, both nursing wounds received in a nightmare of a battle, and here I was badmouthing one of them over a book — a *book!* — while the other, who would never walk right again, looked on in disbelief. I thought, *Lord, wash me thoroughly from my wickedness and cleanse me from my sins.*

"What's happened to you in my absence?" Teddy asked softly.

"I'm sorry, Teddy," I said.

He shook his head slowly. "'Sorry' doesn't do it. Go into the library and sit yourself down in that chair and don't move until I come and get you. Go on now."

It was said kindly, which made it worse. I looked at Louis as I went out, but Louis never interfered when Teddy disciplined me.

I sat in the chair for more than an hour. The wise old

grandfather clock told me it was two hours, and still Teddy didn't come. I alternately cried and hiccupped. I got a headache and my throat hurt. He'd never made me sit two hours.

I thought, *He must wonder at having to bother with me over such a trifling matter when he's seen men getting their heads blown off. He must think, "Is this what I've come home for? There are men getting killed out there on fields and I've got to tell them 'Forward, boys.' That's what I've got to do, not tell this little brat what she can and cannot read." So he's forgotten me.*

It was approaching suppertime. My arms and legs were numb; my head was throbbing. I had no tears left. I was about starved, yet my throat was so scratchy, I didn't know if I could eat. But I'd stay here all night if he didn't come. I'd not leave the chair. I'd pee in my pantalets if I had to, to show him I was still decent, that I still thought him a man to be reckoned with.

My eyes were closing when he came. "Leigh Ann."

My eyes flew open.

"Are you all right? Primus needed me at the stable. We had a new colt born. Why didn't you leave after an hour?"

"You told me to stay until you came and got me."

He nodded appreciatively. "You're a good girl. But what made you talk to me like that before I'll never understand, Leigh Ann. You frightened me. I thought everything I'd taught you had vanished with the first disruption in our lives. You must understand, child, that in difficult times all we have to hold us together is the everyday values and truths we live by. Am I making any sense?"

"Yes, Teddy."

"It's part of what held me together facing battle. All that I'd left in place here. Knowing I'd given you enough to start you on a good life. It's important to me, Leigh Ann." He touched the side of my face. "You don't look good. Are you ailing?"

"I have a headache. And my throat is scratchy. And I'm about starved."

He grinned. "You're going to punish me good for this, aren't you? Go on, clean up for supper."

Viola got in trouble, too.

Jon had told Teddy she'd been drinking sherry. But as despicable as that was, Viola got scolded by Teddy. And lectured. On how decent women from good families did not drink indiscriminately. Or their reputations were ruined. And no man liked a woman who drank, except at a social occasion, and then only one drink, never more.

I listened outside the door. I wanted to tell Teddy how wonderful Viola had been, how she'd worried about them, how she'd dealt with Mother when I was kidnapped, something he knew nothing about. But I dared not.

And then I waited for Viola to tell him about Jon and his wanting to "take liberties" with her. But she'd made me promise not to tell. Did Teddy know how honorable that was? What would he do if he knew about Jon?

"Then there is the matter of the book I caught Leigh

Ann reading. If you have to read such trash," he told her severely, "keep it hidden so Leigh Ann can't get at it."

I heard Viola crying, then heard Teddy say quietly, "Look, Louis and I are aware of how you held things together while we were away. We know what a strain it must have been. But in this family we do not react to strain by drinking. Life is not all peaches and cream, Viola. You're only fifteen, but best you learn it now, especially with this war. We think you did a wonderful job. Come now, give me a kiss."

Teddy always wanted kisses after he scolded. I gave them. Viola would not. I heard her running out of the room and quickly stepped down the hall. She flitted past me, sobbing.

It was the next day that Teddy received the letter from the Confederate secretary of war that put him really in the doldrums.

CHAPTER TWELVE

I WAS VACCINATED against smallpox the next morning. Teddy and Louis had the nasty business done in the army, and so Teddy had Dr. Widmar come around and do it to us.

I did not want it, but Teddy was firm. Louis held me on his lap while Dr. Widmar did the honors. It hurt and I cried and Teddy called me a sissy-boots. Viola did not cry. Teddy was watching and she would not give him the satisfaction. She was still not talking to him. Carol did not cry, either. She had slipped back into her "fussing" with Teddy now that she knew he was recovering.

They vaccinated Careen, too. She and I were given peppermint candy and told to stay quiet, so we went outside under the sweet gum trees. We talked about how she'd been right about Louis being hurt in battle when she'd thrown salt on the fire that day. I saw Jon come back with the mail from town. I was reading one of Percy Bysshe Shelley's poems to Careen when Cannice came out, calling us like the house was on fire.

"Leigh Ann! You're to come right on in, chile. Your brother is having a family meeting and he wants you now!"

They were in the study, Teddy, Louis, and Viola,

waiting for me. Carol was resting after her vaccination. It had rendered her sickly, Teddy said.

With no further ado, he made us sit and then read us the letter he'd received from the secretary of war, LeRoy P. Walker.

It was in a lot of fancy language, but in a nutshell it exempted him from further military service.

His voice shook as he read it.

His name had been dropped from the rolls of the Roswell Guards. He was needed to manage the Roswell Mill. Demands for woolen cloth for the military were increasing, and the mill must run night and day.

There was a lot of other talk about the governor's appreciation of the Conners brothers' performance on the field of battle, but now efforts were needed elsewhere.

Teddy finished reading and looked at us. "You all know who did this, don't you?"

We didn't answer.

"Mother did this," he said.

"What influence has she got with the Confederate secretary of war?" Louis asked.

"Come on, Louis. By now you should know she has influence with everybody when it pleases her. She doesn't give a tinker's damn about the mill. She's getting back at me for something." He looked at Viola. "What happened while I was away? What is it you're not telling me?"

Viola did not answer.

Teddy's jaw was set, like it got when he took me bow-and-arrow hunting and he was intent on getting his prey.

"Damn it, so I scolded you yesterday. Does that mean you won't help me when I need it?"

Louis was standing next to Teddy. "Come here, Leigh Ann," he requested.

Me. So the whole thing fell on me. I went to him.

"Why don't you tell us what happened, sweetie?" He used his best Louis voice on me. Unfair. So unfair. I looked back at Viola.

"Oh, go ahead," she said tearfully, "tell them. They can play you anytime." And she ran out of the room.

I started after her, but Louis grabbed my arm, nearly toppling off his crutches, and held me back.

And so in a hesitant voice I told them about Mother's visit.

Question after question they shot at me, dragging the story out.

How she whipped me, how she kidnapped me, where she lived, how she tied my hands and threatened to send me north, the whole sordid story. How the mayor and my family came to get me and how angry she was that she had to give me up to Teddy.

"Now I know why she's done this to me," Teddy said. "And now I'm going to pay her a visit."

Louis offered to go with Teddy.

"It's my fight," Teddy said.

"We fought together at Manassas," Louis reminded him.

And so they went off together.

When they returned, they told us nothing of what transpired in the visit. But the angels must have marked it down in their golden books that day. Not in the "win" column.

And not as a loss. But in the "debts being settled" column, which for my brothers is a win when going against my mother, anytime.

❧

IN THE END, though, there was nothing for it. Teddy had to go into the mill. He went nights, which he said was more in tune with his moods. He liked walking the eerie lamp-lit aisles. "I suppose," he told us at breakfast, "I have to accept the sound of clacking looms for gunshots and the flying lint and cotton dust for bullets and the acrid smell of oil for gunsmoke."

He always came to breakfast, to make his presence known for the day. We waited for him if he was late, because in the early morning he oversaw the "cloth and pant" goods to Marietta by wagon. From there they went by train to Atlanta.

"At least," he told us, "at night I don't have to see the children working."

He never liked the idea of children working in the mill.

All day he slept. Carol, of course, was furious with his choice to work at night. "It's pushing us further apart," she told him.

"Only if you let it," he returned.

Supper was earlier now, because he got up at five in the afternoon, and after bathing, shaving, and spending time with Carol, he was ready for the family. First, though, he saw Primus and Jon out on the back porch. Then the rest of us at the table. Who had questions? What had happened this day? Was there any trouble? Good news?

We all looked at Louis, who was hiding a smile.

"Come on, brother," Teddy urged, "what is it?"

"A group of men came 'round today," Louis told him. "Mayor Hanley is leaving for the Confederate army. They want me to be mayor."

Teddy raised his eyebrows. "Group of men? Mayor?"

Louis blushed. "All the town fathers."

"Well." Teddy stood up, glass of sherry in hand. "Let's have a toast to my brother, Mayor Louis Conners."

We got to our feet. Teddy went around to Louis's place and poured more sherry into his glass. He filled Pa's, then Carol's, then went to the other side of the table and stood over my sister. "A glass for Viola," he said. "Fetch one, Leigh Ann."

Viola stood, white-faced and stunned.

I fetched the glass.

Teddy filled it halfway, then took his place at the head of the table. His face went solemn. "These are difficult times. But Louis has shown us the way to survive and over-come, in spirit and in deeds. I propose a toast to Louis. May God always be with him."

"Hear, hear!" We shouted. I held up my glass of lemonade.

AND SO LOUIS became mayor of Roswell. He read every newspaper he could get his hands on and told us there was no more fierce fighting since Manassas, except far out in Missouri. And that Lincoln said the Confederate States "were in a state of insurrection against the United States."

"I hope Lincoln gets lots of headaches," I said at breakfast on the day Louis was sworn in as mayor.

Louis told us that some brigadier general named Grant had assumed command in southeastern Missouri. "I hope he falls off his horse and breaks his neck," I said.

"That isn't nice," Louis admonished. "We don't wish bad on others. War does its own job, Leigh Ann."

I giggled. "His arm, then? Is that all right?"

"This afternoon, after Louis's swearing in, I want you to come to the mill with me," Teddy told me quietly.

"But you have to sleep," Carol protested. "How can you take her to the mill?"

"In the army, love, I went without sleep for forty-eight hours or more."

We all attended Louis's swearing in. There was a gala luncheon at the mayor's office. And later Teddy took me gently by the hand and we went to visit the mill. I did not have the faintest idea what was going on.

❧

I HAD NEVER really visited the innards of the mill, and the first thing that hit me was how hot it was. And the noise! The clacking and the screeching and the banging and the clicking! How could any human being abide the noise? I gripped my brother's hand as he drew me down an aisle through two rows of looms that groaned as they reached hungrily back and forth like rabid beasts who would devour the little girls attending them.

I stopped and froze in my tracks. *Little girls!* Why, that's just what they were! All over the place. Some younger than I was. I clutched my brother's big warm hand with my two small cold ones and refused to go on.

He looked down at me. "Well, come on." He fair had to shout because of the noise.

I shook my head no. I planted my feet firmly on the wooden floor.

He jerked me and pulled me forward so that my arm hurt if I resisted, so I went along. Soon I was coughing, for the air was filled with some noxious fumes and floating bits of white that made me sneeze and dust that made me choke when I breathed.

He stopped in front of one loom and pointed to the little girls working at it. "Look," he said.

He made me look. I didn't want to.

The girls seemed like they had come out of a Charles Dickens novel. Their hair was long and unkempt, their faces shallow and dirty, their arms thin, their necks scrawny, their skirts with ragged hems, showing skinny legs. And they had no shoes on their soiled bare feet. But their bodies and hands moved quickly and deftly as they oiled and cleaned the machinery, took off empty bobbins and put on full ones, and removed loose threads from inside dangerous moving parts.

Teddy leaned down so he wouldn't have to shout. "Last week a little girl wasn't fast enough. She lost a finger."

I thought I was going to throw up the vanilla cream pie I'd had at Louis's celebration lunch.

"Last month another little girl had her eye injured by a flying spindle. They always lose hair in the cogs and wheels. Sometimes at the end of the day when they are tired, they get caught up in the belting."

I looked into his face. "Please take me home, Teddy."

"Not yet. They work twelve to fourteen hours a day. Sometimes we have diseases take hold in the factory. Everyone gets the measles. Or dysentery. Have you seen enough?"

"Yes." I was crying. "I can't breathe."

He picked me up and carried me out sobbing on his shoulder.

Outside he set me down. We walked by the millrace, and he pointed out the wild roses that grew along its inclining sides. It was a beautiful place, but I still felt like throwing up.

"Why did you bring me here?" I demanded. "You punished me for something. I don't even know what I did."

He looked down at me, scowling. "You're getting mean," he said, "and vengeful. Wishing headaches on Lincoln. And that General Grant should break his neck. I don't like that in you."

"They're the *enemy*. They made it so Louis could never walk right again. They shot you in the arm!"

"In early August we burned the village of Hampton, Virginia, held by the Yankees, because they were going to use it to keep runaway slaves. It's the business of war, Leigh Ann, and it gets nasty on both sides."

I had no answer for that.

"It shouldn't make our women nasty. We have to have somebody kind and forgiving and loving to come home to or we all lose."

"What do those mill girls have to do with it?"

"I wanted you to see how fortunate you are. You can know that only by seeing those less fortunate. It's your duty, being wellborn, to feel sympathy for others, to try to help their plight, to maintain the sanity, not to contribute to the madness."

It was my *duty*? I had to be kind and forgiving and loving when they came home from the war or everybody lost?

"What about *your* duty?" I flung at him. "Why don't you do something about the poor mill girls? You could, you know."

He just glared at me for a moment and I expected a rebuke for being sassy. But none came. He looked sad, instead. "It's the system," he said. "The mill system. Perhaps someday soon, Leigh Ann, I will be able to do something about it. Now do you understand why I brought you here today, what I've been trying to teach you?"

"That I have to feel sympathy for others and maintain the sanity," I said.

He nodded yes.

He expects all that from me? I felt, sometimes, as if I were insane myself.

"Do you think you can work on that for me?" he asked.

I nodded yes. And then I went over to some nearby bushes and threw up.

CHAPTER THIRTEEN

I DIDN'T WANT to go back to school in the fall, but Teddy insisted on it. We had a contest for a new name for the girls' academy. I entered my selection, the Conners Brothers Academy. My brothers found out and wrote a note withdrawing my bid, embarrassed.

In the end it was called the Bulloch Academy for Young Ladies, after the town's leading family.

It was a bitter winter. The women in our house were "doing their part" for the war. Viola and Carol joined a group who were gathering and rolling linen to be sent to the hospitals for the wounded. Carol no longer taught the mill children. With the new demands for cloth, there was no time for their schooling.

In October I told Teddy that I wanted to do something for the mill children, that I wanted to collect winter clothes for them. He approved wholeheartedly. "Careen will accompany you," he said, "and Jon will drive you about to collect clothing when Pa takes his afternoon nap."

I told him no, I didn't want Jon. He asked me why, halfway suspicious.

"Has he bothered you at all?"

I could truthfully tell him no, although Jon had put his arm on my shoulder and called me "sweetie" a few times.

I'd snapped at him and pulled away. "I'll have Careen put a hex on you," I'd told him.

He'd laughed. "She's nothing but a slave wench, and she'd better never forget it. Your pa doesn't like her. If she doesn't take care, he'll have her put in the fields."

It had frightened me.

"Has he given Viola trouble?"

"No," I lied. Viola didn't want Teddy to know. She could handle this herself, she said. So Jon drove me and Careen around town. We went house to house. As he was helping me out of the carriage at the second house, Jon put his hand on my bottom. I stomped on his foot.

"Ow! You little witch!"

"Don't you *dare* touch me! Ever!"

"Or you'll what? Tell your big brother? What will he do? Challenge me to a duel? Down where I come from I was the best in dueling. How do you think I got this bad arm? I got a shattered bone, yes, but the other fellow died. You want your brother to be the other fellow?"

Careen wanted to say something, but I hushed her. "Then I'll kill you myself," I told him. "I'll get some potion from Cannice and put it in your food."

He didn't answer. But he never put his hands on me again.

We went on, collecting clothes. The residents of Roswell thought what I was doing was wonderful. We collected shoes, stockings, warm dresses, mittens, and capes, everything.

Times I took my own horse, Trojan, and visited Louis at the mayor's office. He was always busy but welcomed me if I sat in a chair and didn't interrupt his work. I liked watching him at his desk. Sometimes he had visitors and would send me out of his office to the waiting room.

Other days he had time to talk. He told me that the rolls of the army were thinning, that men were going home to "fix things" so they could come home in the spring and find all well.

"Will the war be over in the spring, then?" I asked hopefully.

He shook his head no. "They just worry about home," he said sadly. "Many of them have farms and no one to run them. There are food shortages everywhere now. We're all starting to feel the Yankee blockade of our ports. And the army demands a lot of our crops."

As mayor, Louis did not just marry people and do ribbon cuttings. He began to help the wives of mill workers who had died in the war with their applications for Confederate pensions. They soon began to come to him for everything.

But deep inside, my brother Louis was still hoping to return to the field.

We had Christmas. I went with Teddy to cut and bring home a tree, and Viola and I decorated the front parlor with holly and mistletoe and berries of scarlet. We dressed the dining room with red ribbons and garlands and small Confederate flags. We hung stockings on the fireplace, which were to be filled with fruit, and we made hoarhound candy and taffy to put in them. We decorated the tree with a hundred candles in little colored tin candlesticks. And some old and very cunning toys.

I had made, with the help of Viola, a shirt for both Louis and Teddy. Viola gave them each a package of the new Bull Durham cigarettes and a pair of soft leather gloves. Cannice prepared a true Christmas turkey, cranberry sauce, vegetables, candied sweet potatoes, puddings, cake, and such.

I gave Viola muslin handkerchiefs trimmed with lace I had made myself. She needed them. She was always crying over Johnnie, who had not been home since before Manassas.

Teddy gave me two new dresses, one pink and one blue. He and Louis must have put their heads together, because Louis gave me a pair of patent leather boots, two pair of ruffled pantalets, and two petticoats. I needed them. My brothers knew that women's boots were fifteen dollars a pair now, dresses thirty dollars each, and fabric eight dollars a yard.

CHAPTER FOURTEEN

January 1862

IN JANUARY a French national arrived in Roswell. His name was Theophile Roche. He went to work in the mill as a weaver. He had no wife, no family. He was in his late twenties and was well built and handsome. He boarded in a small single-story cottage at 51 Mill Street on the ridge known as Factory Hill. He preferred to live alone, he told Teddy. There was, at the onset, something mysterious about him. The whole town thought so, and his arrival started a series of gossip and imaginings.

The women of the town took turns bringing him cooked food. He never went hungry. A lot of people invited him for Sunday dinner. He always declined.

My schoolmates swooned over him and gathered around whichever girl claimed to have seen him on the street to conjecture over who he'd been back in France.

"A pirate in hiding," Angela Tarberry said.

"A runaway poet with a wife and ten children at home," from Mary Beth Codgell.

"A prince in exile," said Rosemary Brown.

A group of us left school together one February afternoon and, by previous agreement, headed right to 51 Mill Street on Factory Hill. Once we got there we didn't know what we wanted to do, or why we had come. Just to *see* the place where the pirate-in-hiding-runaway-poet-prince-in-exile lived.

Like all the others it was a small, plain cottage. We peeked in the windows. We walked around the back. We tried the back door, and to our surprise, it opened. And before we knew it we were inside the cottage, where we did not plan to be, standing on the bare plank floor in front of the hearth that held no fire. There was a single bed in front of the hearth.

"He must sleep here at night," Rosemary Brown said. "For warmth. Oh, picture a prince in exile in a place like this."

There was a small table with a single bowl of fruit on it. "Fruit in *winter,*" exclaimed Mary Beth Codgell. "Someone sent it to him from Italy."

We were busying ourselves looking around when the back door opened and a woman came in, wiping her hands on her apron. "I'm the next-door neighbor," she said. "What are you girls doing here?"

She said it sternly. No nonsense.

"We were just walking by," Angela Tarberry told her, "when we saw a rat scampering back here. And we came to chase it. The wind blew the door open and the rat came in and we came in to shoo it out. We don't even know who lives here."

Oh, she was a good liar. I wished I could lie as expertly as she.

The neighbor woman was not stupid. "You all are prying about Mr. Roche's place. You all aren't the first fancy-pants girls to do it. And you all know full well he lives here.

It's called treading on private property. But you all have done worse. It's called breaking and entering, and it's against the law."

We looked at one another in dismay.

We'd broken the law!

She looked at me. "You there, in the blue cape. Aren't you the mayor's sister?"

"No," I lied, "you're mistaken. I'm not the mayor's sister."

"You certainly are. I saw you there in his office one day. Well, I'm going to report you all to the mayor's office. Come with me. I want you to write down your names."

There was nothing said by anyone when I got home that day. Supper went on in the usual pleasant way. And afterward I was not summoned by either Louis or Teddy but left to my own terrible imaginings. The next morning, however, a courier brought a summons, a *summons,* to Teddy at breakfast.

"It's from the mayor's office," Teddy said quietly, after reading it. He had no expression on his face. He did not look at me.

Louis wore no expression, either. He just quietly sipped his coffee and delicately wiped his face with his white linen napkin.

"You've apparently gotten into some trouble, sweetie." Now Teddy looked at me mildly. "And your brother Louis is summoning you and your other friends and their parents to his office this afternoon at three thirty. It seems you all have broken some law."

"Teddy, we just . . ."

He held up his hand. "This is not between us this time. This is between you and" — he gestured to Louis — "the mayor. This is official business. And he will handle it. And you'll do whatever he says. Now breaking and entering . . ." He shook his head. "A serious business."

I felt sick. I glanced at Louis, but he did not look at me. Nor did he and Teddy look at each other. *This is all planned*, I told myself. *Teddy knew about this before the summons came, or else he'd be climbing the walls by now. They have combined forces, like they did at Manassas, and they won there, didn't they?*

So, what do I do now? Carol and Viola were looking at me. Pa . . . well, Pa was in his own world, enjoying his breakfast. I bit my bottom lip. Which of them to appeal to?

I got out of my chair and stood next to Teddy. "Please, can't we settle it here?"

"I'm afraid not. This involves the law. Louis has to do his job."

"What did the child do?" As he did at crucial times, Pa came out of his private world to join ours. "What must she face up to? Did she steal something?"

"She didn't steal, Pa," Teddy assured him.

"If she didn't steal, leave her be," he mumbled. "She's just a child. You and Louis got into plenty of trouble when you were children. I never whipped you. Don't you dare whip her. Indians don't whip their children."

"Nobody's going to whip her, Pa," Teddy said. "We never whip her."

Pa settled down. "Indians never whip their children," he kept mumbling. But he settled down and went back into his world again.

"Will you come with me?" I asked Teddy.

"No, I think you can handle this alone. Louis is your brother, remember."

"Suppose he sends me to jail?"

Teddy worked hard to hide a smile. "Then you go to jail."

I looked at Louis at the other end of the table. He was busy eating, perfectly becalmed. I left Teddy and summoned all my courage to go and stand next to Louis.

"Louis," I said.

"Yes, sweetie." He took a sip of coffee and set his cup down.

"What are you going to do to me?"

"Same as I do to the other girls."

"What will that be?"

"The law requires punishment. But you all are still underage, so you won't have to go to Marietta for trial."

I felt as if I were going to faint. I gripped the table.

"So, it is up to my discretion. Whatever I decide is necessary."

I looked into his eyes for the warmth of kindness that was usually there, and found it. He reached out a hand and touched the side of my face.

"You're shivering," he said. "Now listen here. This will not do when you come to my office. This is a bad state of affairs and I hate it as much as you. Still, there's nothing for it but that we get through it. We're dear friends, Leigh Ann, but I am bitterly disappointed in you. Still, that's personal, between us, and it won't affect any decision I make today."

Tears came down my face.

He wiped them with his napkin. "Now, now, we haven't time for that. What's done is done. You have distressed me, yes, but I've forgiven you. What concerns me now is this afternoon. Everyone is going to be scrutinizing my actions because my little sister is one of the offenders. And they'll be watching your behavior. I expect you to be strong and brave and respectful. You've done wrong and you're there to face up to it. Can you do that for me and make me proud?"

I drew myself up. I told him yes, I could.

He looked at Teddy. "All the other parents will be present," he said.

"All right," Teddy said. "I'll be there to give you both moral support, but I must get to sleep now." He excused himself and went upstairs, Carol with him. Louis left for work. Pa was still eating. He did eat tremendous amounts of food, my pa. And he was still mumbling.

"Indians never whip their children. I won't have anyone whipping that child."

CHAPTER FIFTEEN

TEDDY CAME to Louis's office with me and stood with me through the whole session. There were a lot of arguments from the parents of the other girls, especially when Louis imposed his sentence on us.

"I hereby order that each girl serve, every Saturday for the next two months, at the home of an elderly woman who needs help. Either by reading to them, writing letters, having a midday meal with them, or being a companion to them in some way. From the hours of ten in the morning to four in the afternoon. Each girl will be assigned to her woman. By doing this we can hope they will learn compassion and consideration for others, which seem to be lacking in their present makeup."

There was a considerable uproar in the room at that pronouncement. But the parents eventually accepted it and left. After they went out, Louis looked at me.

"I've got more in mind for you," he said. "I want you to bake a cake for Mr. Roche. Then you and I are going to pay him a visit. And you are going to apologize."

"Why must I when the other girls don't have to?"

"Because I said so," he told me mildly.

I didn't protest. He didn't expect me to.

I baked the cake for Theophile Roche that evening. I made my favorite, pound cake with vanilla icing.

Louis came into the kitchen.

"Your elderly lady is Mrs. Stapleton. She lives across town. Tomorrow is Saturday, but your assignment doesn't start until next week. So we'll take the cake to Mr. Roche tomorrow morning. Be ready."

"I can ride my horse to Mrs. Stapleton's," I said.

"No. Teddy and I don't want you coming home in near dark. It's winter, remember. Jon will take and fetch you."

I made a face. "Does it have to be Jon?"

He eyed me wisely. "Teddy says you don't like him. Is there a reason?"

I couldn't lie to Louis. With his Indian powers he saw through lies.

"He touched me."

"Where?"

I blushed. "On my bottom."

Louis's eyes got red flames in them that I'd never seen before. "I'll give him a sound beating."

"No, no. It's why I never told Teddy. Please, Louis, if you love me, please listen before you beat him."

"What is there to listen to?" But he listened.

"I know Teddy would duel him. But in Florida, where Jon comes from, he's the best duelist there is."

"How do you know?"

"He told me and —"

"He *told* you?"

"Yes. He said he dueled and killed three people there. And that's how he got his bad arm. And that's why I wouldn't tell Teddy about it, because I knew Teddy would duel him and he'd kill Teddy. So I told him if he touched me again I'd get a bad root from Cannice and poison his food. And I will if I have to."

"He's lying. He isn't a gentleman. Only gentlemen of honor duel. And Teddy wouldn't stoop to duel him. And neither will I. But to protect your honor I must give him a sound whipping."

"Oh, Louis!"

He swore. My brother took the Lord's name in vain. Twice. He said, "I'm sorry, little sister mine, that you have to put up with all this. He'll never touch you again when I get through with him."

He held me to him. He kissed the top of my head and prayed right there in the kitchen that God would wash him thoroughly from his wickedness and cleanse him from his sins. He acknowledged that his sins were forever before him.

What sins does he have? He was the most sinless person I knew.

I had never seen or heard Louis pray before. He never spoke about God. I was so touched by his reverence and humility that I was afraid to interrupt him. When he finished I looked up at him. "Those are the words Mother made me memorize when she kidnapped me."

He tweaked my nose. He kissed me. "Check the cake. It must be done. Then go to bed. I have an affair of honor to attend to."

After I iced the cake I went to bed, but before that, I peeked out the upstairs hall window in back of the house just in time to see Louis attending to his affair of honor.

He was dragging Jon by one arm out to the barn. Primus had the other arm. *Of course,* I thought. Louis could not do this without help. He walked without crutches now, but he still limped, and in a fracas he would lose his balance. I watched as they brought a struggling Jon into the barn. Then I went to bed.

Jon was not at the breakfast table serving Pa the next morning. Teddy did not ask why. Viola did.

"He's got the measles," Teddy told her. "He's recuperating in the groom's room in the barn. Stay away from him. Primus's wife, Eulah, is caring for him."

We took the cake to Mr. Roche's.

In the carriage, which was driven by Primus, Louis said that he had something to tell me.

"The truth of the matter is that Teddy has been wanting to invite Theophile Roche to dinner," he said, "but he has not found the man approachable."

"Why does he want to invite him to dinner?"

It was then that Louis told me, swearing me to secrecy. "Teddy 'imported' Theophile Roche for a special reason. Not to be a weaver at the mill. But to help out if and when the Yankees come, because Roche is a French national.

Teddy has plans for him. That's all you need to know now. But what you and your friends did has made Roche less approachable. This morning you and I are supposed to help mend things."

I nodded. "Should I invite him?"

"Depends on how he receives you. I'll give you a signal if I think so."

Louis was holding the cake, but he gave it to me when we got out of the carriage. When he knocked at the front door it was answered immediately, and when it opened, Louis said, *"Enfin nous sommes arrivés!"* That meant, as he told me later, "Finally we have arrived."

Louis knew French. I wished I did. Louis introduced me immediately as his sister and one of the girls who had broken into his home. And I was here now to apologize.

I curtsied. And told Mr. Roche I was sorry, that I knew I had done wrong. I handed him the cake, prettily wrapped and tied with a ribbon.

He set it down and stared at me. At first I thought he was going to send me from the house. But he took my hand and kissed it and said, "Oh, my sweet."

He took our wraps. He made us sit on the one couch in the room and offered Louis some French wine and made me a cup of tea. He sliced the cake and served it on plates that looked as if they had come from France. He gave us delicate napkins that were embroidered with his initials.

He was dressed in regular trousers, suspenders, and boots, but his shirt was of the whitest cotton, with ruffles at the wrists and the neck. I could see how broad his shoulders were. And how strong his neck muscles.

On the wall hung a sword in a scabbard. A sword for dueling. I stared. Louis nudged me.

"Do you like it here in America?" Louis was asking him.

"Ah, yes. So much land."

Then he fell silent.

"Well, I hope you'll accept my apology, too, for what my sister did," Louis said.

"Of course, of course." Mr. Roche shrugged. "I do not press charges. Children." More shrugging. "The cake." He put his fingers to his mouth and made a kissing gesture. "It is delicious. Tell your cook I send my compliments."

"She's right here," Louis told him. "Leigh Ann made it."

"Ah!" He raised his eyebrows in surprise. "That you should have such a sister! And so pretty, too. Do you take exception that I say it?"

"No, don't mind at all," Louis said.

Mr. Roche nodded wisely, all the time looking at me.

Louis nudged me and I knew it was the signal.

"Mr. Roche," I said quietly, and with dignity, "my other brother, Teddy, who is night manager of the mill, wants us to invite you to our house for dinner some Sunday in March. Would you like to come?"

"Mr. Teddy," he mused. "Yes, I know him. He hired me. A good man. A good man. I would be honored to come. What is the day and the time?"

"My brother Teddy will work that out with you. It will be at your convenience," Louis said.

When we left, with Louis's permission, Mr. Roche gave me a book, Jane Austen's *Pride and Prejudice.*

And so it was that I met Mr. Theophile Roche, who was to play an important role in trying to save our mill when the Yankees came. And whom, as it turned out, I helped, trying to save it.

CHAPTER SIXTEEN

I DID NOT pay much mind to what was going on with the war. But I did listen around the edges of my brothers' conversations at the table. I came away with some sense of the madness.

In Tennessee it was ten above zero when the fighting was going on and the Yankees took Fort Donelson away from us. *Ten above zero!* How could you even hold a rifle in cold like that?

Twelve-year-old Willie Lincoln died in the White House and they say Mr. Lincoln cried and it took all the joy of winning Fort Donelson away from him. I wondered, *Would he give it back to us if he could have Willie returned to him again?*

The Yankees were doing things on our rivers — the Tennessee, the Cumberland, and the Mississippi — that were not nice. My brothers did not elaborate about what they were doing.

The Virginia House of Delegates wanted to enroll free negroes to fight in the Confederate army. I knew of only two free negroes, and they worked as janitors in the mill. I wagered they'd like to have Primus. Bonded or not, he could whip several Yankees with one hand tied behind his back.

IN FEBRUARY, Governor Joseph Brown must have woken up at night unable to sleep. His wife must have asked him what the matter was.

"Georgia needs twelve more regiments before the fifteenth of March," he likely told her. Because that's what he told the state of Georgia.

Georgia raised thirteen regiments and three battalions by the fifteenth of March.

My brother Louis organized the Roswell Battalion. His ankle still bothered him and he could not mount a horse without help, but he trained them every day.

"I hope you're not planning on going back to the field," Teddy said.

Louis did not answer.

"Some Yankee will pick you off just trying to mount your horse." It was cruel of Teddy, but Teddy could be cruel when he had to be. He had a talent for it.

Louis *had* been planning on it. His men of the Roswell Battalion talked him out of it. The town fathers talked him out of it. Governor Brown wrote him a letter and ordered him out of it. Pa came out of his other world and mumbled him out of it.

Camille got him in the back parlor and kissed him and whispered him out of it.

He and Primus spent an afternoon talking in the barn. In the end, he didn't go, but he spent a lot of time alone. One cold night we couldn't find him, so I went out looking for him with Teddy. There he was, down by the stream.

He had built a small fire. Four long logs jutted out on each side and in the middle of these were smaller pieces of wood. Cooking in the center were pieces of venison. A great deal of smoke curled up overhead.

His only clothing was a leather breechclout to cover his private parts. His legs, folded under him, were bare, as was his chest. Around his neck he wore a large silver medallion. He huddled in an old gray blanket. His hair was wet, as if he had just come out of the stream. He was moving his lips, praying.

And on his shoulder was a hooty owl. It stared at us out of yellow-green eyes. But it never moved.

I became frightened and moved closer to Teddy, who put a protective arm around my shoulder and said, "Don't be afraid."

But I was. This was my beloved Louis, my darling brother, whom I looked up to so. Had he gone mad? I looked up at Teddy.

"Eh, Louis," he said, "you going to include us in your prayers?"

Louis nodded yes. He had heard.

"Look at that," Teddy told me. "There's wind around us. But none around him."

It was true. The bitter February wind that whipped around us stopped in the line bounding Louis. My mouth fell open. Teddy grinned down at me.

"Damn, that venison smells good," he said.

That Teddy was taking this all so lightly made me feel better.

"Is he going to stay here all night?" I asked.

"He better not. Or I'll have Primus fetch him in. Well, good night now, brother. I've got to get to the mill. Can I trust you to tell the Indian powers good night and come in soon to see to the safety of our women?"

Louis looked at us placidly, first at Teddy, then at me. "Go in peace," he said. It was in his regular Louis voice.

We turned and left. I felt a sense of peace come over me, as if everything was going to be all right and I would never have to worry again.

❧

THE ELDERLY LADY I was assigned to by Louis, Mrs. Stapleton, lived alone with a sixteen-year-old grandson. But I never met him. Yet for the first three Saturdays, when I was writing letters to her sister in England, stirring the soup her negro servant had made, and having lunch with her, all she did was talk about him.

It was James this and it was James that.

"I raised him since he was a knee-baby."

And, "He looks just like his father."

And, "His father was killed in a terrible fight in Dranesville, Virginia, on the twentieth of December. Right before Christmas. I haven't been able to get that boy to go to church since."

And, "His mother died when he was a child."

And, "He loves me so, that boy. He couldn't love me more if I were his mother."

Then why, I wondered, *is he never around?* But I did not ask.

She told me anyway. "He is fading away into nothing. He wanted to join the Roswell Troopers. I had to let him. But they discharged him because he is too young. Now he stays away from home a good deal. I don't know where he goes. Someone told me he goes to the town square to watch the young men drill. But after that, where? I hope he isn't falling in with bad company. Sometimes he doesn't even come home for supper. Oh, I am so worried about him."

She fell silent. We were in her solarium and she was knitting him a muffler. Gray. Then she said to me, "Leigh Ann, I would ask a favor of you, child."

"Yes, ma'am."

"If you would just do this one thing for me. Your brother Louis is the commander of the Roswell Battalion, is he not?"

"Yes, ma'am."

She leaned forward and put a hand on my knee. "Leigh Ann, would you ask him if he would please take my James in his battalion? At least ask him if I may send my James around to see him about it. When he meets James I just know he will take him."

"But, ma'am, I don't understand. You lost your son. Aren't you afraid you'll lose James, too?"

A look of peaceful understanding came over her face.

"Oh, child, I've already lost my James. There is more than one way to lose people. If he could go away and fight, at least I know I will find him again. Or at least he'll find himself. And I don't want him to think he has to stay home for an old lady like me."

I hugged her. I told her I would ask Louis. And I did.

⁂

LOUIS LISTENED SOLEMNLY to me about James Stapleton. We lingered over the supper table one night to talk. And I poured out the story of James.

He understood. I saw it in his face. He understood James's need to go to war. James had an ally in my brother Louis.

"Send him to me, here, tomorrow night at eight," he said.

I sent a note around to Mrs. Stapleton.

⁂

AT EIGHT PRECISELY, James knocked on our front door. Careen let him in. She curtsied to him and showed him in to the library, where Louis waited. I was standing in the doorway of the front parlor where I could get a glimpse of him.

He was tall and thin, but someday he would grow into those shoulders just as my brothers had into theirs, and when he did I wanted to be around.

He had a shock of dark brown hair and a well-shaped,

pleasant face, and he stood straight and tall. He nodded graciously at Careen, stopped at seeing me, and bowed, then did something that near broke my heart.

He saluted me, a perfect salute.

I curtsied. And in that brief moment all eternity stopped and I fell in love with this young man.

Louis appeared in the doorway of the library just in time to see this exchange, to see us staring at each other. Just in time to understand what was happening.

"Are you coming in, young man?" he asked.

"Yes, sir." But still James stared at me.

"Is this how you obey orders? Allow yourself to be distracted by a pretty girl?"

James collected himself and went into the library. The door closed behind them.

They were in there a good hour. I stood in the doorway of the front parlor that long. Careen came to me.

"Doan make it so obvious," she told me. "He comes out an' sees you here, he'll know you fancy him from the get-go."

"I don't care," I said. "I've never seen anyone so beautiful. You've been in there. Tell me, what's going on?"

"I just brung them some coffee and cakes. Your brother, he stop talkin' when I come in. You know how they do. But I see he give that young man some rum. Suppose he wanna see how much of a man he be. That James, he come from a good family. That Stapleton family, they go way back. My mama, she know the lady what take care of Mrs. Stapleton."

"I don't care if they're nobody."

"You oughta sit down before you fall down. I gonna get you a cuppa tea."

Careen was my age, but she was physically more mature. She no longer ran around getting into mischief with me. She had a respectable bosom already, at twelve, and had gotten her woman's time of the month. She was now chief house-girl, which meant she answered the doors, showed people in, introduced them to my brothers and Viola, delivered notes and mail, saw to it that visitors' rooms were properly readied, and carried out myriad other responsibilities.

With all this, of course, came the "right" to scold the lot of us on occasion. Lovingly, of course.

She brought me tea and stood over me while I sipped it. "Your brother, he introduce you proper-like," she told me.

"How do you know?"

"'Cause he be a proper-like gentleman. An' when he call you, you doan run. You come on out slow-like, makin' like you couldn't care a fig's worth."

She was right. After another agonizing fifteen minutes, when the door of that library finally opened and they came out and shook hands, Louis called my name.

I came out of the parlor, slow. Like I couldn't care a fig's worth.

"This is my little sister, Leigh Ann," Louis said. "Leigh Ann, this is James Stapleton, the newest member of the Roswell Battalion."

First, respectfully, I hugged Louis and thanked him. James stepped aside.

Then James bowed. I curtsied. He took my hand and kissed it. "Captain Conners," he asked, "may I have the honor of writing to your sister while I am away at war?"

I saw my brother's face. No expression. "Of course," he said, "but I think you ought to also ask my brother, Teddy. He's really her guardian."

"Yes, sir. I will."

Careen was waiting to open the door. I looked at Louis. He glanced at me speculatively, but I went ahead and did what I wanted to do, anyway.

I stood on tiptoe and kissed James on the cheek. "Good luck," I said.

That's all it was. A good luck kiss. Careen rolled her eyes. James left. The door closed behind him.

Louis said nothing except, "I think you ought to go to bed now."

"It's still early."

"I really think you ought to go to bed. Or else I'm going to have to give you a lecture about how to behave with boys. And I really don't feel like it."

CHAPTER SEVENTEEN

M R. ROCHE came to dinner on March ninth, the day of the battle of the Yankee *Monitor* against our *Merrimack,* two ironclad gunboats in Hampton Roads, Virginia.

Teddy had received word of the battle by telegraph, and after dinner he sent Jon down to the telegraph office for the results of the battle.

It was a draw.

I couldn't see why everyone was so worried about two boats, clad in iron, fighting each other. Our armies had taken so many losses lately, all over the place, and we had so many men killed. It looked as if we were losing. My brothers went around grim-faced and sharp-tongued. I stayed out of their way and dared not sass them.

Viola, of course, was in a state of controlled hysteria. The last she'd heard, her Johnnie was with Van Dorn, the commander headed toward Arkansas and Pea Ridge. She'd had no letter yet saying if Johnnie was dead or alive.

Then our brave old Confederate Congress passed a measure saying that authorities should destroy cotton, tobacco, and other property before they fell into enemy hands.

Needless to say, the dinner was a quiet business. Mr. Roche did not even gush over me. And it was concluded quickly, after which Pa, who'd come out of his reverie, and Louis and Teddy went into the library with Mr. Roche. He left soon after.

Louis brought an end to my sentence at the Stapleton house. He didn't want me there, he said, possibly unchaperoned, with James. He would take no buts.

"You haven't got the sense of a guinea hen when it comes to boys, sweetie," he said. He also said that he would personally educate me.

James approached Teddy outside the mill one morning and asked permission to write to me. Teddy came home to glare at me and Louis.

"Who in hell is this boy? He's sixteen? And he wants to write to my sister?"

Louis explained it to him and Teddy gave permission. James left for war with the Roswell Battalion, and we all settled down again. I continued to go and visit Mrs. Stapleton on my own time, at least once a week. We had become friends, and we compared letters from James. By the beginning of April he wrote me from southeast of Richmond, at Yorktown, where he and fifteen thousand other Confederates were holding the line against the Yankee general McClellan.

Viola finally received a letter from Johnnie. He had been wounded at Pea Ridge and he was in a makeshift hospital in Arkansas. She read the letter to us at the supper table.

My arm is shot up, but I am in fine fettle and am being cared for by some wonderful women. They are giving me a lot of beef tea, which is a heap better than the terrible chemical mixture some of the other fellows are being made to swallow. And I am fortunate, love. My frame is not wasted, nor are my vital energies. We have Yankees here, too. But somehow, it doesn't matter when they are lying half dead in the bed next to you. The man next to me was from Maryland, Richard Hammond Key, grandson of Francis Scott Key, who wrote "The Star-Spangled Banner." He had the same pale face and bloodless lips of all who are about to die. Hoping that he would not, they nursed him around the clock and plied him with good brandy. The third day of all this, he gave me trinkets to send to his family and a special button he had made for me. He begged the nurses to bury him apart from others so his family might find him, and then he quietly slipped away. Oh, love, I will not. I promise you. I will come home to you. Even if it's only as far as Richmond, where they are sending me soon, to a hospital. Pray for me. Your beloved, Johnnie.

Viola wept. She got up and made as if to leave the room. Teddy stopped her, went to her, and gathered her in his arms. Together they walked across the hall to the library, where he closed the door. They both missed supper, but they were back for dessert and Viola was smiling.

When Johnnie was shipped to the hospital in Richmond, Viola would be allowed to go and visit him, he told us, providing she was properly chaperoned.

Cannice would go with her. Careen, well taught by her mother, would do the cooking.

I stared at Teddy, my mouth open. He looked sternly back at me, daring me to say a word. I didn't.

WE HAD SOME food shortages.

We were getting short of salt, coffee, tea, sugar, molasses, and bicarbonate of soda for raising bread. All, of course, because of the Yankee blockade.

I don't know what we would have done without Anne Smith, Camille's mother. Since they not only lived in that spacious farmhouse but farmed, they knew the means of survival.

"The ashes of corncobs have the alkaline needed for raising dough," she told us.

Coffee was thirty dollars a pound. "The seeds of the okra plant, nicely browned, for coffee," she advised. "For tea, use raspberry leaves. If you run out of kerosene, the oil of cotton seed and ground pease, together with the oil of compressed lard, will do. Any more questions?"

"Has Louis asked Camille to marry him yet?" I asked.

"Leigh Ann, that's none of your affair!" Viola gripped my shoulder.

"It's all right," Anne Smith said. "I'm hoping, too."

Primus knew how to get salt, for now. I watched him pour hot water over the smooth oak planks inside the little house where the beef and pork were salted. Out in the sun a white foam bubbled on their surface; then the water disappeared and a white sand dried into salt.

For medicines, also in short supply, we depended on Cannice. She showed me and Careen her secrets.

I learned how to gather the berries of the dogwood tree. They had the properties to make quinine for pain. The bark of the tree was used for chills and agues. We dug up blackberry roots to make a soothing cordial for dysentery. The leaves and roots of the mullein plant, globe flower, and wild cherry tree bark, smashed and cooked and mixed together, made a syrup for coughs.

Jon came upon me one day while I was out gathering roots. After Louis gave him that beating, Teddy gave him a choice. He could leave, or stay and behave himself. He stayed. Simply because he had no place else to go. But he was ever so sullen.

"It was because of you I got that beating," he said.

We were alone. Careen had gone into the house with her mother to cook supper.

"It is a Southern gentleman's duty to protect his sister's honor," I said.

"I'm watching you. Always. First thing you do against your brothers' wishes, I'm going to inform them."

I said nothing.

"You'll be sorry you ever informed on me."
I went on digging up blackberry roots. He left.

❧

VIOLA AND CANNICE left for Richmond on the seventh of
April to visit Johnnie in the hospital there.

"Best go now," Teddy advised, "before the Yankees close
in on it."

The Yankees were in Yorktown, Virginia, where James
had been. And on the Tennessee River. And in Laurel Valley, North Carolina. Not to mention St. Andrew's Bay,
Florida, and Medicine Creek, Missouri. And, it seemed,
everywhere.

So Cannice and Viola left. And Careen, my friend
who used to light torches and help me smoke snakes out
of a pile of rocks down by the stream, did the cooking.
And oh, she did a fine job of it. Her mother had taught
her well.

Teddy and Louis were well pleased. Pa did not even
know the difference. And fussy, uppity Carol approved,
heartily, though she had never approved of Careen herself.

In the middle of all this change going on, Louis found
time to educate me about "how to behave with boys."

I had already received four letters from James. Unlike
Viola, I had kept them all to myself. They were in my room,
tied with a pink ribbon, the way all the heroines in French
novels kept letters from their lovers.

We sat in the library, Louis and I. It was after supper. He tried to appear placid. He sipped some rum.

"You've received letters from James, I hear," he said.

"How do you know?"

"Jon picks up the mail. He said one of the letters fell open one day and he read it. He said maybe Teddy or I should read it."

"Oh, *damn* Jon! He opened my letter!"

"Eh, eh, language. *Watch the language!*"

But I was fuming. "You're going to let him open our mail?"

"That matter has been taken care of. May I see the letters?" And when I didn't answer: "Go and get me the letters, please."

I went upstairs and brought them down to him and sat there blushing inside while he read them with no expression on his face. He would, of course, read what James wrote in closing. *All my love* — not *fondly,* or *until we meet again,* but *all my love.*

Then he smiled. "This is pretty good," he said. "Our Major General Magruder using logs painted black to resemble cannon to create the impression of more strength. We call them Quaker guns." He looked up at me to see if I was enjoying the humor of it.

I did not enjoy the humor of it. There were tears in my eyes.

He set the letters aside. "Look, sweetie, I know it hurts, but I have to do this."

"Why?"

"We can't let Teddy do it. He'd forbid you ever to write to James again. Now this is just what I'm concerned with. He shouldn't be writing *all my love* to you. You are only twelve years old. He should know better. But it isn't all his fault. You led him on."

I stared at him angrily.

"Go on, you can hate me. I can take it. But you have to know. You don't kiss a boy, *not even on his cheek,* not the first time you meet him, not the sixth or seventh, or eighth time you're together. A girl never initiates intimacy. It gives a young man ideas. You gave him ideas the day you kissed him."

"What kind of ideas?"

Louis groaned. "Oh, God. Don't you know about boys at all? I thought you said you knew all about how and why women gave men babies?"

"What has that got to do with me kissing James on the cheek?"

So he told me. About boys and how they become aroused. I got embarrassed, but he didn't care. "That kiss was a sign," he said. "It is not fair to give such encouragement to a boy unless you are willing to carry through with it. Do you know what I mean by 'carry through with it'?"

Oh, sweet God in heaven, will he never stop?

He sighed. "It means to let him go further," he said. "Much further. And touch you in other ways."

Please don't let him tell me the ways!

"Now, a young man of honor cannot act upon his impulses, but once aroused must suffer instead. And when a girl acts like that she is known as a 'tease' and there is nothing worse to be known as among boys than a tease.

"Word gets around. Fast. And young men will stay away from you. And if it ever gets back to me that my sister is a tease, well . . ." He paused. "Don't ever do that to me, Leigh Ann," he said with great sadness. "Just don't ever do that to me. Please, sweetie."

I said that no, I wouldn't.

There was silence from him for a moment while he contemplated the whole of it.

It was all he could do and he knew it. The talk was over, thank God and His angels. He picked up my letters and asked my permission to burn them in the fireplace. Tears came into my eyes again.

"If Teddy ever sees these . . ." he said, shaking his head sadly.

Tears came down my face.

"I hate conspiring against Teddy," he said. "But in this case I'm helping him. And you. Don't think I'm ever going to do it again." He handed the letters to me. "Next time you take your punishment from Teddy. In full."

Could it be any worse than this?

I stepped forward and put the letters in the fire. They made a pretty blue flame.

Then he told me he was going to write to James and say how proud he was of him and ask him, kindly, not to call his sister "my love" in his letters. To remember that she was only twelve years old. And the friendship between them was just that, friendship.

I left him there in the library, writing the letter. Just as I got to the door he called after me. "It could be worse, you know. I could ask to see the letters you write to him before they are mailed off."

I stopped dead in my tracks and looked back at him. He was smiling innocently, his eyes twinkling. He winked at me. I ran off.

CHAPTER EIGHTEEN

V IOLA AND CANNICE came home on the twenty-third
of April.

The moment I saw Viola I knew something was wrong
with her.

Or, at the least, something different.

Her face had a faint flush, like a fever was coming on.
Didn't Teddy see it? He always saw such signs.

Her eyes had a distant look in them, as if she'd left part
of herself back there in Richmond. *But of course she has,
fool,* I told myself.

But no, it was more than that.

I stood back as Teddy took her face in his two hands
and kissed her. Then watched Louis hug and kiss her, then
Camille and Carol. I kissed her and grinned.

"How's my daughter's cookin' been?" Cannice asked.

There were murmurs of approval — no, of praise. We
moved to the carriage. I walked close to Viola. "You look
different," I whispered.

She tossed her head and held her chin high. "Do I?
Well, you haven't seen me happy in a long time."

All through the welcome-home supper I watched her.
She scarce ate. She played with her food. Now Teddy took
notice.

"You're thinner, Viola," he said. "No food in Richmond? Or does love not need food?"

He was teasing her. She blushed painfully. He drew back, noticing that, too. "You look tired," he said. "We'll leave you alone tonight, but tomorrow you must tell us all about conditions in Richmond."

When she said she was retiring early, Teddy told me to leave her be, not to be a pest to her. But before she went upstairs I saw my sister in a confab with Cannice in the hall just outside the kitchen.

"You gots to tell Teddy," Cannice was saying in a loud whisper.

"Why?"

"'Cause he be head o' the family, thas why. He be responsible for you. Jus' like he be for Leigh Ann."

"I'm seventeen, Cannice."

"You still be under his authority. Your pa make it that way. An' Teddy, he made me responsible for you when we were gone. So I duty-bound to tell him if'n you don't."

"You're going to tell on me? Is that what you're saying, Cannice? There will be hell to pay if you tell on me. Because I did it without Teddy's permission."

Silence for a minute. *What has she done? What has my sister done?*

I heard the heavy breathing of Cannice, saw her put her hand on Viola's arm. "No, honey, I ain't gonna tell on you. I don't do that. I keep all kinds of secrets in this here bosom for all of you chillens in this family. But I'm countin' on you tellin' him before long. Now go along to bed. Go on."

I hid in a corner so Viola couldn't see me as she went through the hall and up the stairs to her room. Soon afterward I followed.

She was lying in bed in her silk wrapper, on her side, propped up on pillows and reading a book by the light of candles. I opened the door a crack.

"Come on in," she invited.

"Teddy said I'm not to bother you."

"Oh"— she waved a hand disdainfully —"posh Teddy."

All right, posh Teddy. I went in and climbed up on the bed next to her. She smiled at me and I saw a secret in her eyes, a secret she was bursting to tell me. We had shared so many secrets in the past.

"What have you done?" I asked.

She smoothed my hair back off my face. Teddy and Louis often did this, but nobody could do it like Viola. "If you tell anybody, if it gets out to Teddy, I'm going to be disowned, nothing less," she told me.

I shook my head no, vigorously. I crossed my heart. "I would never betray you, Viola."

"You're so loyal to Teddy. He sweet-talks you. So does Louis."

"Never," I promised. "Hope to die. Teddy can put me in that chair for two days and I won't tell."

She smiled. "I'm married," she said, "to Johnnie Cummack."

I sat up straight. Did she say *married?* The word flew around me like a white dove beating its wings until I accepted it, and then it settled down in some small corner of my brain.

"How did that happen?" I asked.

"It's wartime," she told me. "In Richmond it isn't like here. You know it's wartime in Richmond. Trains do not run on time, and when they do they are full of wounded and dying soldiers. There are so many hospitals full of wounded and dying soldiers. Death is everywhere. And so are women nurses, working themselves to death and getting no credit for it. All the dying men want are two things. Whiskey and that last letter written for them. While Johnnie was sleeping, I wrote many letters and fetched lots of cups of whiskey and saw a lot of men die.

"Meanwhile, around the edges of all this, the regular people are partying like their lives depend on it. Like their world will end tomorrow. One lady approached me and wanted me to hire out Cannice to work at her party. I said no.

"I tell you, Leigh Ann, when you come from an atmosphere like that, the petty rules around here mean nothing. Most of life means nothing. And all that meant anything to me was my time with Johnnie and that it would soon end. I knew I must do something about it. Johnnie knew, too. I knew he would soon be going back to the field."

She stopped. Then, "People are getting married all over the place."

"But who married you? And where? And what did Cannice say?"

"We were married by a minister in a special part of Chimborazo Hospital, where Johnnie was being treated. The surgeon-in-chief, who was a very kindhearted man, asked the matron to give us the loan of her parlor for one night. She lived in a long, low whitewashed building, and she didn't come in until first light, anyway. They set up a hospital bed for us there." She stopped.

I stared. "So you are really married."

"Yes."

"What about Cannice?"

"She saw the world as I did in Richmond, too. Everything stood out stark, like in a Dutch painting. So she went along with what I wanted to do."

"And you're not going to tell Teddy?"

"No. I can't take any scoldings now. I'm still basking in my happiness. I'm a woman. I'm a wife. I can't be banished back into the world of a naughty little girl."

I kissed her good night. I left, thinking what courage she had. Then I thought, *What if she finds she's with child? She'll tell Teddy then,* I told myself. *He'll have kittens, but she will.*

CHAPTER NINETEEN

May 1863

TEDDY HAD GIVEN somebody fifty percent interest in the mill.

I wasn't supposed to know this. Teddy and Louis tried to keep all mill business private.

The way I found out was, I was at the other end of the long dining room table one Sunday night when my brothers lingered over their coffee at supper. We were saving on kerosene so we used candlelight. It flickered romantically. It also conveniently hid things.

Like me.

I was also hidden by the bouquet of roses that Viola had put in the middle of the table this sweet night in May.

"He relieved me of any liability to him in case the property is destroyed," Teddy was saying.

"What is the date of the certificate of interest?" Louis asked.

"March ninth, 1863. I want you to have a copy of it."

"As your brother? Or as mayor?" In spite of the gathering twilight I could see Louis's eyes twinkle.

"As my brother," Teddy said solemnly. "He's promised to stay in the mill to the last moment if the Yankees come. In case they're set on burning it like they burned the Trion cotton factory in Rome. He says that owning half the mill, he's going to demand that the rights of neutrals be respected. He plans on flying a French flag on the roof."

Theophile Roche! They have given Theophile Roche fifty percent interest in the mill! So that's why Teddy brought him here!

Louis nodded his head approvingly. "It's chancy, but it could work. There's just one drawback."

"What's that?"

"He's afraid of heights," Louis said. "He told me. He's terrified of heights. He'll never go on the roof of the mill to put a flag up."

"He'll get someone else to do it for him," Teddy concluded.

I was the only one left at the table, finishing my cake. I ate it very slowly, very quietly. I had learned, of late, how to become almost invisible around my brothers, ever since they had become grim and grumpy because the war news was bad.

Only now Cicero was sitting right next to me because I was feeding him bits of cake on the sly. But then I stopped feeding him and he whined for more.

Teddy looked up, saw me, and scowled. "How long have you been here?"

"I'm finishing my dessert."

"Good Lord, she's heard everything," he told Louis.

They looked at each other.

"Can you keep quiet about this?" Louis asked.

I nodded yes.

"Didn't I tell you not to feed Cicero at the table?" Teddy said. "Didn't I?"

"You do," I flung back at him.

This was not about feeding Cicero at the table and I knew it.

"Come over here," he said sternly.

I had sassed him. But this was not about my sassing him, either. He was afraid because I had heard the conversation.

I went and stood in front of him.

He took my hand. "Why do you want to sass me?" he asked sadly.

I shrugged and looked shamefaced.

Gently, he brushed some tendrils of hair back from my face. "This business we're discussing is of the utmost importance. To our family's welfare and to the survival of the mill. Pa built the mill. Bad times are coming. We're trying to save it. We must do everything we can to save it. Mr. Roche is going to help. You talk about anything you heard here tonight, and it's lost. Can I make it any plainer?"

"No, Teddy."

"All right." He kissed my forehead. "Now go. Get out of here."

CHAPTER TWENTY

RUMOR WAS GOING around amidst the girls I knew about a Mrs. Kate Latimer Nichols, wife of Captain James H. Nichols of the Phillips Georgia Legion — Louis knew him from college.

Mrs. Nichols was in her sickbed when she was raped by two Yankee soldiers who came into her bedroom with guns.

"She went mad," Angela Tarberry told me. "Her husband had to put her into an insane asylum."

I felt horrified. And put out. "He's my brother Louis's friend," I told the girls.

"Well, then, you should have known it," Angela said.

How could I tell my friends? Louis would never talk about it. I asked Teddy. "Is it true?"

"I don't like you knowing about this." He wore his grim Teddy face. But he told me. "Yes, it's true." It was then that he confided in me that he was studying on sending his womenfolk north to Philadelphia, to Grandma's, if the Yankees came.

"I don't want to go north," I protested.

He did not even acknowledge my argument. It seemed it was not worth a reply.

As of the last of May, my James wrote to me from the Rappahannock River, where he was with Lee.

Though he'd first enlisted in the Roswell Battalion and they were still here in Roswell, James, by special approval of my brother Louis, had been detached to serve under Lee.

As of May everyone feared a possible attack on Atlanta. The South had won at Chancellorsville but things were not good otherwise.

Meanwhile, Mrs. Lincoln was having séances in the White House, trying to get in touch with her dead son Willie.

The Union troops were threatening our borders. Camille's father and mother were talking about leaving Roswell. Her father, Archibald Smith, buried his important papers and possessions under a walnut tree in his backyard. Louis helped him. They had a young son, Robert, at the Georgia Military Institute on the hill outside Marietta, and they hated to leave him. But Mr. Smith wanted to get his wife and daughter to safety in Valdosta, a home they had in the southernmost part of Georgia.

Upon hearing this, Louis immediately proposed to Camille. They were married in our church by Reverend Pratt in late May. A small wedding. I stood up for Camille and Teddy was best man. Louis promised Mr. Smith he would look after Robert, and the Smiths left.

A few days later the Georgia Military Institute cadets boarded the trains for the frontlines.

Camille and Louis lived with us. He didn't want to leave her alone in that log farmhouse way outside of town all day, he said. It was nice to have another sister in the house, especially since this was one I liked.

In July we had Gettysburg. There is nothing that can be said about that except that the news reports that came to us were shattering. Louis and Teddy pored over them. They went to the telegraph office every day with all the other people to search the list of names posted of the wounded and the dead. Many of the dead were past acquaintances. People of the town had relatives who were killed there.

My brothers felt ashamed because they hadn't been at Gettysburg. Even Louis, who still could not walk without aid of a cane. Teddy's anger simmered slowly because he'd been cashiered out of the army.

My James was at Gettysburg, but his name was never on the list. He wrote to me afterward, saying his job had been to hold some of the lower works on Culp's Hill. He met North Carolina boys who didn't want to be there, he wrote, who were glad to be captured, who never wanted to be part of the war in the first place.

I let Teddy and Louis read the letter. Teddy nodded grimly. "North Carolina did not secede soon enough to please some of the other Southern states," he said. "I heard some of those boys were treated badly because of it."

At the end of the year, we started to hear a considerable lot about a Yankee fellow, a general by the name of William T. Sherman.

CHAPTER TWENTY-ONE

1864

O<small>N THE FIRST</small> of April, just as we were at supper, we had a visit from the vegetable lady, whom we hadn't seen in more than a year.

Careen came into the dining room. "Viola, that lady with the veggies, she be here agin."

Viola started to get up.

Teddy stopped her. "Just a minute. Who is here? Just who is important enough to interrupt our dinner?"

Viola explained.

"The telegraph wire's been cut," Louis reminded him.

"Tell her to come in here," Teddy ordered.

"She won't," Viola said. "She's very secretive about her business."

"Tell her to come in here, Careen," Teddy said again.

Careen left and came back in short order. "She say please, Massa Teddy. She say please, she gotta see Miss Viola. She got 'portant message."

Again Viola started to get up. Again Teddy tried to stop her, but Viola ran into the kitchen. Teddy flung down his napkin, pushed back his chair, and followed.

We all stopped eating, except Pa. In a minute, we heard a scream from Viola. And then she ran back to us with a letter in her hand. Tears were coming down her face.

"Oh," she cried, "oh, Johnnie's coming home. My Johnnie, oh, my Johnnie. Oh, at long last, he's coming home."

⤜✦⤛

HE CAME HOME on April eighth, a Friday. Johnnie Cummack, with the shot-up but healed arm and the old-man's look in his twenty-four-year-old eyes, was a lieutenant now. He had received a battlefield commission serving under General James Longstreet at Chickamauga the previous fall.

Viola could not wait to get him off alone. She was starry-eyed. She hung on his arm, and I saw Louis and Teddy exchange many a concerned look between them.

"Why don't you two get married?" Teddy said mildly when we were sitting in the parlor having coffee.

My heart leaped with gladness. Maybe now they would tell him and all would be well.

"We agreed to wait until the war is over, sir," Johnnie said. "And you don't have to worry. I respect Viola too much to dishonor her, or you all, in any way."

Teddy nodded, satisfied. I was not. Suppose Viola got pregnant. What kind of game were they playing? They had Teddy's permission to get married!

Somehow Viola and Johnnie managed to get their time alone. The Yankees had been threatening our borders since December. Louis, as mayor and as commander of the Roswell Battalion, had been getting letters from Colonel Marcus Wright, who was heading up troops in

Atlanta, reminding him that Louis's battalion covered an important line of approach to that city.

Wright would give Louis no peace. Louis had to account to him about the doings of his four pieces of artillery, his fifty cavalrymen, and his one hundred armed infantrymen.

So Louis was busy, between that and meeting with citizens who planned to leave Roswell and wanted a safe escort out.

He had no time to oversee the honor of his sister Viola.

Neither did Teddy. He was seeing to the constant running of the mill. Mr. Eldridge had already left town with his children for far-off safety. And Teddy also had the mill books to worry about. He was getting ready to ship them, along with hundreds of bales of cotton, heaps and heaps of yarn, and thousands of yards of cloth to storage houses somewhere in the deeper South. He hadn't made up his mind where yet.

So, what with all this and Johnnie's mother having gone to Staunton, Virginia, to her sister's, and his father, the colonel, still being in the field, he had no one to report to. And so he was at our place quite a bit.

And he and Viola had their time alone.

"Why?" I asked my sister when Johnnie was out one day watching Louis post the Roswell Battalion at the bridge that crossed the Chattahoochee River. "Why won't you tell Teddy you are married? Are you that afraid of him?"

"No," she said. "Johnnie is that afraid of his parents."

"Why?"

"His mother always wanted him to marry his cousin Mary Berkeley of Staunton, Virginia. She's staying there now. And she's furious that Johnnie isn't visiting her there. The Berkeleys go way back in our history and have a magnificent plantation. But Johnnie doesn't love Mary. He loves me. So we can't let out that we're married."

"But you have to. Someday."

"After the war we will. After the war everything will be different. Johnnie says the territory of the Confederacy is dwindling. That many soldiers are uncertain as to the meaning of the war anymore. That Longstreet isn't that good a general, that he's slow to act on orders and, though he's fearless, can't take independent command."

She hesitated and looked down at the dress she was mending. Clothes were getting in short supply. We had to make do with what we had. I often wore some of Viola's hand-me-downs.

"Johnnie says our army has depleted numbers and inferior equipment. And that we're going to lose the war, Leigh Ann. When that happens, Johnnie's parents won't care who he married. That plantation in Virginia won't be worth a Confederate dollar. The slaves will own it."

"Stop!"

"It's the truth. Somebody has to tell you."

"Why doesn't Teddy? Or Louis?"

"Because they don't want to frighten you."

"What will happen to us?"

"We have money. Yankee money. If Teddy is smart he'll take Carol and Pa and you west. There's miles of land out there. And nobody cares if you're a Rebel or not. Everybody starts new out west."

"And Louis?"

"Louis is too much Indian not to know what to do next."

"But the mill! What about the mill?"

"If the Yankees come, they'll destroy it."

"No, Viola, no. Teddy says we have to do everything we can to save it. Pa made the mill."

"We have to do everything we can to save ourselves, Leigh Ann. That's what we have to do. Pa made *us*. You're no longer a little girl. You're fourteen. When I was fifteen they put me in charge of you. We're in the middle of a nasty war. Everything is changing. You have to grow up. Promise me you'll grow up."

I promised. But inside I knew I was still a little girl.

CHAPTER TWENTY-TWO

O NE MORNING, the third week in April, I was having a dream about Louis, about him taking me to the confectionery in town for ice cream and me wanting peaches on top of it. I was just about to put a spoonful of peaches into my mouth when that hooty owl of Louis's flew in the door and perched on his shoulder and Louis said, "Wait, we have to pray now. We have a lot to pray about."

It was a warm, pleasant dream. I find the dreams I have right before I wake always are. I opened my eyes. From my bed I could see out the front windows that it was all gray and misty outside, so it had to be very early. Still, I heard voices from below on the verandah. I got out of bed and knelt by my window. There, below, were Johnnie and Viola, saying goodbye. He was all spiffed up in his cleaned and ironed uniform. She was in her blue silk morning wrapper.

He was leaving us today. Ordered to help defend Richmond. Their words were muffled in the misty air. Then they kissed, a long and agonizing kiss. Johnnie took the reins of his horse from the groom, mounted, and swiftly rode off down the drive. Viola stood there, one hand to her mouth, watching him go.

I thought how cruel love is. I thought how Mother and Father hated each other. How Teddy and Carol could have conducted their marriage by telegraph, for all the love that lay between them. Oh, there was physical attraction. I could see the yearning between them for that. I was old enough to know that my brother Teddy, besides being attractive to women, had manly strengths and needs, and vigor. And Carol was as a kitten in his arms. I knew he loved *her*. I sensed that she had already broken his heart, because he could not make her love *him*. And Teddy did not like losing disputes.

But these days his problem with Carol took a back seat to other concerns.

I know he wrote to Grandmother in Philadelphia, telling her to be prepared, one of these days, for the arrival of his sisters, his wife, and perhaps even the wife of his brother, Louis. That he was corresponding with the owners of warehouses in Augusta, Newnan, Griffin, and Macon, inquiring as to who had room for his goods.

He and Louis had already shipped their prized horses to a friend of Louis's in northern Maryland, a Yankee who had a horse farm there. My brothers had, in the last couple of years, purchased thoroughbreds from Savannah, with the intention of raising horses after the war.

And Teddy was still courting Theophile Roche. The Frenchman had been invited to supper a few times since December. Teddy was counting on him to keep the mill running at full capacity even when the Yankees came.

I had not seen Mr. Roche for many weeks, though Teddy spoke of him often. He came at last, bowing and bearing gifts for my sister and sisters-in-law: perfume he'd had imported from France, or powder. He'd kiss their hands. Me? He'd turn and bow most exquisitely and kiss my hand and say something in French that Louis told me later meant "ah, my precious little princess." And, with Teddy's permission he'd give me a book.

One time he gave me *The Raven* by Edgar Allan Poe, another time *Frankenstein* by Mary Shelley, and still another, *Christine* by Alexandre Dumas.

"*Père,*" Roche said to me. "He fought his first duel at twenty-three. In it his trousers fell down."

Everyone laughed. Teddy did not. I don't think Teddy liked the attention Roche paid to me, or the books he gave me, especially the one by the Frenchman whose trousers fell down.

❧

As May came into its third week, Teddy called me and Viola, Carol, and Camille before him in his study, and we stood there like delinquent schoolgirls.

Louis, apparently knowing what Teddy was about, stood in the hall just outside the door.

"I want you all to pack up some clothes," Teddy said, "for me to send on to Philadelphia. Necessities and one dress apiece will do. You can buy what you need there. Grandmother will help you."

We looked at each other, aghast. Nobody spoke.

Then Viola did. "I don't want to go, Teddy," she told him.

He was ready for this. He was calm but firm. "The Union army is not far away. That means Sherman's men, and we've all heard enough horror stories about them. Now Louis and I have an obligation to protect our women. I'm sorry, but what you all want doesn't come into it right now. Please do as I say."

Camille looked at her husband. "Louis?" Her voice cracked.

He stepped into the room. "Yes."

"Do you want me to go?"

Everyone was silent for a moment.

Louis's face had about it that Indian mask that you could not read. It was a long enough moment for him to contact his inner spirit.

"I don't know what I'm going to be doing yet," Louis told us. "A lot of citizens have come to me, wanting to leave town, to go to places like Milledgville, Valdosta, Jacksonville, Waynesboro, and Macon. They want me, as mayor, to escort them. Colonel Marcus Wright from Atlanta wants me to continue leading the Roswell Battalion to hold this town and the line to Atlanta. Teddy says I should turn the battalion over to Captain Will Clark and escort the citizens to their destinations."

He hesitated a moment, then recommenced speaking. "If I do that, Camille comes with me. If I stay, Camille, you'll have to go to Philadelphia with the others."

She ran to him and threw herself in his arms. He hugged her. They said no words.

We all spoke at once, all except Teddy. We all told Louis to go and take Camille. They loved each other so much. Teddy gave a small smile and nodded yes.

"All right," he said, quieting us, "all right, it's Louis's decision. Leave him be. Now the rest of you, go pack your things. One valise, no more. You have half an hour before the stage leaves for Marietta."

Camille sent a valise, too, just in case Louis decided to stay. She wanted to please him.

❦

MONDAY OF THE third week in May, Louis announced at breakfast that he had decided to escort the citizens out of town.

"We'll be leaving by the middle of June," he said.

We were all tremendously happy about that. But happiness in such times lasted only two minutes. I had learned already not to trust happiness.

In the next moment Teddy told Viola, Carol, and me that we should dress for our trip, that this afternoon we were taking the stage to Marietta, and from there the train to Philadelphia.

"Scouts say that Sherman's within a hundred miles," he told us.

I froze in my seat. My breakfast went cold on my plate. "I want to go with Louis," I said. "I don't want to go to Philadelphia."

Silence. So loud that Sherman could likely hear it a hundred miles away.

Teddy compressed his lips and looked down the table at his brother from beneath lowered eyelids.

Louis tightened his jaw and did not look back at Teddy. *They have been expecting this.*

"I think I'll wear my flowered suit," Carol said lightly. "It's always comfortable to travel in."

"I want to go with Louis," I said again.

"Why don't you ask him," Teddy said.

So he would let Louis do the dirty work. I looked at Louis, who was sipping his coffee.

"Can I go with you, Louis?" I appealed.

He set down his cup. "I can't take you, sweetie, much as I'd like to."

"Why?"

"Because you belong to Teddy. He's legally responsible for you."

"Bullcrap," I said.

"That's enough, Leigh Ann," Teddy snapped. "I'll not have such language at the table. Now you are excused. You can go and eat breakfast in the kitchen."

"If we're leaving this afternoon, it's my last meal here," I protested.

"You should have thought of that before." Teddy did not look at me. "Leave, please."

I got up and ran, tears coming down my face.

Cannice, who'd heard it all, brought my plate and tea and set it down before me on the kitchen table. "You'd best eat, lamb," she said.

"I hate him. Why did he have to send me in here when it's my last meal with Louis and Camille and all?"

" 'Cause you been naughty. You know he doan like to hear you cuss. Why you hafta go and plague him so? You know how upset he be, you all leavin' today."

I sat there pouting, but I did not eat. They were all talking and laughing in the dining room like it was just a regular day. *How can they be that way?* I started to cry.

I don't know how much time passed, but Cannice went out the back door to the kitchen garden. And then Teddy came in.

"You didn't eat," he said. "Don't you know you'll be hungry on that stage to Marietta? Now stop that crying and put some food in your mouth."

But I couldn't do either one. "I can't wait to go away this afternoon," I said between sobs. "I can't wait to get away from you."

"I can't wait to get shed of you, either. You're nothing but a little brat who's always given me nothing but trouble."

"In Philadelphia I'm going to do just what I want. I'm going to stay up late and read racy books and use cuss words and you'll never know it. I'm going to kiss boys."

"I hope you have a good time."

He pulled up a chair, sat down, and, with a napkin, wiped the tears from my face. Then he picked up a fork-ful of scrambled eggs. I opened my mouth and he shoved it in, like I was a knee-baby.

It went on like that for three or four forkfuls, with neither of us saying a word. Cannice came in, looked at us, put her hands on her hips, shook her head, and made a throaty sound.

"You got a fierce bark," she told my brother, "but you sure do spoil her. You want a fresh cuppa coffee, Massa Teddy?"

He said yes. That sounded good.

He gave the fork over to me and I ate and he sipped his coffee and no words were necessary. All had been said. Except, from Teddy: "You remember what I taught you."

But before we got on the stage for Marietta that day, Louis got a telegram at the mayor's office. As of that day, the last Monday in May, train travel was forbidden to all civilians.

We were going nowhere after all.

CHAPTER TWENTY-THREE

THAT VERY NIGHT, at dusk, when Teddy had gone to the mill and Louis was still at the mayor's office, a telegram was delivered to the house for Viola.

Johnnie had been killed on the eleventh at the Richmond defenses.

Viola collapsed in a faint. When we revived her she got hysterical. Camille gave her rum. Carol put cold cloths on her forehead. Cannice told me to ride and get Teddy at the mill.

As I mounted my horse, Trojan, Careen told me that Viola was pregnant. I carried that thought with me, a sour taste in my mouth, as I rode to the mill.

Johnnie dead. Louis soon to leave. Viola pregnant. Yankees soon to come. Me saying vile words at the table, and Teddy sending me into the kitchen.

What had happened to my world?

In no time, it seemed, I was at the mill. Inside, the din that had always terrified me now validated the confusion in my mind. Quickly, I found Teddy's office. The door was closed, but behind the glass was a light. I knocked and saw the figure behind the desk come to the door and open it.

Teddy stood there in shirtsleeves, scowling. "What's wrong?"

"Johnnie's been killed defending Richmond. Viola's hysterical. They told me to come and get you."

I did not tell him that Viola was pregnant. He would not hear that from me. He had enough to cause him pain these days. I vowed to myself that I would not be the reason for any more of it.

Within a few minutes we were on the way home, where Teddy took charge.

Viola was on the Persian carpet in the front parlor. Neither Carol nor Camille could get her up. She wouldn't let anybody come near her, not even Cannice.

Why not Cannice? I wondered as we came into the parlor. She always trusted our beloved housekeeper. Everybody did. But there Cannice stood, in a far circle that had formed around my sister, which included Careen. All kept their distance.

And then I saw why.

Viola had a gun, Teddy's .32 Colt navy revolver. She held it carelessly in one hand.

I gasped, standing beside Teddy. He put out his arm and held me from going any farther into the room. "Stay where you are, everybody," he directed. "Don't move."

He took a cautious step forward. "Hello, honey," he said to Viola. "I'm sorry for what's happened."

"Come near me and I'll kill you," she told him viciously.

Teddy squatted down. "The mill's powerful busy, but I've come home just for you."

"You don't care for me. Always want to scold me. That's all you want to do."

Teddy nodded. "I've done my share of scolding, I admit, but it was always 'cause I loved you and wanted to see you grow up and become a sister I could be proud of. And you are."

He shuffled a mite closer to her. "Damned proud of you, I am."

She raised the gun. "I said I'd kill you if you came closer."

"I know you did. But then, what would more killing do? You're not in charge of your senses, Viola, and if anybody around here has senses to be in charge of, it's you. Sometimes you've got more sense than all the rest of us put together. And if you kill me, why, then they'll have to take you away and hang you. You can't just kill people, even though there's a war on."

He stopped. Someone had come in the front door and was coming down the hall. We listened to the steady steps that halted at the doorway of the parlor.

Louis.

He stood there, taking it all in. From behind Teddy, and out of range of Viola's eyes, I signaled to him to stay where he was. He nodded at me.

"And then," Teddy was saying, "with me dead and you dead, and Louis gone away, who would take care of the family? Who, Viola?"

"I don't care," she said. "Johnnie's dead, so I don't give a damn about anything. I may even kill myself now. Save everybody the trouble."

She raised the revolver so the barrel was pointed at her face.

Everybody muffled screams.

Only Careen didn't muffle what she wanted to say but yelled it out: "Don't, don't, Miz Viola," she screamed. "'Member, you be's pregnant. You be's pregnant!"

In that moment Teddy leaped toward his sister, throwing himself at her. Everything happened at once then.

Teddy landed on top of Viola and his action pointed the gun away from her, over her shoulder. The revolver went off and the shot exploded loudly and went through the window. The glass shattered like ice, and servants came running from all directions, thinking the Yankees had arrived.

Teddy enfolded Viola in his arms and held her while she bawled out her misery. Louis quieted the servants and sent them back to their posts, saying no, there were no Yankees, that Leigh Ann had been playing with one of Teddy's guns and it went off accidentally and, yes, she would be punished. And Viola was crying because her betrothed had been killed. And yes, Johnnie's body would be shipped home and they could come to the funeral and sing some of their spirituals.

Viola stopped crying, finally, and told everybody how sorry she was. Especially, she told Teddy. "I was out of my senses," she said. "You should have slapped me."

"I've never slapped my sisters," he said, "and I never will."
Everybody calmed down then.

Cannice gave Viola a concoction to quiet her nerves.
Carol and Camille readied her for bed. Teddy went back
to the mill. I slept with Viola. Louis, being home, told me
to wake him if she gave me any trouble.

Nobody said anything for many days after about Viola's
being pregnant. All were hoping she would come through
this and be all right. We just pampered her and fussed over
her. Nobody wanted to upset her.

In early June the Yankees took Marietta.

CHAPTER TWENTY-FOUR

JOHNNIE CUMMACK'S MOTHER did not come home from Virginia for the funeral of her son. Having heard that the Yankees were in Marietta, no civilians were allowed to travel on the trains, and most citizens were leaving Roswell, she was afraid to come.

His father, Colonel John Cummack, came. He was a scraggly-faced man with hard blue eyes and a short white beard. Louis and Teddy called him "sir." He was with the Confederate Infantry of R. H. Anderson's Corps that had attacked Sheridan's Cavalry near Cold Harbor.

He told us about it. Oh, the names. The corps, the infantries, the brigades, the attacks. I was sick of hearing about all of them. All they meant were more dead Johnnies.

My own James hadn't written a letter in weeks. And when one finally came it was from north of the Chickahominy. James was with Lee, moving southeast toward Cold Harbor, Virginia. All was still well. He was not wounded.

I was in a state of terror now, after what had happened to Johnnie. I'd been visiting James's grandmother, Mrs. Stapleton, at least once a week, and we compared letters. And after supper we prayed together for him.

Colonel Cummack allowed our negroes to come to Johnnie's funeral and sing their spirituals. Johnnie was buried in the cemetery behind the Roswell Presbyterian Church. A lot of the townfolk came. I thought, *How can a mother not come to her own son's funeral? How can you be afraid to come to town? How can you be afraid of anything after you have lost a son?*

And then I thought, *How can I criticize others? I have not seen my own mother in more than a year.*

Viola wore black and a widow's veil.

Colonel Cummack looked at her strangely, but she did not care.

He left to go back to the field right after the funeral. He would not even come back to our house for a repast.

JUNE WENT BY in a haze. I did some swimming in the stream. Viola stayed pretty much in her room, or else she sat on the front verandah, rocking next to Pa, who never came out of his reverie anymore but was content to stay in his own little world. Viola would just sit there with a book in her hands, gazing off into some middle distance.

Sometimes Jon would sit with them. He would talk to her. And he would always make sure someone would see him doing this.

Viola did not seem to mind. It was as if she did not even know he was there.

One day, the third week in June, when Teddy was upstairs sleeping, Carol with him, when Viola was out on the verandah and Louis and Camille were meeting in the mayor's office with the people they were leaving with the next day, Theophile Roche came around.

From my room upstairs I saw him riding up the front drive and going 'round the back to the rear entrance. What did he want? Had he come to see Teddy? There was an iron rule in the house. Nobody woke Teddy from his sleep during the day. If the Yankees came, they must be told to wait until it was time for him to get up.

I waited for about seven minutes, then crept downstairs.

Roche was in the kitchen with Cannice. I could see he was drinking tea and eating cake she had given him.

"So, I do not know what to do," I heard him telling her in his French accent.

He was confiding in Cannice, like everyone else did, sooner or later.

About what? Women? The mill? Was he sick? Had he come for a remedy?

I casually sauntered into the kitchen. "I smell cake," I said.

"You know you'll ruin your appetite now for supper," Cannice said.

"Just a little piece? I won't tell anybody you gave it to me."

She set it down on the table and I pulled out a chair and sat down.

"I have come to see your brother," Mr. Roche told me. "I forget that he is sleeping. Cannice here is kind enough to offer me tea and cake. So I confide in her. It is time to put the French flag on the roof of the mill, but alas"— and he raised both hands —"this poor Frenchman is too frightened to go up there. It is so *high*." He made the sign of the cross and rolled his eyes to heaven. "I am afraid. What am I to do? I have promised your brother I will fly the flag to show that the mill is under neutral ownership. And now I can get no one to go up there and place it for me! All are afraid!"

He was truly distressed.

I looked at Cannice and she at me. I thought for a moment.

We must do anything we can to save the mill.

I could hear Teddy saying the words inside my head, even now. And then I had a thought so brilliant that it struck me like lightning, leaving me in shock.

"When does the flag have to go up?" I asked Roche.

"Soon," he said. "The more soon the better."

I nodded. I finished my cake and told Cannice how excellent it was. I gulped my tea. "You could," I told Roche, "offer one of the workers extra money to take the flag on the roof. I'm sure my brother wouldn't mind."

He shook his head no, sadly. "They are all afraid."

I got up. "I can help you. I can go with you and offer one of them extra money. They will talk to me. Come on. Cannice, if anyone asks for me, tell them what I'm about.

No, don't, not yet. I may fail and I don't want anyone to know it. I'll be back in plenty of time for supper."

Cannice said yes. She wouldn't tell anyone. And I went off to the mill with Roche.

*

OF COURSE, I had no intention of asking any of the mill workers to bring the French flag up on the roof. If one of them did, and fell and got killed, Teddy would be in all kinds of trouble.

I was determined to do it myself.

Here was my way to make amends to my brother for all the trouble I'd given him over the years. Here was my chance to do something important for my family. For the war. I was not afraid to go up there on the roof. When I was ten I'd climbed to the uppermost limb of our cherry tree in our backyard, hadn't I?

"Show me the flag," I said to Roche once we got inside the mill.

He took me to a storeroom on the third floor.

Oh, it was a magnificent flag, blue and white and red, but not as pretty as our Confederate banner. "I'll have to take our Confederate flag down, won't I?"

"You?" He said something in garbled French. "You are going to do this? I thought you said you'd get a worker?"

"Oh, Mr. Roche, don't be a silly-boots. You knew I was going to do it all along, didn't you?"

"But, pretty little miss. Your brother will — how you say? — kill me."

"My brother is so busy worrying about the Yankees coming, he won't have time to kill you. Anyway, you don't have to tell him. Not right away, anyway."

He made the sign of the cross and said a prayer, his lips moving quickly. Did that mean he would let me do it? "I have a little sister at home," he told me. "I would not let her do it. And if I found out she did such, I would — how you say? — spank her."

"Teddy doesn't spank. Now show me: how do I get up there?"

He led me down a small hallway to where he reached up and pulled down a ladder. Above it in the ceiling was a trapdoor that led to the roof. Just like in an English romance novel.

He went up first and opened the trapdoor to reveal an expanse of blue sky. Then he came down and bowed and extended his arm graciously.

Gripping the staff of the flag, I climbed the steps.

The roof was slanted. The Confederate flag waved gaily a good distance from me at the other end of the roof. My heart leaped in my throat.

I would have to walk all the way to there? I looked down at Roche, smiling, determined not to appear frightened.

"You can do it, yes?" he asked.

"I can do it, yes," I returned.

"Excellent." He clasped his hands together. "I wait right here. You don't forget. Bring back the Confederate flag. It must not be seen on the roof. The whole idea is that once the French flag is up, this mill is neutral territory."

"Yes," I said. And I proceeded to plant my feet firmly on the roof and get my breath.

One step at a time, Leigh Ann, I told myself. *Slowly, go slowly. There, one foot on each side of the peak. Keep your balance. Oh, the roof is hot! I should have worn my boots instead of these silken morning slippers. What's wrong with me? I should have taken the time to change! Oh, don't look down, even though you can see the whole town from here and it's so beautiful. Even though the water is there that powers the mill, the cool, cool water. Oh, how I wish I could put my feet in the water!*

Careful. Oh, I almost tripped! There, I'll use the staff of the flag to lean on. See, I'm not stupid. I'll make it, and someday I'll tell my grandchildren about how I did this.

Oh, I'm more than halfway across. I want to stop, but I won't let myself. Let me think, was that Jon I saw listening in the hall outside the kitchen when I was talking to Roche? I wonder why he's been languishing around Viola so much lately. Oh, damned flag, you almost got me killed, blowing in front of my face like that. I should have bound you up.

Here, here, a few more feet and I'm at the Confederate flag. Now what to do?

Kneel down is what, if I can manage it. Oh, don't drop the flag or all will be for naught. Just hold it tight and kneel. No, wrong. Can't hold the damned flag and pull the Confederate one out of the receptacle at the same time. Try getting up again and putting the French flag between your knees and kneeling down again. Should have worn boys' pants, too. All right, that's better.

Now, reach and grab the Confederate flag.

Damn, what did they do, lock it in? Yes, it's screwed in, I can see that. Now what? Have to undo that screw.

Ohhh, I've cut my finger. Damn, it hurts. Just a few more turns now and, there, it's loose. Lift it up now and, oh, it's heavy and tipping over and, hell, I've got to let it go or it will take me with it.

Well, there goes one perfectly good Confederate flag tumbling down the roof and splashing into the water. Darned shame. Maybe we can rescue it later. Hope it doesn't mess up the works. Now I've got to get the French flag up from between my knees and set it in the receptacle, like this. Oh, the darned wind. I'm fighting the wind.

There, I've set it in, but Roche gave me nothing to screw it in with. Well, I've done my best. Yankees come, they'll likely shoot it down anyway. I don't believe they'll accept this claptrap about neutral territory. Those Yankees are animals from what I hear. Now I have to get up and turn around and start back.

Oh, no, I can't do this again. It's so far back. How did I ever come all this way? And the roof is burning hot. It was one thing making my way here, but I never considered going back. I just can't do it.

My head hurts. I feel like throwing up. I'm thirsty. Let me just close my eyes for a minute. Oh, what are all those swirling lights? And why is my breath coming in heavy spurts?

God, I've got to get away from here! You can't abandon me now!

I started forward, one step, two steps, but everything was going around and around. I stopped again and closed my eyes and sat down.

"Leigh Ann! What in the name of the devil's wife are you doing up here?"

That's what Teddy would say. I heard it inside my head. He said things like that. Oh, how I wished I could hear it now.

"When I get you back down I'm going to hang you by your thumbs until the Yankees come and then let them have you."

Yes, he said colorful things like that all the time.

But then I heard footsteps coming toward me and I opened my eyes.

Teddy. A good distance from me, but not so far that I couldn't see the steam coming out of his head.

"You've done it now, little girl. This is it. This is the end. Now you can go with Louis and good riddance to you."

He meant it.

"Teddy," I started toward him.

"Shut up and don't move!"

I did both. He made his way toward me like he was a circus performer. When he got to me he maneuvered me around in front of him and held on to me, guiding me all the way back to the trapdoor. He let me go down first, and I stood there and waited while he came down, locked the door shut, and snapped the ladder into place.

Waiting for us in the hall was Jon. He grinned at me. I kicked him in the shins. Teddy pulled me away. "If he hadn't warned me, you could have been killed," he said. "Now get the hell home."

When I left he was bawling out Roche.

❧

AND THAT WAS truly the end of it with me and Teddy. His disgust with me that day knew no bounds, and he showed it in the only way he knew how to convey it.

He did not make me sit in a chair for an hour to contemplate my sins. He did not hang me up by my thumbs. He did not spank me as Roche said he did with his sister. I would have preferred any of these things.

He simply would not speak to me except to issue sharp orders. And when he did this, he would not look at me. He would not have to do with me in any way. He went inside himself so far, I could not find him again.

But the French flag flew on the roof of our cotton mill. And I had put it there. And someday I would be able to tell my grandchildren about it.

❧

THE NEXT MORNING, without saying a word to anyone, I dressed and left the house before breakfast. Teddy had not yet come home from the mill. Louis had left early for the mayor's office to close things up. I mounted Trojan and rode to Louis's office and went in.

He looked up from his desk in surprise. We'd already said our goodbyes the night before. "What's wrong?" he asked. He eyed me solemnly.

"You've got to take me with you."

"Look, I know things are bad between you, but . . ."

"It's more than that, Louis. He doesn't want me around anymore."

"Oh, I'm sure it's not that. He's just worried about the Yankees coming."

"He doesn't want me around anymore. Why won't you believe that?"

He rubbed his face with his hand. "What you did"— he shrugged his shoulders —"is pretty serious, Leigh Ann." He shook his head. "No words can mend it."

"He might as well kick me out. He won't talk to me, look at me, or anything."

Louis nodded. "It's his way of punishing you."

"So you'll take me with you, then? I can go home and pack?"

Louis bit his bottom lip. "Honey, if I take you, you'll never mend it with him."

"He doesn't want to mend it."

"Yes, he does. He told me. But he's just so angry. You did a stupid thing, Leigh Ann. I'm sorry, sweetie, but I have to tell you. He said you were frozen in fear up on that roof. He can't get around that. This time you've gone too far. He can't forgive you right now. You have to give him time."

"If you were in charge of me, what would you do?"

"Not fair," he said kindly. "But it wouldn't be pretty between us, either."

"No wonder he and Carol don't have any kind of a marriage. I'd sooner marry a crocodile."

"Now, it isn't your place to talk about his marriage. You overstep yourself. If I take you away, you'll grow up during the most important years of your life without him. And he's your guardian. He has a lot to contribute to your upbringing."

"You could be my guardian."

He smiled. "Sweetie, I told you, I'd spoil the hell out of you. But right now I'm more concerned about Viola. Has Teddy said anything yet about her being pregnant?"

"No. Anyway, she's married."

He raised his eyebrows. "You know this?"

"Yes. She told me. It's a secret. She and Johnnie were married when she went to Richmond. She didn't want the Cummacks to know, because they wanted him to marry someone else."

"You must tell Teddy this."

I looked at the floor. "How, when he doesn't talk to me?"

"Leigh Ann, if push comes to shove, you must tell Teddy. Even if Viola doesn't. You are obligated. Promise me."

When Louis said *promise me* like that, you promised.

He pulled some paper out of a drawer and scribbled a note, then put it in an envelope but did not seal it. The envelope had the mark of the mayor's office on it.

He handed it to me. "My last official act as mayor." He winked at me and came around his desk to kiss and hug me. "Leave this on Teddy's desk when you go home. Don't forget about that silver we buried."

"When will I see you again?"

"Next time you need a lecture about boys."

I got out of there fast, because I was crying. When I got home I read the note, as I supposed Louis had intended me to, because he had not sealed it.

Dear Brother:

She wants to go with me. I would love to take her, but I will not let myself. She belongs with you. You have always done right by her and I trust you always will. Right now, she's brokenhearted because she thinks you don't love her anymore. Enough of this discipline will make her strong; too much will kill her spirit. I pray you will know the difference. I wish you luck with the Yankees. Don't be too brave. Be back soon.

Love, Louis

CHAPTER TWENTY-FIVE

Two days later I came upon Viola crying in her bedroom after breakfast. On her bed was laid out her best summer dress.

"Where are you going?" I asked.

"Nowhere." She blew her nose. "I've got to marry Jon."

I stood rooted in my place. My head whirled, worse than when I'd been on the cotton mill roof.

"Jon?" I repeated the name like the village idiot. "Jon? Why?"

"Because he went and told Teddy he's the father of my child."

"Jon did that?" For a moment I had doubt. I counted the weeks. "Viola, he isn't, is he?"

"Of course not," she snapped. "You think I'd cohabitate with that low-down reprobate? He'd do anything to be part of this family. It's all he's ever wanted. He told me so."

I wasn't sure what *cohabitate* meant, but it sounded like it covered the situation.

"Then why marry him?" I asked.

"Because I've got to do the right thing and save the family name. Do you realize what a disgrace I'll be, walking around pregnant with no husband?"

"Why don't you tell Teddy you're already married?"

"Because Colonel and Mrs. Cummack have money and I don't want them to think that I want it for my baby."

"You have a marriage license."

"Yes, but the Cummacks will still think I'm after their money."

"When are you getting married?"

"Tomorrow evening. Reverend Pratt is coming here."

"You can't, Viola. Please!"

"I'm doing it. My baby needs a father."

There was no sense in arguing with her, no sense in getting her in a state again. I turned, remembering the promise I'd made to Louis. I scampered across the hall and knocked on Teddy's door, hoping he'd not yet retired for the day.

Carol answered. She was in her nightdress, a flimsy thing. It made me embarrassed, seeing her like that. There wasn't much that was hidden underneath it.

"Yes, Leigh Ann." Clearly she was annoyed. "What is it?"

"I have to see Teddy. Just for a minute. Please?"

"When are you going to get the message that he doesn't want to see you? Don't you know what you've done to that man? He's absolutely dispirited these days. He's put so much into you, and after the other day, he feels he's failed with you and he can try no more. He's down in his study, if you dare approach him. And if you do, please don't upset him. I'm waiting for him, so don't put him in a bad mood."

She closed the door in my face.

I ran downstairs and hesitated outside the study door. Then I knocked softly. There was no response. I turned the knob, opened the door slowly, and went in.

Teddy was at his desk, poring over the newspaper. He did not look up. "Who said you could come in here?"

"I have to talk to you, just for a minute."

"Did I say I wanted to talk to you?"

"Please — I know you don't want to talk to me."

"Then get out, please." He was still reading the damned newspaper, and he never raised his voice.

I took a deep breath and started again. *I'm doing this because I promised Louis,* I told myself. *And for Viola.* What I really wanted to do was throw something at him, the damned crocodile.

"Just listen to me for one minute," I said politely, "and you don't ever have to again."

He turned the page of the newspaper. "Leave, please."

"I won't. I don't care if you hang me by my thumbs. I don't care if you hit me."

More reading. "I want you out of here in two seconds or I'll drag you out. I mean it."

"Teddy, this isn't for me. It's for Viola."

He got up, came around his desk, threw down the newspaper, grabbed me by the arm, and dragged me out of the room. I fought him. I kicked him in the shins, and he yelled, "Ow!" I even hit him. In the face. I hit him good.

"Damned crocodile," I shouted at him.

He said nothing. He never hit me back. But before I knew it I was out in the hall and the door was slammed behind me.

I stood outside, my heart beating rapidly. I tried the doorknob. It was locked. *Oh God, what to do. Louis,* I thought, *this was all your idea. Tell me, what do I do now?*

I must think! "Teddy," I called out. "Teddy, please listen. Just this once let me in and I'll never bother you again."

If Viola marries Jon tomorrow, I thought, *it's all my fault. And I won't stay around here. I'll run away.*

"Teddy!" I called again.

No answer. I started to cry, bitterly. I slumped to the floor, leaning against the door.

Then I had a thought.

"Teddy, I know you don't want me around. Carol told me what I've done to you. So, how about this? If you hear me out, I'll leave. I'll go and live with Mrs. Stapleton, James's grandmother. She said she'd be glad to have me. Only all I ask is one minute of your time. Then I'll go."

No answer. So even that didn't work. Well then, I might as well go and live with Mrs. Stapleton, for all he cared. I might as well go and pack my things right now.

I leaned with my forehead against the door, accepting it all, even while I couldn't believe what had come about. Then suddenly the door opened and I fell in against my brother's shoes.

"Get up."

I scrambled to my feet and wiped the tears from my face. Tears were a sign of weakness.

He glared at me. "What's this about going to live with Mrs. Stapleton?"

"She said I could. So I thought . . ."

He put a hand on the back of my neck, roughly, not lovingly, and pulled me into the room. "You told her about us, eh? You went over there and complained about me?"

"No, Teddy. I asked if she was frightened with the Yankees coming and she said yes. I offered to stay with her and she said she'd like that."

"Without my permission."

Oh, God, I was in more trouble. "I figured you didn't want me around, Teddy."

"I don't, but I'm stuck with you."

Did he know it was a knife in my heart?

"Now what's all this blubbering about? What have you got to tell me that will only take one minute?"

"You can't let Viola marry Jon."

"Oh, you're telling me what to do now?"

I shook my head no.

"He came to me like a man and told me he's the father. Does he not measure up to your high standards?"

"He isn't the father."

"You are privy to this information?"

Tears were coming to my eyes again. His voice was so scathing, so bruising. "I wish you wouldn't be so mean to me."

"I know you do." But it meant no nevermind to him.

I had to be done with this or I would soon die. "She's already married. To Johnnie Cummack. He's the father." *There, I've done it.*

I could say no more. Sobs came from my chest and I turned to leave.

He pulled me back, put his hands on my shoulders, and shoved me down roughly in a chair. "Stop that damned crying." There was disgust in his voice.

Somehow I managed to. He walked away and looked out the window, silent, his hands clasped behind his back. "Why didn't Viola tell me?" he asked.

I told him why.

"You damned girls will put me in an insane asylum yet." He turned around. "You can go now. I've broken my vow of silence with you, but I'm renewing it."

I walked to the door. There I turned. "Can I go and live with Mrs. Stapleton?"

"No. Now get out of here and don't bother me again."

I left.

CHAPTER TWENTY-SIX

O<small>N THE FIFTH</small> of July, around noontime, the Yankees
came within two and a half miles of Roswell.

Teddy was at the mill. He had not come home that
morning. He sent around a note telling Carol that he was
riding with Roche out to General Kenner Garrard's headquarters at Sope Creek. And that all of us were to stay inside the house.

The sun was hot that day. I wanted to go down to the
stream and swim. But Carol, considering herself in charge
now, said no. "You know your brother's orders. Don't you
dare disobey him now."

Viola and I were not even allowed out on the front
verandah to enjoy the occasional breeze. We commiser-
ated with each other in the front parlor. I closed the drapes
against the sun. She slept and I fanned her.

At five o'clock Teddy came home, morose and as glum
as I'd ever seen him. Primus, waiting for him out front,
took his horse.

"Out of his sight," Carol directed me, as if I had the
pox. She stood there at the front door, waiting with a tall
glass of iced tea in her hand. He took off his hat, wiped his
brow with his sleeve, and gulped down the tea.

I hid behind the door of the back parlor, listening.

"Thanks," he said.

"What happened?" she asked.

"You won't believe it."

"Try me."

"My mother was at Garrard's headquarters. My damned *mother.*"

"What was she doing there?"

He slumped down in a chair in the hall, rested his elbows on his knees, and put his head in his hands. "Seems she's been corresponding with him for weeks, advising him what's going on here."

"What did Garrard have to say to you and Roche?"

"Told Roche he has no order from Sherman for the destruction of the mill."

"Well, that's encouraging."

"I don't believe a damned word of it. Says he's considering Roche's claim of neutrality. I don't believe that, either. Says he wants the French flag in hand before reaching any decision."

I gasped. *The flag I had put on the roof?*

"Cannice is running a bath upstairs for you. Or do you want to eat first?"

"He kicked me out of the mill."

"What?"

"Garrard. He kicked me out of the mill. It was my mother's doing. She's in cahoots with him. Couldn't think of any other way to hurt me, I guess. He's taking suggestions from her. He intends to arrest every man in town as a traitor when he gets here, and he's coming in a day or two. Mother claims she's done me a favor. Garrard says if I'm arrested I'm to be sent to prison. It's that or stay here and run the plantation. Keep it going. For Mother."

"For your *mother?*"

"Yes. So she gets what she wants, after all."

Silence. *Oh, God,* I thought, *this must be killing Teddy. First she gets him kicked out of the army, then the mill. And now he's to keep the plantation going. For her.*

I wished I could run out into the hall and throw myself at him and put my arms around him. I couldn't, of course. He wanted naught to do with me.

Carol fed Teddy and then took him upstairs for a bath.

I went and told Viola what had happened. She cried.

"We're all finished," she said. "I'll wager Teddy runs off and joins the Confederate army."

The thought never occurred to me. But it was the only thing he could do if he wished to remain a man.

"What will we do without him?" I asked.

She gave a sad smile. "Don't tell me you haven't noticed that he doesn't give an owl's hoot for us anymore, Leigh Ann."

"Well, then *you* can take care of me," I said, "and I'll take care of you."

We hugged and it was a promise.

THE NEXT MORNING we had breakfast as usual, as if nothing had happened. But something had happened.

There was a new servant, a middle-aged white man taking care of Pa. Teddy introduced him to us. "This is Andrew," he said simply. "He'll be caring for Pa from now on. I expect you all to be polite and decent to him." That was all.

Viola and I just looked at each other. All traces of Jon were gone.

Teddy and Carol spoke quietly to each other. Teddy did not even cast an eye in my direction. He did not have much to say to Viola, either, but he always asked her how she felt. She would say she was doing fine and he would go back to his meal.

I did not exist for him.

Why he insisted I be present at the table I did not know. If I had my druthers I'd eat in the kitchen, but I dared not mention it.

My family was broken. Oh, if only Louis and Camille were home!

At four thirty that afternoon, when Carol was napping and Teddy was in his study, there came a knock on the front door. I was just coming down the stairs, so I opened it.

There stood a soldier, a Yankee, tall and regal and superior as St. Michael after driving the devil out of heaven.

"I am Captain Robert Kennedy, General Garrard's assistant adjutant general," he said. "Is this the Conners' residence?"

"Yessir."

"Is your brother Theodore Conners here?"

"What the hell?" Teddy came out of his study, storming up behind me. "What are you doing opening the door like that, Leigh Ann? Didn't I tell you not to? Didn't I?"

He pulled me aside, roughly. "Go on, get out of here."

Embarrassed, I ran down the hall, but not before hearing the Yankee captain saying, "Conners? We've done an inspection of the mill. It's revealed that the factory was, indeed, supplying cloth to the Confederate government. General Garrard has issued orders for the immediate destruction of the Roswell Mill."

THEY DID IT that very afternoon.

Teddy went, but only to ensure that the workers were all safely evacuated, women and children. Once he was satisfied about that, he rode back home and stood, wordlessly, on the verandah, Cicero next to him. From there the terrible flames and smoke could be seen belching into the sky. Every once in a while an explosion was heard, and I saw Teddy's shoulders shudder, as if he were on the battlefield. And Cicero would howl.

Sitting in a chair nearby, Pa shouted. "Arson, Teddy, arson! Like back when! Arrest the rotten bugger! Send him to Marietta to jail!"

"All right, Pa," Teddy said soothingly, "all right. It's being taken care of. The mill will be fine." Silent tears were coming down his face.

Carol stood next to her husband. Viola and I stood a ways back. Cannice and Careen were with us. Cannice was weeping.

THE NEXT AFTERNOON, four riders were coming up the front drive at a slow trot. Cicero barked on the verandah. Teddy folded his arms across his chest. He knew what was coming.

That morning, Teddy and Primus had buried a considerable lot of his rifles and revolvers out back under the pine trees on the other side of the stream.

The riders drew up in front of the verandah, raising dust. Cicero's bark became more indignant. Teddy shushed him.

The officer got down from his sleek Yankee horse. His movements were slow but sure. He handed the reins over to another man in blue without even turning to see if the other man was there. He expected him to be there.

He looked around for a moment, taking everything in.

He was a tall man, and wiry, and his shoulders were more than sufficient in their spread. His uniform was somewhat dusty, but fit him like a second skin.

Like my brothers, he wore no beard. I always felt that men who wore beards were hiding something — past scars, ugly expressions, grim mouths, something.

He was freshly shaved.

He nodded at Teddy and came up to the verandah and put one dusty boot on the first step. "I am Major J. C. McCoy, Sherman's aide-de-camp. My escort is a detachment from the 7th Pennsylvania," he said. His voice was clear and decisive. "Mr. Theodore Conners?"

"You've found him," Teddy said.

Major McCoy nodded again, this time thoughtfully, saw Carol and Viola and me, and with his gloved hand touched the edge of his broad-brimmed hat and raised it just a bit.

"Ladies," he said, and bowed his head.

Each of us in our own way acknowledged his greeting. I gave a small curtsy.

He looked back at Teddy. "I am here to tell you, as owner of the mill, that it's beyond the point of rescue. The walls are very stout and will likely remain standing. No workers were harmed in the fire. We'll extinguish the last of the flames. The cloth that was made yesterday morning was saved and will be used for our hospitals."

Teddy nodded his head.

"General Garrard has given orders that we're to occupy the town and use unoccupied houses as headquarters. All people, male and female, connected with the mill are to be arrested as traitors.

"Now we are to enter this residence and collect all firearms. We understand, Mr. Conners, that you are well esteemed in town. Your actions will be an example to others. It will be better for all concerned if you cooperate."

Major McCoy then removed his yellow leather gloves and tucked them in the sash of his uniform, mounted the steps of the verandah, and offered his hand to my brother.

Teddy, ever the Southern gentleman, took it for a brief handshake.

"I hear you and your brother were heroes at First Manassas," he said.

"There were a lot of heroes there," Teddy told him.

McCoy absorbed that and looked at the rest of us. "Who are these people?"

"My family."

McCoy gestured to one of his aides, who quickly came forward with a notebook.

"If you don't mind, I'd like the names, please," he said.

"My wife, Carol," Teddy told him. "My father, over here, Hunter Conners, who built the mill. My sister Viola Cummack."

"Where is her husband?"

"He was killed, defending Richmond."

McCoy nodded again and his aide scribbled. Then the major's eyes went over me and he gave a sort of small smile. "And who is this?"

"My sister Leigh Ann. She's only fourteen."

At the sound of my name, McCoy quickened. "She the one who put the French flag on the roof of the mill?"

Teddy sighed.

"Your mother told us all about your family, Mr. Conners," McCoy advised him.

"Yes," Teddy said. "It was a childish prank."

"I have a little sister," McCoy said. "I know about pranks. But prank or not, that French flag was part of a conspiracy to make us think the mill was in neutral hands. Don't be surprised if she's put under arrest. Garrard is, even as we speak, writing up an order to put all the mill workers under arrest for treason and marching them to Marietta, where they'll be sent by rail to the north."

A bolt of fear went through me. Arrest? Could Garrard do that?

I saw Teddy's shoulders go rigid, saw his face set so that he gave away no expression. "I'm Leigh Ann's guardian," he told McCoy. "I'm legally responsible for her. I take the blame for her actions."

Again McCoy gave a small smile. "Very commendable, but I'm sure Garrard won't see it that way. He's sending mill workers younger than she to Marietta."

"I'd like a meeting with him on the matter."

"I'll request it," McCoy promised. "Now, where is your brother, Louis, the mayor?"

"He's gone out of town, escorting families who wanted to leave."

"How many slaves do you have?" McCoy went on with his questioning and Teddy answered. Slaves, horses, cattle, acres planted in corn, wheat, and so forth.

When they were finished, McCoy said, "Now, I'm sorry, but we have to search the house for firearms. I'll take just one man with me, Mr. Conners, and I promise nothing will be disturbed. You may accompany us to make sure."

So Teddy took them through the house and they collected firearms.

When they came back out with the few guns Teddy had left for them lest they get suspicious, McCoy told him, "I'm leaving a detachment of men. I've been given orders that this place is to be left under guard. My men will bivouac in the front yard. I expect them to be fed and treated decently. They have orders not to enter the house or disrupt the family in any way. Do we understand each other?"

"Understood," Teddy said.

They shook hands again. "Nice plantation you have here," McCoy said with a hint of envy in his voice. "Look, Mr. Conners, you're a decent fellow. If I were in your shoes I'd want to take off and rejoin the army. I heard about how and why you got cashiered out. But any ideas you got about that, I'd advise against it, or you'll bring devastation down on your family."

Before he left the verandah he put his hand to the brim of his hat again and said, "Ladies."

And he smiled at me.

Then he shook hands with Teddy, mounted his beautiful horse, and looked back. It appeared as if he wanted to say more, but he had said all he could. He saluted and rode away, leaving his four men, who promptly set up their two tents. I stood watching until I felt Teddy's firm hand on my shoulder, ushering me into the house.

"How can you get in touch with the vegetable lady?" Teddy asked Viola.

He sat behind his desk in his study, his elbows propped up on it, his head in his hands. Carol and I and Viola had been summoned before him. McCoy had just left.

The door of the study was closed and locked.

"I have to put a quilt over the fence in front," Viola told him.

"And she'll come? Just like that?"

"She has people in the area who will see it and let her know," Viola explained.

"Then do it," Teddy told her, "right now. And don't talk to those men out there. And come right back in. We have things to discuss."

Viola ran. Teddy reached for a newspaper. "You see the trouble you've gotten yourself into?" he scolded. "Now go sit in that chair."

I went. Carol sat down, too. He gave her part of the newspaper and both read until Viola came back. Then we all stood before him again.

"It's this way," he told us. "Soon's I can get a message to the vegetable lady, it'll be to inform Grandmother in Philadelphia to send someone down to Marietta to pick up Leigh Ann and get her out of there. I'm adding a message to the bearer of the note to telegraph it to Grandmother once out of Yankee lines. There will be time, before Garrard gets situated, gathers up all the mill women and children, and marches them off. The trip to Marietta, by foot, ought to take a few days. How does that sound?"

"Terrible for Leigh Ann," Viola said. "Poor thing, walking all those miles."

"Fit punishment," Teddy said.

"Teddy," and Viola pulled herself up straight, "I have to tell you. I think you've been a terrible brother to her lately. I just have to tell you that, is all."

He glared at her. "All right. You've told me."

Silence, then Viola spoke again. "You're breaking her spirit."

It was the same thing Louis had warned of in his note.

"And she worships you, Teddy," Viola appealed. "If you don't know that by now . . ." Her voice faded off helplessly.

Did she have to say *that?* Oh, I wished she would stop. *Please stop!*

Teddy's jaw clenched. "Thank you, Viola, for that information." Then he tried to go on, but Viola interrupted again.

"And if Leigh Ann goes on this trip, I'm going with her."

Teddy scowled. "You are not."

"I am. Leigh Ann and I had a talk. We realize you are disgusted with both of us. We know we've given you some bad times lately and we don't blame you. So we've promised to take care of each other. And this is my way of fulfilling my promise. I'm not letting her go on that trip alone."

He leaned back in his chair and looked from one of us to the other. Then just at me. "Is all this true?

All *what?* What was I pleading to? Worshiping him? I would not answer. I would not give him the satisfaction.

"I'd like an answer, please."

"Yes," I murmured.

He nodded his head slowly. "You'll lose the baby if you go," he told Viola.

"No, I won't. I'm strong. Leigh Ann will take care of me."

He looked at me again. And again I looked at the floor.

"How are you going to convince Garrard to let you go, Viola?"

"I'll tell him my husband died for the Confederacy."

Teddy compressed his lips and said nothing. "So then I tell Grandmother to look for two girls in Marietta," he said.

My heart was breaking. My yes had made no never-mind to him.

"Aren't you even —" Viola was fearless with him. "Aren't you even going to *fight* for Leigh Ann? You're just going to let them take her away? What kind of guardian are you?"

"The kind," Teddy answered, "that provides for the future. Of course I'm going to fight for her. Didn't you hear me say I wanted a meeting with Garrard? What do you think that was for? But if I lose I have to set things in motion now so that plans are in place for someone to be there to meet you all in Marietta!"

He was getting angry now. He was not accustomed to explaining himself.

"I'm sorry," Viola said.

He nodded. "Now wait while I scribble this note. Then you both keep a lookout for some variation of the vegetable lady. But be discreet. Don't loiter outside. Stay away from those Yankees. And, Leigh Ann, I swear if you disobey me in this I'll —" He broke off and eyed me menacingly. "Well, just don't," he finished.

He signed the note with a flair, folded it, put it in an envelope, and gave it to Viola. This meeting had fixed nothing between us. I went out with my sister.

CHAPTER TWENTY-SEVEN

W E HAD TO feed the four Yankee soldiers who were bivouacked on our front lawn. Cannice did it. She would not allow Careen to have anything to do with the chore.

"They gots eyes for the women, Massa Teddy," she said. "An' somethin' tells me they don't care whether that women be white or black. I seen them eyein' my Careen already. You keep your wife an' sisters outta their way."

Careen was beautiful. And, taking the lead role in the house that her mother used to have, she wore pleasing clothes, the fabric of which she had once, before such fabric became scarce, woven herself.

It was when Cannice was bringing the Yankees their supper that first night that a black woman came to the front gate bearing vegetables.

"I don't know whether the mistress of the house is in need," Cannice told the woman, "but it be so hot, you best go to the back door for a cool drink, anyway."

And so, right under the nose of the Yankees, the note was delivered.

Cannice took the quilt off the fence.

Late that night, General Garrard took up residence in town, at Barrington Hall. First thing in the morning his order to arrest and deport factory workers went out.

Just before breakfast, one was delivered to the house for my arrest.

The sergeant who delivered it told Teddy that women and children were already being assembled on the town square. Theophile Roche was also arrested.

We had a silent breakfast. I could scarce eat. Teddy did not talk at all, and he paid no mind to me. I looked at him appealingly several times, but he did not respond.

What was he going to do? Just let soldiers come to the house and take me away? Was he not even going to say a proper goodbye, advise me as how to act?

Viola and I exchanged several looks. She was going, too — I knew she was, if she had to attach herself to me. Had he no last-minute words for her?

Immediately after breakfast, Teddy and Carol retired to his study and closed the door.

"I'm going to throw up," I told my sister.

"No, you're not. Come on, now. It'll be all right."

"How can it be? I need him now. And he doesn't even care about me."

"He cares."

"Well, he's got a downright odd way of showing it."

The grandfather clock in the hall struck nine. I started to cry. My shoulders shook. Viola came over and sat in the chair next to me and pulled me close to her. She wrapped her arms around me.

"I'm going with you. I'll be there," she said.

Her words comforted me and I stopped crying. "I hate him," I said.

"Do whatever makes you feel better."

Of a sudden we heard voices from across the hall. Teddy, talking angrily. We looked at each other and went to the doorway of the dining room, where we hid behind it to listen.

"If Garrard thinks . . . if that low-down, womanizing chigger thinks that I'm just going to hand my sister over on his say-so, he's crazier than a skunk in daylight."

"What will you do?" Carol was asking.

Viola and I looked at each other. She winked at me and smiled. She was about to say something when there was a knock on the door.

Teddy came out of his study to answer it.

There stood a Yankee soldier. "I'm Lieutenant Darius Livermore of General Garrard's staff, sir. Are you Mr. Conners?"

Teddy replied that yes, indeed he was.

"The general requests the honor of a meeting with you at ten thirty this morning at his headquarters in Barrington Hall. May I have the courtesy of a reply?"

"Tell the general I will be there."

The lieutenant saluted and left.

To Viola's and my surprise, Teddy was already dressed for such a meeting. And he had some papers ready for it. "Hand me my portfolio," he requested of Carol.

In the next minute he yelled, "Leigh Ann!"

"Yes?"

"You can come out into the open now. I know you've been listening. Come across the hall."

I did so.

He stood there with his portfolio in his hands. He looked at me appraisingly. "Go and put on a different dress. Something churchy but plain. No frills. You have ten minutes."

I ran upstairs. As I did so, I heard Viola asking him if she could go, too. He said no, this wasn't the time. If he lost this battle with Garrard, that would be the time.

Primus drove us in the carriage. Teddy would have it no other way.

We passed the skeleton of the burned mill, only the brick walls remaining, smoke still rising, like out of a dying dream.

Teddy would not look at the spectacle.

The town was full of men in blue uniforms, cavalry troops and horses, wagons raising dust, federal flags flying from posts, women carrying carpetbags and being ushered along by Yankees with drawn bayonets to the town square.

There stood what seemed like hundreds of women and children, all waiting in the heat, unsheltered. Children were crying. Soldiers guarded them with guns.

When we pulled up in front of Barrington Hall, Teddy, who had not uttered a word all the way, spoke finally.

"When we go in here, keep quiet, unless Garrard speaks to you. Then be polite. No sass. You hear me?"

"Yes, Teddy."

"Tell the truth. If you've got any decent reason why you did what you did, in God's name, tell him. You never did tell me."

"I —"

"No, I don't want to know now. It's too late. Just help yourself, however you can. Now let's go. Oh, one last thing. Mother will likely be in there. He and she have something going. Please don't let either of them know we haven't been getting on and we're ready to kill each other."

It tore at my heart, his saying that.

We got out of the carriage and walked past the guards in front. The house had five enormous pillars and there were more guards at the door. We were ushered in and down the wide hall to a commodious room with highly polished floors and all the accouterments of wealth and power.

We were announced by the same lieutenant who had come to our house earlier.

General Garrard was seated behind a large desk covered with papers. If he stood, he would be tall. His hat was off and his hair was sandy. His beard was full. I did not like men who wore full beards.

Major McCoy had told us Garrard was a West Point graduate. Teddy had once said you didn't fool around with West Point graduates, because they were all fools. Couldn't think beyond what those gray walls had taught them, Teddy said.

Garrard had gray eyes and I did not like gray eyes, either. They could not make up their mind what they wanted to be, like brown or blue ones could, but kept you speculating.

Major McCoy stood next to a fireplace. And my mother was there, seated in a Victorian-style chair, her taffeta skirts billowing about her as she sipped a glass of something red and sparkling. She smiled wickedly when we came in.

Major McCoy introduced Teddy to the general, whose only acknowledgment was a nod of the head and a gesture that my brother should sit on the couch.

"And his sister Leigh Ann," the major finished.

The general's eyes went over me. "Ah," he said. "The young lady who walks on roofs."

I curtsied.

He smiled, approvingly, and pointed to the couch.

I sat next to Teddy.

"Of course, you need no introduction to this lady," Garrard said.

Teddy poked me in the ribs.

"Hello, Mother," I murmured.

"You're growing up, Leigh Ann." She looked at Teddy.

My brother stood briefly and gave a short bow. "How are you, ma'am?" he inquired.

"Quite well, Teddy, thank you."

"Now, as to the matter at hand," Garrard began briskly. "As I understand it, you are here, Mr. Conners, to plead your sister's case, she being under arrest for her part in the conspiracy of the French flag, as we have come to call it. That flag was put on the roof of the mill to lead us to think that said mill was under neutral ownership and as such could not be destroyed. Am I correct?"

"Mr. Roche owns fifty percent of the mill," Teddy informed him. "I have papers here stating such."

"Fifty percent is not total ownership. And such papers were likely drawn up in anticipation of our arrival. And so you sent your sister up on the roof to plant the French flag. Involving her in the conspiracy."

"I did not send her up there," Teddy said evenly. "I would not do such a thing."

Garrard looked at me. "Then why did you go up, young lady?"

"Because she's a brat," Mother put in.

Garrard rolled his eyes. "Please, love," he said. Then he looked at me again. "Well?"

I drew in my breath, then let it out again. Everyone was looking at me. "Because I haven't been very nice lately," I told him. "I've been bad. I've been giving my brother a powerful lot of trouble. So when Mr. Roche said he was afraid to go up on the roof to plant the flag because he's scared of heights, I offered to do it."

Everybody was still staring at me. "I didn't tell anybody. Especially not Teddy. Jon told him, the boy who cares for my pa. And Teddy came and got me down and he was mad as all get-out."

Still nobody said anything. I went on. "I did it because I wanted to make things up to my brother. I wanted to make him proud of me."

Silence, pure and thick, so thick you could pour it. From his position by the fireplace, McCoy was looking at me, and I thought I saw tears welling in his eyes.

Garrard was eyeing me, too. "You got yourself in a lot of trouble there, missy."

I nodded my head. "Yessir, I know."

"You love your brother that much, eh?"

I did not answer.

"Of course she does," Mother answered. "Why shouldn't she? He allows her to run free. He never disciplines her. If she were in my care, which she should be, she'd never attempt such a thing."

"Why isn't she in your care?" Garrard asked.

"She was taken away from me. I was deemed not a fit mother."

"Well"— and Garrard gave a short laugh —"recalling the last few days, love, I'd call you anything but a fit mother. You got papers to prove you're legally in charge of her, Conners?"

"Yes," Teddy answered. "Got them right here, too."

Garrard waved his hand. "Never mind. I believe you. Nevertheless, they won't do a damned thing to prevent her arrest, or my sending her on to Marietta. I've got orders from General Sherman to arrest all connected with the mill as traitors and send them north. The men will be sent right to prison. Can't disobey orders. Sorry, Conners. You were in the army. Heard you were a hero at First Manassas. Surely you understand about obeying orders."

"Sir." It was Major McCoy.

"Yes, McCoy."

"Respectfully, sir."

"Go ahead."

"The child's motivation was pure, sir. She had no knowledge of a conspiracy. And then there's this, sir, if Mr. Conners will forgive me. She's a, well, a downright beautiful girl, sir. There will be all kinds of soldiers who haven't seen women in a while on that march. It'd be like sending a lamb to slaughter."

"You're letting your emotions get in the way of your thinking, McCoy. What in hell are you thinking, anyway?"

"Afraid I was thinking of my own little sister, sir."

"Yeah, well, there will be a lot of other women on that march, too. And girls younger than she is. Why is this one any different?"

"She's from an esteemed family, sir, if I may. Refined and innocent."

"So what do you want me to do? Let her off the hook?"

"No, sir. But I have an idea. Respectfully."

"Let's have it, McCoy. Respectfully."

"Make her a bummer, sir."

"A bummer? Are you crazy?"

"It'll save her, sir. Put her in boys' clothing. Give her to Mulholland. Don't let him know she's a girl."

"Bummers forage," Teddy said.

"Does she know how to shoot a gun?" Garrard asked.

"Yes," Teddy answered. "I taught her."

"Somebody could ask me. I'm right here," I put in.

"Quiet," Teddy ordered. "Don't be disrespectful."

"Kid's got sand," Garrard said. "I like that."

"You taught her to shoot a gun?" Mother flung at him. "I won't have it. She's my child. I simply won't have it. Kenner, I'll let her go on the march, but I want her sent on to New York to this private boarding school where I always wanted her to go, where she will learn true Yankee values and get her away from these decrepit Southern ways."

"What's the name of it?" Garrard asked.

Mother told him.

"What? And lose her sand? No, sorry, love. Even if I wanted to accommodate you, once these women and children leave Marietta, I'm finished with them. I can't be concerned with individual destinations."

"Not even after all I've done for you?" Mother actually *purred* it. In front of everybody.

I was ashamed of her.

Garrard softened. "Why don't we let the little girl decide. Well, what's it to be, missy? You want to go on the march as a bummer? And take your chances that someday you may come back and see your brother again? Or you want to be cared for special on the march, by my orders, and shipped on to New York to a nice boarding school and be safe, then come back to your mother?"

There was no decision to make.

"I'll take my chances and be a bummer and make it home to be with my brother," I said.

The meeting was over.

We stood up to leave. We were dismissed. *Crestfallen* was not the word for what Teddy was. He had lost, and he was not good at losing.

"I'll see them out, sir," McCoy said.

Garrard just waved him off.

On the verandah, McCoy shook Teddy's hand again. "Sorry," he said.

"Thanks for your help," my brother told him.

"She'll be all right. Like Garrard said, she's got sand. Boys' clothes will help. She's a dear little thing."

McCoy looked at me. "Escape any chance you get. Steal a horse. These soldiers are drunk most of the time."

"Yessir."

He reached into his pocket and took out two ten-dollar gold eagles and a compass, held them in his open hand, looked at Teddy for permission, and, receiving a nod from my brother, gave them to me. "Travel off the beaten path," he told me. "And God bless you."

Then he leaned down and kissed my forehead and went back inside.

Teddy was just helping me into the carriage when Mother came out.

"You think you won again, don't you?" she lashed at him. "Because she chose you over me?"

Teddy said nothing.

"Well, you didn't. I've got one more card to play, Teddy boy. And let me tell you. You're going to be sorry this time, you are. Wait and see. Just wait and see."

We did not talk again, all the way home.

CHAPTER TWENTY-EIGHT

Viola and I worked the rest of that day, making over Teddy's and Louis's old trousers and shirts to fit me. Careen helped. We got the clothes down from the attic and set up shop in the back parlor. The size of the outfits indicated they were from when my brothers were about thirteen or fourteen.

Careen cut and I measured and we all did the sewing. We found suspenders and old hats, too. And even boots. By afternoon we had two outfits.

We even found boys' underwear.

"Do I have to wear these?" I held up the small clothes.

"You'd best," Viola advised. "Just in case push comes to shove."

"Well, I'm sure glad I didn't get my woman's time of the month yet."

It had been a source of embarrassment to me at first, that I hadn't yet gotten it. But then Viola told me she hadn't gotten hers until she was fifteen. Now I considered myself blessed. I had just turned fourteen. God was good to me.

And then, just before supper, when I was upstairs washing up and Viola and Carol were napping, a carriage pulled up in front, a fancy carriage.

Mother's carriage.

Her footman opened the door. She got out, came up the verandah steps, and pounded the door knocker.

Cannice answered.

I stood at the top of the stairs.

"I have come to see my son," she said. "Is he here?"

"He's in his study, ma'am," Cannice said.

Mother pushed her way into the hall and into Teddy's study. She did not bother closing the door all the way.

I crept downstairs and listened outside.

"What's this I hear about you sending around a note to Garrard asking him to let Viola go along on the march?"

"If it's any of your business, she wants to go to look after Leigh Ann."

"I told him you were sending her because she's pregnant. And not married. And a disgrace to the family. So he's going to let her go."

I could see through the door, which was ajar, Teddy standing behind his desk holding an open newspaper. And Mother holding her riding whip.

"How dare you say such," Teddy said with contempt.

"I'll say what I please."

"*You* were in the family way with Louis a few months before you married Pa, I'm given to understand. How could you demean your daughter so?"

"She's not your concern!" Mother screamed at him.

Teddy said she was, as much as I was, especially now that she'd taken up with that Garrard popinjay who was addicted to liquor and women.

She called Teddy a no-count rogue.

He called her a Northern witch.

At which juncture she raised her riding crop and swung it expertly.

It hit his shoulder, ripping his shirt, then continued on its journey to the side of his face, slashing it.

He laughed, though it made his shoulder and face bleed.

At that point I burst through the door and ran toward her. "Don't you *dare,*" I screamed. I took her unawares and, doing so, wrested the riding crop from her and threw it across the room. "Don't you dare come in here and treat Teddy like that. You have no right. You left us! You don't care about any of us! You have no right!"

I was bawling, unashamedly. I began to hit her with both my hands.

"Leigh Ann!" Teddy came out from behind his desk and seized me. I fought him, but he got both my hands behind me and secured my wrists until they hurt.

I was sobbing.

Mother held her face where I'd hit her. "So this is the kind of child you're raising. The kind that hits her mother."

Still holding my wrists, Teddy said, "Apologize to your mother."

"I won't."

He gave me a couple of shakes. "Do as I *say,* for God's sake." There was pleading in his voice, even a hint of desperation.

I knew I had to, for his sake. But by all the gods above, I did not want to.

"I'm sorry," I said.

Teddy released me. "Now go. Get out of here."

"Can I just say one thing? Please?"

Teddy closed his eyes. That was my answer.

"Viola is married," I told my mother. "Her husband was killed at Richmond. And Major McCoy knows it. It's in his records. And if he knows it, General Garrard knows it."

I looked at Teddy. He nodded his head approvingly. His face was bleeding. I curtsied to my mother and left the room.

⁂

THAT NIGHT I'd just put myself to bed when there was a knock on my door and Teddy came in.

"Get dressed in your boys' clothes and come out back," he said. That was all.

I did so, quickly. What was going on? *Anything,* I told myself. *Anything might be going on.* Was he going to sneak me away?

The house was quiet, and something warned me to be quiet, too. I sneaked out the back door, deciding whether to take one of the many lanterns that were at the ready there. But I did not need one. The moon was full and cast a light as clear as day.

Sure enough, a distance away from the house, down by the grape arbor, there were two figures waiting. I crept through the already dew-wet grass toward them.

Viola and Teddy.

Teddy held a lantern. He had a plaster on his face where Mother had hit him.

Viola held a pair of scissors and a comb in one hand and a hand mirror in the other.

Between them was a chair.

I stopped a few feet from them. "No," I said. "No, Teddy, please. I'm sorry I've been naughty. I'm sorry I hit Mother."

"Sit down in the chair, please," he said quietly. "Viola is tired and needs to go to bed."

I stood rigid.

He came over and took me gently by the arm and sat me down in the chair.

"This could save your life, honey," Viola told me. "We have to do it. It isn't on account of anything you did. Teddy wouldn't punish you this way. It'll grow back, prettier than ever. Sometimes, especially in this heat, I wish I could cut mine."

I sat in a daze. Viola undid the braid that I put my hair in at night and combed out my long, curly hair. Tears came quietly down my face.

Teddy stood next to her with the lantern so she would have good light.

Inside, my heart was breaking as Viola combed and snipped and combed and snipped. I could feel rather than see the hair falling to the ground.

My hair. It had always been my vanity! It reached well below my shoulders and was naturally curly. I usually wore it pulled high off my forehead and tied with a ribbon on top, with some of it falling down on the sides of my face. Everyone said that with such hair, my upturned nose, my large brown eyes, and the dimple in my chin, I was a beautiful child.

Teddy worried about me being a beautiful child. I think that was why he was so strict with me.

By now Viola was cutting up to my cheekbones. She stopped and looked at Teddy. "Lots of boys wear it to about here," she told him. "Especially ruffians. They don't bother cutting their hair."

He considered that. He put his hand under my chin and turned my face to look at him. Did I look enough of a boy to please him? Enough of a boy not to be a beautiful child anymore?

He released me. "All right," he said, "that's good. Thank you, Viola. You'd best get to bed now."

Viola stood in front of me with the hand mirror. "You look kind of saucy. You want to see?"

"No," I said.

She kissed me on the forehead. "Don't be angry with me. You'll be glad we did this, you'll see. Now come on, let's go to bed."

I started to get out of the chair, but Teddy put his hand on my shoulder and held me back. "You go on, Viola. We have something else to attend to."

She looked from him to me. "Is everything all right?"

"It's fine," he assured her. "I just want to show Leigh Ann a few moves to protect herself if she has to."

Viola nodded and started toward the house.

Teddy extinguished the lantern, set it on the ground, then turned and gestured that I should follow.

I did. *What now?* I followed him across the grass. What was this damned crocodile of a brother of mine about now?

Of a sudden he halted and turned around. "Now," he said in not so friendly a tone, "I'm going to teach you how to defend yourself in case they discover you're a girl and some man comes at you with devious intentions. Do you know what I mean by devious intentions?"

"Yes," I said in an equally unfriendly tone. "If he can't control himself and wants to touch me in all kinds of ways. And maybe do more." I said it with satisfaction. "Louis explained all that to me."

He nodded, a little surprised. "All right. I'm coming at you now. I'm going to grab your arm. Fight me off. Hit me, kick me, do anything you can to defend yourself."

I stood staring at him, uncertain.

"Come on. I mean it. You can do it. Have at it. I know you're angry with me. Get it out. I give you permission."

He came forward and grabbed my arm roughly and pulled me toward him.

I did the only thing I knew how to do. The thing that Viola had once told me to do.

I lifted one leg swiftly, and with my heavy, laced-up brogan, I kicked him in the groin.

There, I thought, *that's for cutting off my hair.*

He yelled and crumpled to his knees, clutching himself.

I stood there, paralyzed with fear. *Oh God,* I thought, *what have I done? Oh, God, he'll kill me now.*

"Where"— his breath was coming in short gasps — "where in hell did you learn to do that?"

"Viola taught me. She said that would stop any man."

He was breathing heavily. *What should I do?*

"Yeah, well, she's right."

"Do you need help? You want me to get somebody?"

"You do and I'll skin you alive. You tell anybody about this and I'll . . ."

More heavy breathing. He was leaning over, like he was going to throw up.

"Go in the house," he ordered. "Now."

I ran. Inside the back door I turned and looked.

He was throwing up. *Well,* I decided, *that does it. He'll never speak to me again. As of now, we are definitely finished.*

CHAPTER TWENTY-NINE

B UT THE NEXT morning it was as if nothing had happened to him. He was bright-eyed, vigorous, clean-shaven, and immaculately dressed as usual, and attending to a dozen things all at once. The last of which was meeting with Primus in his study to talk about plantation matters while the rest of us sipped tea and waited for him to come into the dining room to start breakfast.

Cannice and Careen complimented me on my new hair fashion. So did Carol, to my surprise.

I could not get accustomed to the feeling of no hair on my neck and shoulders, but I was more concerned with meeting Teddy's eyes. Or would he not look at me at all?

And here I was, leaving tomorrow.

Someone knocked on the front door. My heart fell and I saw Viola bite her lip and Carol almost choke on her tea. It was the way we all reacted these days when someone knocked on the front door. You'd think it was the Angel of Death come calling.

Cannice answered. "Massa Teddy?" she called.

Bad, I thought, *bad, when she called him like that.*

He came out of his study, saying some last-minute words to Primus, who went out through the kitchen. We heard voices, low, in the hallway. Then Teddy's: "What the hell!"

Viola put her elbow on the table and covered her eyes with her hand. Carol closed her eyes. Pa just sat there, oblivious. Andrew continued holding Pa's cup and spooning tea into his mouth. I started to tremble.

"Sorry, sir," the voice answered, "but those are the orders. She's to report with the others to the town square first thing in the morning. Oh, and some good news. They won't be walking to Marietta. General Garrard has got wagons, dozens of them. They will ride. Some of the women have already been driven off this morning."

"That's *good news?*" Teddy asked. "That's like telling me their destination has been changed to hell, but the good news is that the temperature has been lowered ten degrees! I want to see Garrard!"

"I'm sorry, sir. He has an interview with a correspondent from the *Louisville Journal* this morning. And after that the *Nashville Dispatch.*"

"Just tell me," Teddy asked wearily, "what has my wife done to be connected with the mill?"

I gasped and covered my mouth with my hands.

Carol burst into tears. Viola, sitting next to her, put her arms around her sister-in-law.

"It says right on the arrest notice, sir. She taught school for the mill children. See? It says so, right there."

Silence.

"My mother did this," Teddy mumbled.

"Pardon me, sir? I don't quite understand."

"Neither do I, sergeant. Neither do I."

"Would you sign this paper, sir, acknowledging that you have received the arrest notice and will comply with the order?"

"And if I don't?"

"Sir, the general told me to inform you that if you do not sign and comply, he is going to send a contingent of men from company H of the 3rd Ohio around to take her forcible. They are, how shall I say, excellent soldiers, sir, intent on obeying orders. It won't be pretty. The general also said I should tell you that if he has to resort to such tactics, your wife and your two sisters might find the trip considerable dangerous and uncomfortable. But if you do comply, your wife and your two sisters will find the trip — how shall I put it? — agreeable and safe. Do we understand each other, sir?"

Before Teddy could answer, Carol got up out of her chair and went into the hall, and we heard her say, "I will go along on the trip, Teddy. Tell the . . . lieutenant, is it?"

"Sergeant, ma'am."

"Tell the sergeant that we comply."

"Carol." The pain in Teddy's voice could not be described. How there could be so much pain in just the saying of a name, I did not know.

"It's all right, Teddy. If my going keeps your sisters from harm and perhaps more, I shall go."

Viola and I looked at each other in disbelief. Was this *Carol* talking?

There was silence again in the hall. Teddy likely signed the paper. Then we heard the door close and a horse ride off. But Teddy and Carol did not come into the dining room for a long minute

"They're kissing," I whispered.

"It takes something like this," Viola whispered back.

When they did come in, Carol looked as if she'd been crying. Teddy looked stoic. Sometimes I think he had as much of that Indian quality in him as Louis had.

"You heard?" he asked us.

We both nodded yes.

Careen came in and served breakfast.

"Leave us, Andrew," Teddy ordered. "Take Pa into the kitchen and feed him." He waited until Andrew did as he said, and then he told us.

"It's my fault. Mother did this to punish me because Leigh Ann chose to take her chances and go on the trip as a bummer and make her way back to me rather than go on to that boarding school in New York and return to her."

He sipped his coffee. "She told me she had one more card to play and I would be sorry. Well, she's played it. She took my wife."

He looked down the table at me. Right at me. "You did what was in your heart. It isn't your fault. Nobody is blaming you."

It was said matter-of-factly. Not with love or forgiveness by any means. But it was said, nevertheless.

AFTER BREAKFAST, Viola and I helped Carol pack. Then she and Teddy spent the rest of the day together. She went

along with him while he attended to plantation matters. Viola and I let them be. We sat ourselves down in the kitchen to eat supper so they could be alone at the dining room table, but Teddy came in and stood there looking at us.

"What is this all about?" he asked grimly. "I want you two in the dining room. We're still a family, aren't we?"

He was torn to pieces. And even Viola, who sassed him most of the time, did not know what to do.

At the table Viola scarce spoke, and I did not speak at all. Finally he could take no more.

"Would it be too much to ask you two to say something?"

Viola took the lead. "I'll look after Carol, Teddy. I promise."

Carol put her hand over his on the table. "We'll all be together, Teddy. Family. Like you want."

"And you, chatterbox," he said to me, "you who never learn to keep a still tongue in your head. What have you to say?"

Say something brilliant, I told myself. *Oh, there is so much I want to say, but I can't say it here and now. And I never did tell him about the silver Louis and I buried.*

"I'm going to look after Carol and Viola. Best I can. I promise."

That seemed to mollify him for the moment. We finished supper. He and Carol lingered at the table. He directed Viola and me to go to bed early.

The July light lingered longer than it had a right to. From my window I could see the strange sky, yellow at the edges on top of the trees, then piled high with banks of clouds going in all different directions, as if God were playing with building blocks. When what He was really doing was playing with people's lives.

That was blasphemous. Louis would scold. Louis. Where was he now? Oh, how I wished he were here! He'd have words of wisdom for me, words of peace.

Louis! I never did tell Teddy about the silver we'd buried out back! And early tomorrow we were leaving!

I got out of bed, put on my robe, went into the hall, and looked over the banister. Where was Teddy? Had he gone to bed with Carol? No, not yet, thank heaven. Gaslights were lighted in the downstairs hall.

I crept down and knocked on the closed door of his study, where from under the door there shone some light.

When it opened, he stood there with a scowling and forbidding face. "What do you want?"

Lord in His heaven, I thought, *will this man never forgive anything? Will he never forgive himself?*

For a moment I felt sorry for him even as I wanted to flee, but I stood my ground. This was not for me, and this was not frivolous. This was for a promise to Louis.

"I have to tell you something before I leave tomorrow."

"I told you, it isn't your fault what Mother did about Carol to get back at me. So go to bed."

"It's not about that! You're a crocodile, you know that?"

"Well, I've been called worse." He touched his face where Mother had hit it. He still had a plaster there.

Oh, good. A sense of humor. That was good.

"This is about a secret Louis and I have. He said if things get bad, I should tell you."

He stepped back. "Well, things can't get any worse, so come on in."

And so I told him the secret Louis had left with me. The secret I had promised to keep and tell no one but Teddy, and then only if things got bad. He listened. He nodded his head solemnly. Then, just as solemnly, he told me I'd done well. High praise, considering his attitude toward me over the last six weeks or so. But he did not kiss me as he would in the past, or as he should because I was leaving tomorrow. He did not say he was proud of me. Things I wanted, I needed, more than anything else in the world.

He just sent me to bed.

CHAPTER THIRTY

W E WOKE the next morning at first light. Carol and I and Viola had to be at the town square, ready to leave, at eight. We'd already eaten breakfast at six thirty, a solemn and forced affair, scarce looking at one another.

I'd said my goodbyes to Cannice and Careen. I'd given Careen a letter to mail to James in which I'd told him about my arrest. I dressed in my boys' clothing. Teddy gave each of us last-minute instructions at breakfast but said nothing else to me except "Go upstairs and get your things. There soon will be soldiers outside." His voice broke. "I'll be along to see you all go."

Upstairs I took one last grief-stricken look around my room, at the dressing table with my powders and brushes and combs, ribbons and the bonnets on a peg next to it. *Bonnets and ribbons.* Would I ever wear such trappings of girlhood again? What would happen to me now? How had my life taken such a turn?

Just last year this time I'd be dressing in a riding skirt and hat and going on horseback with Teddy to learn how to use the bow and arrow.

Impulsively, I went over to the chair where my dolls sat and kissed them. Tears were coming down my face as I went downstairs.

The front door was open.

The soldiers were already waiting outside.

Carol and Viola were there, with them.

I stood in the doorway of Teddy's study where he sat at his desk in front of the turreted window.

"I'm going," I said.

He looked at me and saw my large drawstring bag. "What have you got in there?"

I shrugged.

He motioned me over.

I brought it to him. He opened it and rifled through it in an impersonal manner. "No extra brogans? Yours get wet, it's a great way to catch cold. No preparations for your woman's time of month?"

I blushed. With Teddy, his sense of responsibility came before his sensitivity.

"I didn't get it yet," I admitted.

His eyebrows raised. "Oh. Too much of a hooligan, eh?"

"Viola said not to worry. She didn't get hers till she was fifteen."

"Well, you'd better bring something along just in case. And what is *this?*" He pulled out my book by Shelley.

"Shelley's heart wouldn't burn when they cremated him. And Mary Shelley carried it around in a silken shroud for the rest of her life. That's why he's my favorite writer."

His face went expressionless. I knew the look. He was fighting to hide his feelings.

"Go upstairs and get the things I told you to include. And hurry. The soldiers are waiting."

I picked up my bag and did as I was told. Then I dragged my bag downstairs again. "All right now? Can I go?"

"No, you can't. Not yet."

So I stood there in the doorway of his study. What did he want now?

He just sat there, looking at me and I at him across the expanse of his study floor.

"It's been some ride, Leigh Ann," he said.

"I'm sorry I kicked you the other night."

He shrugged. "At least I know you can take care of yourself."

I wanted to run to him, to sit on his lap, to hug him the way I used to. But I dared not.

"Leigh Ann!" Viola called from outside. "We have to leave!"

Suppose I ran to him and he pushed me away? I would die!

Oh, the donkey's hind end to it! I ran to him. He looked up, surprised. I fell into his lap and he did not push me away. He held me close, embracing me tightly. He rested his chin on top of my head. He kissed me and because he hadn't shaved yet, the side of his face scraped mine.

"You're not mad at me then?" I asked.

"Tell you something. My damned heart wouldn't burn now, either."

"Oh, God, Teddy."

"Remember all I taught you," he said roughly. "And say goodbye to Pa. He's on the verandah. Now go."

He pushed me off his lap.

In the next minute I was gone.

CHAPTER THIRTY-ONE

WE STOOD, Carol and Viola and I, on the village square with about a hundred or so other women and children, I in my boys' clothes.

I was Sam Conners, Viola's little brother. I had run errands for my big brother Teddy in the mill.

At least fifty empty supply wagons were lined up on the side of the road ready to take us away. Yankee soldiers from company E of the 7th Pennsylvania stood ready.

We assembled in the morning sun, then waited. In the middle distance, across the street a ways, I saw Teddy watching. I nudged Carol and she smiled and waved.

At first he didn't see us. He was talking with Major McCoy. They were studying some papers. Then I saw them shake hands. They were conspiring over something. McCoy came toward us. Teddy nodded in our direction and I heard McCoy saying,

"Just a moment there, boy. You there, is your name Conners?"

He was talking to me!

"Yessir," I answered.

"What are you doing here with all these women?" His voice was stern. He was acting as if he did not even know me.

"They are my sisters, sir."

He grabbed me roughly by the arm and pulled me along with him to another Confederate soldier a distance away, who was lounging against one of the wagons.

"Sergeant Mulholland!"

The sergeant immediately straightened up and saluted. "Sir!"

"I've got a bummer for you. Name's Conners. What's your first name, boy?"

"Sam, sir," I told McCoy.

"Sam Conners. Brother owned the mill. He can shoot a gun."

"Good. I can use another bummer. Get in the wagon, boy."

"Not just yet," McCoy told him. "He's got two sisters on this trip. I'd like him to ride with them, at least to Marietta. They're under Garrard's so-called special protection."

Mulholland uttered an oath.

McCoy corrected him. "Enough of that! You'll have Sam whenever you need him on stops along the way. And I'll not have him mistreated, either. Got it, Mulholland?"

"Yessir."

McCoy was still gripping my arm. Now he let go. "All right, back to your sisters, boy."

I walked back. He followed me. When I got there, he demanded to look into my bag and I handed it over. Then, discreetly, while pretending to inspect the contents, he slipped in two pieces of paper. Having done so, he pulled the strings to close the bag, set it on the ground, put his hand on my shoulder, and gripped it. Then he winked at me and walked away.

❧

SLOWLY AND CAREFULLY the wagons moved out of town, even as I could not believe we were finally going. As we passed Teddy standing there watching, Carol was crying, and so was I.

He nodded his head and waved, and we kept our eyes glued to him until he was out of sight.

Then Carol broke down and I held her, weeping, on my shoulder.

We were not the only women in the wagon, to be sure. There were at least ten others, all mill women, all dressed in plain brown calico, all weeping copiously.

"We've got to stick together," one named Muriel Meadows said. "No matter what. It's all we've got."

All agreed.

"Well," another put in, "I heard they're sending us across the river, to Ohio. And they hate us in the North. What will we do?"

"Don't panic," still another put in. "I for one am glad to get away from that damned mill. I hated it. And I hated that damned Teddy Conners. Who in hell did he think he was? That whole family was a bunch of swells. I'm glad the mill burned."

Instantly, there was a chorus of hushes and whispers and some pointed at us.

"Oh," said the woman who hated Teddy. "So some of the family got their comeuppance, eh? Well, I'll say it to your faces. I hated Teddy Conners. So there."

It got silent then. Carol's sobbing had subsided somewhat. Then she whispered to me.

"Leigh Ann, I've got to tell you something."

"What?"

"I'm pregnant."

Would there be no peace, ever, in my world again? The words slammed in my face, gave me a headache. "What?"

"Yes. Can you believe it? After all these years? When we thought we'd never have a child?"

No, I could not believe it. "How far are you?"

"Two months."

"Does Teddy know?"

"No. I couldn't tell him with all the trouble going on. At first I thought I'd wait until things calmed down. But they never did. And then I decided I'd better tell him before he figured it out for himself. And I was just about to when the arrest notice came around for me. And then I couldn't. How could I? He'd never let me go. He'd do, oh . . ." She clutched the front of my shirt. "He'd do something terrible, Leigh Ann. You know your brother."

I certainly did. Likely he'd shoot Garrard and get himself shot in return.

"Don't worry." I patted her. "It'll be all right We'll take care of you."

"You sound a lot like Teddy."

Viola was sleeping already. So she hadn't heard. With the rocking of the wagon, a lot of the women had fallen asleep.

I figured it was safe enough to open my bag and read the notes McCoy had given me.

The first was directly to me and said:

Dear Child:

    God be with you. Remember what I said. When you come through this, and I know you will, write to me and let me know.

                Your friend, J. C. McCoy, 112 Canterbury Rd.,
                                    Akron, Ohio.

The second one read:

    I, Major J. C. McCoy, General William T. Sherman's aide-de-camp, do hereby direct the recipient of this notice to honor my wishes not to harm the bearer of said notice, or companions, in any way, either by starvation or beatings, and furthermore to aid and assist the same in any way possible.

    If I, Major J. C. McCoy, hear anything to the contrary, severe disciplinary action will be taken against the offender.

It was signed with a flourish.

These must have been the papers McCoy and Teddy had been poring over near the town square. McCoy had shown my brother the protection order to ease his mind.

And the note to me, asking me to write to him. McCoy had asked Teddy's permission for this first. So, it was more than his just asking for a note to know I was safe. And Teddy had obviously given his permission.

What was it then, if not just his need to know I was safe?

My head spun with the idea of it. How old was McCoy? Younger than Teddy, who was twenty-seven, to be sure. How old did you have to be to be a major?

I would ask Viola. She would know. She knew everything. The wagon continued to rock and I fell asleep.

CHAPTER THIRTY-TWO

THE RIDE was bumpy. When I woke, the rest of the women were still sleeping. Carol was leaning on my shoulder, and the thought hit me like a wet towel in the face: *Carol is pregnant.*

At first I thought I'd dreamed it. But no, it went with the whole ritual of the journey, part of it now, like the great indigo bird that just then went screaming over our heads, warning us to beware.

I had been to Marietta before, with Viola and Louis and Teddy, but none of this landscape was familiar to me. We had to be on a different route. Most likely, in case any of us thought to escape. We would never find our way back along this off-the-beaten-path route.

Or it could be because some of our own people might take it in their head to pursue us, and they would never find us through this floundering way.

But it was pretty. We passed through some very wild country with a rolling surface. It was pleasantly wooded and filled with azaleas, andromedas, stalmins, and other flowering shrubs I could not name.

Then of a sudden we passed fields and fields of cotton, where negroes chopped incessantly at the weeds in the hot sun, and we heard them singing. Some of the smaller ones ran over to the fence along the road to stare at us as we went by.

"I'd like to know who's the slave here and who's free," said the woman who hated Teddy, startling me. I'd learned that her name was Sadie Moline.

The women were all waking up now, stretching and moaning about needing water. We'd all been given canteens when we left Roswell, but they were empty now, and the July sun was nearing its highest time of day.

Coming into view to the right of us was a tributary of the Chattahoochee River. You could smell the water. And when they saw it the women all started yelling out at once for water and banging their canteens on the side of the wagon and hanging out the back of it, so that the Yankee soldier who rode alongside of us did not know what all to do and had to ride up to the front of the caravan and speak to his commanding officer.

In short order he came back, telling us he'd gotten permission for the wagons to stop. We were to be allowed to get out, under guard, and in an orderly manner fill our canteens with water, then in like manner come back immediately to the wagon. All up and down the line, women were being allowed to do the same thing.

One by one we got out and made our way down the grassy slope to the water. As I stepped carefully down, guiding Carol, with Viola on the other side of me, I saw Sadie Moline eyeing me hatefully.

This woman means trouble for me, I told myself. *I must never turn my back on this woman.*

If Teddy had taught me anything it was to recognize an enemy when I saw one.

But oh, the water looked so delicious and inviting! I longed to strip down to my chemise and pantalets as I did at home, or in this case, my skivvies, and plunge in. I looked at Viola and she at me, and she knew what I was thinking.

She smiled wistfully. "Those days are gone, Sam," she said. "At least for now, anyway."

We hugged briefly, and then the three of us filled our canteens and started back up the slope.

Halfway up, I was so busy helping Carol and worrying that Viola should not slip and fall that I did not see Sadie coming at me.

She came so fast, like a noxious reptile, and grabbed for my canteen. Before I knew it she had it in her hands, had undone the cover, and poured the contents on the ground.

I reached out to grab it. Too late. There went my precious water, all over the place. I reached out to grab her, but Viola held me back.

"Don't, Sam, don't." She grabbed my arm as Teddy would have done. "You'll only make more trouble. We have a ways to go with her yet."

"But she had no right."

"None of us has any rights at the moment," Viola reminded me.

We were almost at the top of the slope. Our Yankee guard had seen the whole thing and was waiting for us at the top.

"Is there trouble?" he asked.

I knew better than to tell. Did I ever tell Teddy what the matter was when Viola and I had been fighting?

"I dropped my canteen and spilled my water," I said. "May I please get more, sir?"

"No," he answered. "You had one shot and you blew it. You'll just have to make do."

Back in the wagon, however, I looked Sadie Moline right in the eye. "Why did you do that?" I asked her.

She eyed me viciously. "Just settling some scores, is all," she said.

❧

THE FOOD they gave us for lunch was not to be borne. At home I would not give such food to Cicero. It consisted of hardtack and stale corn bread. The only redeeming factor was the coffee. The Yankees had real coffee. And plenty of it.

Carol tried to eat the food but became nauseated and had to throw up over the back of the wagon.

Sadie Moline enjoyed this spectacle immensely. "What's wrong? She miss her creamed chicken?"

"Leave her alone," I snapped. "She's pregnant."

This I will not abide, I told myself, *this rattlesnake harping on Carol or Viola. She can torment me all she wants, but I will not tolerate her picking on my sisters.*

"You don't want to tangle with my little brother," Viola advised her. "He can be a terror when he sets his mind to it."

"I see you're pregnant, too," Sadie commented. "What kind of water do they have up in that big plantation house?"

"I said *shut up!*" I stood now and shouted it at her. "Don't you just know how to shut up?"

Everybody got quiet of a sudden and the ride plodded on.

Now I concentrated again on the scenery. We passed sandy patches on the side of the road where I saw some giant tortoises basking in the sun. Then came cornfields and plantation houses. They were not like ours, but two- and three-story clapboard with dormers and porches in front, lots of wings stretching out on the sides, and board fences all around.

This was more like the "Gothic Georgia" Louis sometimes talked about, the Georgia without culture, grace, the arts, and elegance. Louis had traveled through much of it and said it had its own charm.

About one o'clock the wagons came to a halt. Our Yankee guard came along with none other than the esteemed Sergeant Mulholland.

"I want my bummer," he said.

I stood up and went to the back of the wagon and got out.

"This is wild turkey country," he said. "I want you to get out there and shoot us one." He gestured to the right side of the road where there was a spread of thick woods. "They're all over the place."

He handed me an Enfield rifle. "Go on now. Show us what you're made of. We want a big fat one for supper. As for you ladies, get on out here and gather some kindling and the makings for a fire. There's a small brook across the road. We've got a tripod here. Set things up so you can cook the turkey he brings back."

At first I stared dumbly at Mulholland, then the rifle, then the woods. Could I do it? Of course I could, I decided. How many times had I gone hunting with Teddy? The thought generated confidence in me.

I felt tolerably well about the whole thing as I stepped into the thick woods and disappeared into them to find my wild turkey.

CHAPTER THIRTY-THREE

A N ODD THING happened to me as soon as I plunged into the thicket of trees. I lost any trace of fear I should rightly have had in the strange forest in which I found myself.

I suppose I was too busy trying to sort it all out. At first I was on a narrow dirt footpath obviously made by humans, which led through what consisted mostly of pinewoods. Deer bounded through the trees and across my path in front of me. Rabbits and squirrels went about their business. But I saw no wild turkeys.

Then, of a sudden, there were some magnificent evergreen oak trees and a small wooden bridge that crossed a spring of pure water.

I stopped to fill my canteen and in the distance saw what appeared to be a peach orchard. Beyond that I could have sworn I saw some wigwams.

I stood up to better focus my vision. I was right! Just on the other side of the peach orchard were at least six wigwams that seemed to be built out of bark and evergreen boughs.

I felt a curious attraction inside, a drawing of myself toward them.

Were they really there? Or did I just fancy they were?

I had to find out.

I picked up my Enfield and walked on through the peach orchard and toward the small settlement. Never had I expected to come upon human habitation in this wilderness. As for Indians, I thought they had been driven out ages ago.

As I came closer to them I counted, indeed, six wigwams, and each had a tripod in front from which hung a kettle. There were also frying pans and all the other accouterments that Indians used.

There were only women present, no men.

In the ashes of the fires some cakes were cooking.

On one tripod hung a huge kettle in which something was cooking, and the smell was so fragrant, it made me realize how hungry I was. But it not only did that. It near hypnotized me. It brought me into their world. It made me unafraid.

Was it all real? Or was I dreaming? I thought of Louis. Had he guided me here? Did he have something to do with this? Was he helping me, even now? Would these women know where I could find a turkey?

Had I entered his world?

The women looked up as I approached and smiled. And what I had feared, that they would be afraid of my rifle, did not happen.

Though they were all busy, either sewing beads on moccasins or ornamenting deerskin pouches or frying bacon, they looked up and smiled as I approached. They nodded their heads.

"You've come at last," one said.

At last? Had they been waiting for me? Known of me?

"Yes," I said. "I suppose I lost my way. But now I have found you. Have you been waiting for me a long time?"

"Long enough," another said. "We were told by the owl that a little girl of our people would soon come and she would be in trouble and we were to help her. From where do you come, little one?"

So they knew I was a girl, in spite of my boys' clothes. "Roswell," I said.

They nodded to one another. They said something in Indian language. What language. *Cherokee?* Oh, why had I never asked Louis to teach me Cherokee?

And then, in the middle of the Indian language I caught his name. *Louis.*

So I was right. He had guided me here. They knew of him.

"Do you travel with the Yankees?" the one who was beading the moccasins asked me.

I told them yes, I traveled with the Yankees. I was being sent to Marietta with the other women who had been arrested.

"Well, you are not to worry," the one who was frying bacon said. "Your Father in heaven will protect you. And the two who travel with you. Last evening we saw it in the smoke of our fire. Now, how can we help you today?"

I told them about the turkey.

They laughed. "No wild turkeys around," said the one who was stirring the fragrant soup in the pot. "Mulholland Bad Face fooled you. He waits for you to return with no turkey so he can whip you. But we tell you now, that if you go to the other side of the bridge that goes over the stream that is pure, you will see one standing there and waiting for you. Shoot him. Then kneel over him and tell him you are sorry. And thank him for his life. And bring him back to Mulholland Bad Face."

"Oh, thank you," I said.

One by one, I went to them and embraced them. Before I took my leave they said some Indian prayers over me. Then out of the ashes, they gave me a cake wrapped in a cabbage leaf. I did not really want to leave, there was such a sense of peace here, but I knew that I had to. So I picked up my Enfield and walked slowly away.

When I got to the other side of the peach orchard, I turned to look back.

They were no more.

They were gone.

But the ash cake wrapped in the cabbage leaf was very real in my hand. And I unwrapped it and ate it. Oh, it was delicious! I did not question its origin or what had just happened to me. There are some things in life that you just do not question, Louis had once told me. You just accept them for what they are.

And when I came to the small wooden bridge that went over the water that was pure and saw the large fat turkey that was just standing there waiting for me on the other side, I did not question that, either.

I aimed my rifle as Teddy had taught me. I fired it. The sound echoed and reechoed in the silent forest and the turkey fell to the ground.

I set down my gun and went over to kneel beside the turkey. I told it how sorry I was that I had to shoot it. I thanked it for its life. Then I picked it up, retrieved my rifle, and started back along the path to Mulholland Bad Face.

CHAPTER THIRTY-FOUR

WHEN I GOT back to the wagon they were waiting for me. The women had the fire going and were sitting around it.

I handed the turkey to Mulholland Bad Face. He looked down at me with a mixture of surprise and disdain.

"Where'd you get it?"

"In the forest. It was there, waiting for me. Like you said it would be."

He took it and handed it over to the women, with orders to pluck it and cook it, right off. Then he took my Enfield from me and gave it to our Yankee guard. At this juncture, as I was about to help the women, he grabbed me by the wrist and took me back into the thicket of pine trees, dragging me a good ways in from the others.

"Where are you taking him?" It was Viola's voice.

"To see if we can find any more turkeys," he yelled back.

But I knew it was not so, and fear overtook me. He was handling me roughly. As soon as we were covered by a goodly number of pine trees, he let my wrist go.

"You lie," he said. "There are no turkeys about. This part of the country has been without them for two years. Now, where did you get that turkey?"

"I told you. I found him near the stream a ways over there. I shot him as you wanted. I'm not lying. Why did you send me there if you knew there were no turkeys?"

He was taking off his wide Yankee belt. "I'll teach you to lie to me, you little Southern bugger," he said.

And so saying, he grabbed me by the arm and proceeded to whip me with the belt. Oh, merciful God; I thought I would die! It was worse than when Mother had whipped me with her riding crop, and there was no one about to help. I wanted to scream but wouldn't give him the satisfaction.

And then, of a sudden, there was someone. Oh, there was a blessed someone!

From out of nowhere came a bird, screeching and clawing at him, attacking him.

An owl!

It hovered about his head. It bit his ears. It went for his eyes, and he had to release me to protect himself.

I stood back, breathlessly, watching in awe its tremendous wingspread, its terrible claws, its insistent anger. I thought, *It's just like Louis's owl. It looks just the same as Louis's owl did that night.*

And I knew that if I did not say something it would not cease its attack; it would blind him or bloody his face to pieces. So I sang out, "It's all right, Owl, it's all right now. He won't hurt me anymore. Thank you, thank you. It's all right now."

The owl hovered around us another minute or so. Then

it alighted on my shoulder and gathered in its wings. I stood very still.

Mulholland stared at me while he righted himself. "You crazy or something?" he said to me. "You talk to birds? That how you got that turkey? I heard all you Southerners are crazy. Learn it from the negroes, I hear."

The owl made a warbling noise on my shoulder.

"You can go back to Louis now," I whispered.

It took flight and I watched it go.

Mulholland was breathing heavily. "You tell anybody about this and I'll whip you again," he threatened, "inside a building, where that damned owl can't get to you."

I was hurting from this whipping. Before the owl had come he'd gotten in enough stripes to make my bottom smart. And anyway, I didn't want anybody knowing about it, either.

We had the turkey that night for supper, and it was most delicious. There was enough for all, with some left over.

The Yankees decided to stay right there and sleep. But no sooner had we settled in than they started with their festivities. About ten o'clock someone began playing the harmonica and the banjo, which wasn't all that objectionable, because I do love music and at home either Carol was playing the piano or Louis was picking at his guitar.

But the music was just part of it. Soon the Yankees were passing a bottle around, and be it brandy or rum or whatever it was, they could not hold their liquor. And one of the greatest sins in a man, according to my brothers, is that he not be able to hold his liquor.

Soon enough some were wandering around to seek out women to dance.

A very handsome but in-his-cups Yankee with an equally agreeable companion came over to our wagon to cast an eye on the women.

Our Yankee guard ordered us all out. Even me, in my boys' clothing.

Most of the women mumbled. They were tired and wanted to sleep. They were not dressed fetchingly enough. They wanted no truck with the Yankees.

Sadie Moline, however, was clear-eyed and enticing, and the in-his-cups Yankee immediately selected her.

"How about somebody for my friend here?" he asked.

Sadie grinned at me and reached out and pulled Carol forth by the hand.

"No." I stood in front of Carol and the agreeable Yankee soldier. "Not my sister. Pick somebody else."

He scowled at me. "Very commendable, little buddy, but I like your sister. She's the prettiest one here. Now out of the way before I box your ears."

I turned from him to Sadie. I pulled her aside. Quickly I reached into the pocket of my trousers and pulled out the two ten-dollar gold eagles that Major McCoy had given me. "Please," I begged. "Just leave us alone."

Sadie nodded and took the money, then turned to the agreeable Yankee and said, "You don't want her. She's pregnant." Then she pulled forth another woman named Ella

Powers, who was not near as pretty as Carol but was presentable enough to hold her own. And they went off to tear up the night with rowdiness and screaming laughter and what they thought passed for singing and Lord knew what else.

In the morning the women were still not back. And nobody commented. But I was glad I had had those two ten-dollar gold eagles that Major McCoy had given me. For after that Sadie Moline did not exactly become my friend, but she did leave us alone.

And, speaking of McCoy, Viola told me that he was twenty-three years old and unmarried. I don't know how my sister found such things out, but she always did know everything.

She also told me the reason Carol had offered to come with us, had suddenly voiced such concern for us, was because she wanted to make it up to Teddy for all the bad times she'd given him.

"She told me this," Viola said. "And after all, it isn't as if we're going to be sent farther north with the others. We're going to Grandmother's in Philadelphia, aren't we?"

CHAPTER THIRTY-FIVE

THE NEXT DAY there was leftover turkey enough to give to Carol for her midday meal. The rest of us made do with the coarse fare that the Yankees fed us.

We were passing a part of the country steeped in poverty. It was truly a dilapidated part of the wilderness. Tumbledown houses, if one could glorify them with that name, appeared on both sides of the road. Here we saw women in ragged clothes, some chopping wood, some attending to halfhearted gardens. There were lots of dirty, half-naked children running about.

"Our negroes live better at home," Viola whispered.

"I wonder where the men are?" a woman named Elinor asked.

"At war," another called Betsy said.

"For which side?" Rose asked.

"Which do you think?" Sadie put to us. And nobody dared answer. For none of us knew and none of us dared guess. Which side, Yankee or Confederate, would allow their women to live like this?

And to mention which side, here and now, would cause an argument to break out.

Quickly, but not quickly enough, it seemed, we passed this ungodly settlement and soon came upon another sight even more ungodly.

Up ahead to the left of us was a slave gang, all chained together, sitting around a fire, resting. What appeared to be the slave trader and his assistant were standing under a nearby tree, with guns, drinking and watching them.

I had never seen a gang of slaves in chains.

All I knew of negroes were Cannice and Careen and Primus and the other house and field servants. We never called them slaves. Surely they had never had beginnings like this!

I had never really thought of them as having been purchased anywhere. They had just always been there, around me. Friends. *Part of the family.*

If I sassed Cannice, Teddy would punish me.

I came out of my reverie then because our Yankee guard was saying something.

"Lookee here, you people. Here's what your loved ones are fighting for. Don't it make you proud? See that bunch of slaves? On their way to New Orleans to be sold to the highest bidder. What gets me is you people never give up. Here we are and the war is nearly over. You're losing. And you're still selling slaves!"

Then there was the barking of orders and I saw an officer on a horse and men with guns at the ready, forming up and going to surround the slave trader and his assistant. The officer ordered him to immediately unlock the chains of the slaves.

There was a heated exchange of words. The slave trader not only refused, but he and his assistant fired at the Yankees, who immediately fired back. In a minute they both lay dead on the ground.

In the wagon the women all screamed and were shouted at by the Yankee guard to quiet down.

We watched in horrified fascination as the Yankee soldiers secured the keys from the dead slave trader and unlocked the chains of all the slaves. For a moment or two, the slaves just sat there, though unchained. They raised their arms in surrender. They mumbled things like, "No trouble, boss. I gives no trouble," and "I stays put, suh. You doan gotta worry."

It took a lot of coaxing from the soldiers to convince them it was all right to get up. They offered their own canteens of water. They squatted down and made themselves eye-level with the slaves and spoke quietly with them for several minutes. Other soldiers came across the road with goodies to offer. Some pieces of bread, it looked like. And ham.

We all watched, speechlessly.

Eventually, one by one, the slaves got up. There were six of them. They were properly dressed, in osnaberg trousers and white shirts, hose and shoes that they had trouble walking in. They went with the soldiers over to one of the wagons, to continue on with them.

"Now they're free and we're not," Sadie said.

A detail of men with their horses was left to bury the bodies.

We continued with our travels, and later on in the day we reached Marietta. Too early by half for Grandmother's emissary from Philadelphia to meet us.

What would happen to him when he came? How would he find us? More important, how would we find him? I already considered it my responsibility to make the connection, but suppose I was off on some mission for Mulholland Bad Face. Would the Yankees have shipped Carol and Viola off north to Nashville by then?

Marietta had once been the prettiest of little college towns, with beautiful homes, tall trees on the main street, and a train station that looked like something out of a painting.

Oh, the homes and trees and train station were all still there, but now it was an army town, a conquered and fortified military city. The courthouse was a military prison. The fine old houses were hospitals. Nine trains arrived and departed at the depot each day, bringing supplies for the Yankee armies as they readied their advance toward Atlanta.

The infantry was housed in buildings on the square. All deserters and stragglers were immediately arrested. The mill workers were taken to the Georgia Military Institute on the hill.

Somehow I got permission from Mulholland Bad Face to accompany my sisters there while he found a place for his bummers. We walked up the lovely, rolling grounds full of soldiers and tents and horses and were ushered into the barracks to the side, which were once occupied by the cadets.

Here there were women already, some from Roswell and others from the mill at Sweetwater, which had also been burned by the Yankees. The rooms seemed to go on forever, with rows and rows of cots. Women waved at us, came forward, and hugged us as if we were friends.

There were crying children. The women spoke of the horrid food. Of the even more horrid Yankee guards. They said we would have to wait two days before the first train came that would ship us out.

I noticed that it was terrible hot in here. And that the women had already taken sheets from the bed and draped them over the windows to shield themselves from the sun, which shone directly in this time of day.

Immediately Viola lay down on her cot. I knew she was not feeling well. I also knew I could not stay long, or Mulholland Bad Face would beat me again.

"I'll look after her, don't worry," Carol promised.

So I left, halfheartedly, promising to be back, though I didn't see how I could.

Outside, on my way down the front path, I thought I saw in the distance an owl on a tree limb. I was so intent on looking at it that I bumped into a tall, fine-looking Yankee officer. I mean I ran right into him. And fell onto the ground.

"Oh, I'm sorry, sir," I said.

"*You're* sorry! Are you hurt?"

I had scraped my elbow somewhat. "No," I said, though I'd turned my wrist.

"Here, I'm a doctor. And I feel responsible. Wasn't looking where I was going. Habit of mine." He took the hurt wrist to help me up.

"Ow!"

"You *are* hurt."

"No, sir, I'm fine."

He squatted down like Teddy would and flexed the wrist, which made the elbow hurt.

"Sir, please don't."

"Why do people lie to doctors?" Quickly and expertly, he felt me in more places. *If Louis were here,* I thought, *he would have to beat him up.*

He ran his tongue inside his cheek. "You're not a boy, are you?" he said.

I blushed. "Please, you mustn't tell anyone, sir. My life depends on it."

He took me by the waist and pulled me to my feet.

"Doctors don't tell. They know how to keep secrets. I would like to bandage your wrist and elbow, though. I work in that big house over there. It's a field hospital."

I got suspicious.

"What's the matter?" he asked.

"My brother Teddy told me always to be suspicious."

"I see. Go on."

"Why should I go into a big house with a good-looking Yankee who just put his hands all over me and claims to be a doctor?"

He threw back his head and laughed. "Good girl. Good advice. I like your brother Teddy already. And I'm flattered to be called a good-looking Yankee. I take it you just came in from Roswell?"

"Yes, sir."

"Then you should hate all Yankees."

"I've decided only some of them are devils. I haven't made my mind up yet about you."

His blue eyes sparkled. He shook his head in disbelief. "I don't know who raised you, but they did a good job."

"My brother Teddy."

"Ah, so I see. Look, you don't have to come to the field hospital with me if you don't want to. I just thought to bandage your hurts. But what you can do for me is help me right now. The reason I'm here, you see, is because I'm looking for some women to help out at the field hospital. I'm Assistant Surgeon Captain John Ashton of the 7th Iowa Infantry, and I've been asked by Major General Grenville Dodge to hire some of these women as nurses."

I came alert. "Nurses?"

"Yes. So they don't have to get shipped out to God knows where. And perhaps never see home again. You came out of there." He gestured to the door of the barracks. "You know anybody inside?"

I glanced briefly at the tree where I'd seen the owl. He was still there, perched on a limb. I took Captain Ashton inside and introduced him to my sisters.

Immediately, he leaned over Viola and asked her if she thought she was up to being a nurse. She told him she would be, after a good day's rest.

He helped her to her feet. His consideration was beyond even that of a doctor.

He signed out Viola and Carol and two other women and took them with him.

As we left I tapped his arm. "Captain?"

"Yes?"

"I'm sorry I doubted you. I don't want you to think all Southerners have the temperaments of hedgehogs. And I thank you for taking my sisters."

He looked down at me and smiled. "Do you think Teddy would let you come with me now and attend to your hurts?"

I knew I shouldn't go. I knew Mulholland would punish me. But I did hurt, and the captain's voice was so kind.

"Yessir," I said.

Before we left the premises I cast another look at the tree. The owl was gone.

CHAPTER THIRTY-SIX

ALTHOUGH THE supply trains came in regularly at Marietta with food for the army, Mulholland Bad Face still sent his bummers out to forage in the surrounding countryside.

The supplies that came in by train, he said, were for the armies that were going to Atlanta. And he wanted to keep his bummers in practice.

"Besides which," he told me, "Sherman wants the Southerners in his path to feel the wrath of his destruction. And I want you to feel the wrath of my anger, 'cause I'm mad as hell at you for comin' in so late t'other night, Conners. And I ain't finished punishin' you yet."

I hadn't used my protection notice yet because something told me I'd be needing it for a more important moment. Ashton had bandaged up my hurts and given me powders for my headaches, and although he had written a note to Mulholland explaining the reason for my lateness, old Bad Face had whipped me again on my return. Inside the small brick building where he and his bummers stayed. So there was no owl about.

I fought him. I tried to kick him in the groin, but he knocked me about so that, besides a hurt bottom, I came away with a bruised cheekbone.

The man was what Louis would call a clodplate, one who had no soul, no spirit, one who had never heard of fanciful things, of books like *Gulliver's Travels* or *Jack and the Beanstalk*, one who had never traveled by using the North Star.

So on the second day of our sojourn in Marietta, he sent me out alone on another impossible task, to a nearby farm to steal chickens.

I was frightened this time, not reassured, like when I went looking for the turkey. I didn't even have my Enfield rifle. I was not supposed to shoot the chickens. I was supposed to wring their necks. Three of them, and bring them back to Mulholland for supper.

I had never wrung the neck of a chicken in my life. I had seen Cannice do it. I don't think Careen had ever done it, either.

It was not in the geography of my makeup to wring the neck of anything.

By the time I got to the farm I decided that I would not do it. I would run away, even though Mulholland had told me that if I did not return by three o'clock that afternoon he would personally track me down and shoot me dead.

The farm was a pretty place and I found the part of it where the hen house was without difficulty. Once there I sat down outside the fence and commenced crying.

I wanted to go home. I wanted my brother Teddy. I wanted to be a child again, to let everybody else make the decisions for me. I had not asked for any of this. It had all been thrust upon me, and the unfairness of it now gripped my soul so that it felt as if I had no soul left at all.

And then, as I was looking up into the vast blue sky for inspiration, through the branches of a nearby pine tree, my soul came alive again. For I saw, there on a high branch, looking down at me, the owl.

I stopped crying, knowing it was Louis's owl, because owls never came out in daylight. Everything would be all right now. What the owl would do to remedy my miserable situation, I did not know. But it would do something.

I sat watching it for a while, having a tête-à-tête with my fancies.

And then, in no time at all, he did it.

He swooped down low into the yard of the hen house, and before the chickens could even raise a fuss he grabbed one by the neck, did something that rendered it helpless, scooped it up, and carried it over to me, where he set it on the ground and then flew back to repeat this performance twice more.

When I had three dead chickens on the ground in front of me, he perched on the limb of the tree again and sat there staring at me with his unblinking eyes.

I stood up. "Thank you," I said. "Oh, thank you. You have rescued me again. Tell Louis thank you, dear owl." I held my arm straight out.

It took only a second or two for him to lift his wings and come and perch on my arm. He was gentle with his talons. He stayed just a moment, then bobbed his head and flew away.

I picked up the three chickens and started walking back to camp.

WE STAYED at Marietta for two more days and then they started shipping the women out on the trains. It was all great confusion, with some of them crying, some of them refusing to go, and soldiers pushing them on board and threatening them with guns.

And where, I wondered, was the emissary from Grandmother in Philadelphia? He should certainly be here by now. But how would I know him? He would be in a wagon, of course, but didn't they say that all stragglers would be arrested?

And weren't there Yankee soldiers all over the place, guarding the entrances and exits of the town? If he'd come, likely he'd been turned away, I decided. So it was a good thing — no, a blessed thing — that Carol and Viola had gotten those jobs as nurses in that field hospital. But what would happen to me? Would I be shipped on with Mulholland's bummers to Nashville? Or would I go to Atlanta?

And then we went out to forage on the plantation where I found the dog, and Mulholland discovered that I was a girl, and he took me to his brother's office. And it was agreed that I and Viola and Carol were to be sent home.

"THE FIRST THING I must do," I told Sergeant Mulholland, "is go to the field hospital over there and get my sisters."

"You do that. I have to get a replacement to tend to my bummers, fetch the horses, and get the rations. I need two hours, at least. We meet at the foot of the hill down there, Sam Conners, or — what did you say your name was, anyway?"

"Leigh Ann. Come on with me, Buster."

"Who's Buster?"

"The dog. I've decided to call him Buster. He's mine now. I'm taking him home."

"You remember one thing, Sam, or Leigh, or whoever you are. We get to your plantation and your brother don't have the money to ransom his wife, all of you come right back here, you got it?"

I nodded yes. We had the money. I wasn't worried about that.

I was worried about what Viola and Carol would say about the conditions I had agreed to that allowed us to go home. And then, before I had weaved in and out between the soldiers' tents that occupied the lawn between the military institute and the field hospital, the dog trailing behind me, I had decided what I would do.

I had to tell Carol and Viola that Mulholland wanted money for Carol's return. Carol would never forgive me if I did not. But I would not disclose the amount.

Mulholland and his brother, Major Tom, wanted at least five thousand dollars.

I did not know whether Teddy had that much money

lying about doing nothing. But I did know that the silver Louis and I had buried that day under the tree was worth quite a lot. And hadn't Louis told me to use it, if push came to shove, to save the family?

And with Carol expecting a child, wasn't this saving the family?

I did not know which door to go in at the field hospital, but there were Yankee guards all over the place and soon enough I was called to account by one of them.

What was I doing on the grounds? Explain myself.

"I-I'm looking for Captain Ashton," I stammered. "My sisters work for him. It is important that I see him right away."

I was scowled at, patted down, and scowled at some more. I had to give my name.

"Sam Conners."

What was I doing with this dog? He could not go inside. Didn't I know that? This was a hospital, not a kennel.

"Please, sir, is there some place safe you could keep him for me? He's my dog, and I'm taking him home. And I've come to get my sisters because they're going home, too."

"By whose orders?"

"Major Thomas Mulholland, sir."

That becalmed them somewhat. There were three of them tormenting me by now. One of them went inside to inquire whether Dr. Ashton did indeed know a scruffy, paltry excuse for a boy named Sam Conners. And in a short time he came out and said yes, the doctor did, and furthermore the doctor said the boy was to be treated with the utmost courtesy and respect. And was to be taken inside to the coffee room into the presence of his sisters.

Which put the three Yankee guards in a considerably contrary mood. Still, the doctor's words must have carried some weight, because they put a rope leash on Buster and brought him into a small unused office for safekeeping. Then they ushered me inside and down a main hall.

It was a hospital and it was not a hospital. It was easy to see that it had once been an enormous mansion. Rooms off the main hall were emptied of all furniture and filled with beds on which were sick men. Nurses moved between them. It had three stories, so I assumed the same scene was repeated on each floor as well as in the sunroom. From the kitchen came smells of good cooking. And I saw stacks and stacks of doctors' supplies in what must have been the office as I passed.

They took me to a small pantry with a table and chairs. The coffee room. The eating place.

There were Carol and Viola, waiting.

They jumped up and we hugged. "You finally came to see us," Viola said. Then she drew back and took my measure. She touched my face, tenderly. "Mulholland hit you again?"

"I fought him, but he was too strong for me. He knocked me about. I'm in fine fettle, though."

"We've got to get you out of his hands," Carol said.

I grinned. "I am. I'm no longer a bummer. I'm going home. This very afternoon."

They both gasped. Carol got tears in her eyes.

"So are the both of you. It's all arranged." And I proceeded to tell them how I had arranged it.

They listened in silence. Their eyes grew wider with every word.

"How much?" Carol asked.

"Whatever he and Teddy agree to," I said.

Carol nodded in understanding and I felt a sense of relief, but I should have known better. Any sense of relief I felt these days lasted only two seconds.

"I can't go home," Viola told me.

I stared at her as if she had said she had just decided to become a Yankee. "Why?"

She lowered her head. She folded her hands on the table in front of her as if she had committed some sin and was afraid to tell me. But I knew what it was. I had known all along, hadn't I? Even before I had come in here?

She and the doctor-captain were in love with each other. I knew that from the first day he had leaned over her cot and looked down at her so tenderly. And from the way she had looked up at him.

I had seen enough looks of love pass between Louis and Camille, hadn't I? And, in the end, just before she left, between Carol and Teddy? And hadn't I, God forgive me, seen the way Major McCoy had looked at me?

"I've got complications with my baby," Viola said softly, still not looking at me. Then she saw a nurse passing by out in the hall, got up and whispered to her, and came back to us. "I've sent for John. He'll be along momentarily and he'll tell you why I can't go home."

John, is it? I thought. *Well, you've told me already, Viola.*

He came. Momentarily. He came in an apron stained with blood, which he immediately whipped off on coming into the room.

His eyes twinkled when he saw me. "Ah, the little brother who isn't," he said.

I got up and went to him to shake his hand, but he gave me a quick hug instead. Then he looked at my face. "Been in a fight? What does the other guy look like?"

But he was not happy about my face, I could see that. He went immediately over to the sink in the small room, wet a towel under cold water, and held it to my face.

"Mulholland knocked her about again," Viola told him.

He sat down and drew me toward him as Teddy would have done. "You've got to stop with this boy business," he said. "Viola told me the why of it. Now I'm telling you the no of it. I'm going to put a stop to it here and now. Use my authority. This is unconscionable."

"Your authority as what?" I asked.

"Leigh Ann, don't be impertinent," Viola scolded.

But the doctor-captain only grinned at me. "As your future brother-in-law," he told me. "Your sister Viola and I are to be married. This weekend."

Well, so soon? I was not surprised. Now I know how Teddy feels half the time, dealing with us.

What would Teddy say, I pondered. I looked up at the doctor-captain. "Sir, I don't mean to be saucy, but you do love my sister, don't you?"

"Leigh Ann, shame on you!" Viola scolded.

"It's all right, Viola, really," the doctor-captain said. "The child is concerned about you. I'm a Yankee, remember. Yes, Leigh Ann, I love your sister, dearly. And I want to take care of her. I don't want to lose her. I realize we've only known each other about a week, but it's wartime and we're in love and a week is worth six months."

"Well then, you'd best explain to her why I can't make the trip home with her as she wants," Viola told him. And she proceeded to tell the doctor-captain about my plans.

"She's telling the truth about her condition," he said after Viola had finished. "She has complications carrying her child. The ride home would not only cause her to lose it, but endanger her own life as well. You don't want that to happen, do you?"

"And if she stays here? Will she be all right?"

"I'll make sure she is. We'll marry. And as my wife, she'll no longer be under arrest. She'll live in my quarters and be properly attended to before, during, and after the baby's birth."

Tears came into my eyes. "Will she ever"— my voice broke —"come home again?"

The doctor-captain took me on his lap, just as Teddy would have done, and held me while I cried. "I'll bring her home," he promised, "as soon as she and the baby can travel."

CHAPTER THIRTY-SEVEN

WHEN IT WAS time to go, Dr. Ashton walked down the hill of the Georgia Military Institute with me and Carol and Buster, to where Mulholland Bad Face was waiting with four horses all laden with supplies.

The doctor was dressed in his full military uniform. He held my hand all the way down the drive and let it go only when he stood before Mulholland, so he could draw himself up to his full height, which was considerable and which allowed Mulholland to observe at close quarters that he was a man to be reckoned with.

He introduced himself and Mulholland came to attention.

"I am here as a superior officer, as a friend, a soon-to-be-relative, and a spokesman for these women," he told Mulholland. "I do not know the intimate details of your mission, other than that you are to see them safely home. Whatever subversive reason you and your brother have for letting them free, I do not wish to know the details. I assume you will iron them out with this little girl's brother. And, from what I have heard of him, I wish you luck on that score. Especially if he finds out how you have treated her."

Mulholland offered no reply to that. What answer could he possibly give?

"But I will tell you this," the doctor-captain went on in the same even, steady, and authoritative voice. "I am keeping an eye out for the results. I have my spies. And if I hear that you so much as lay a finger on this little girl again, or in any way disrespect her or her sister-in-law Carol on the trip home, I will come after you with the full force of my authority. And I will have you placed under military arrest, stripped of your rank, and sent to prison. Do you understand?"

"Yes, sir," Mulholland said meekly.

"I should whip you now," the doctor-captain said, "for what you have done to her already. It would give me great pleasure. The only reason I don't is that it would ruin my hands for surgery."

Then he turned to me, leaned down, and kissed me on the cheek and winked at me. He put his arms around Carol and gave her some last-minute advice about taking care of herself.

"Where's the other one?" Mulholland asked. "I was told there were to be three."

"The other one stays with me," the doctor-captain said. "She is to be my wife. Thus I am family."

He helped Carol mount one of the horses. "I'll take the other horse and rations," he told Mulholland. "You just get on your way. And remember what I said."

Before he waved us off, he stuffed a letter in my saddlebag. "This is for your brother Teddy," he said. "The least

I can do, taking away one of his sisters, is to introduce myself and tell him of my experiences with all of you."

❧

THEY HAD GIVEN me a tea-colored filly and Carol a long-tailed gray with a smooth gait.

We each had a bag of rations and plenty of water. Buster trotted faithfully along beside me, and Mulholland had given me my Enfield. I hoped he did not expect me to go into the woods to seek out any more mystical turkeys.

As we left Marietta, I perceived that this was another way I did not recognize. How many routes were there between Marietta and Roswell? About half an hour into our trip it started to rain, but the air had been sultry, not at all agreeable, so I was glad of it. Anyway, they had thoughtfully given us oilskins and hats, and Carol and I immediately put them on. I felt sorry for Buster, but he seemed to enjoy the rain.

The road, of course, became muddy. It rained copiously for about ten minutes; then, just as suddenly as it had started, it stopped and the Georgia sun came out again, but now the air had cooled and we took off our oilskins. Buster shook his ragged golden hair in a sort of celebration, then barked.

When we came to a curve in the road there was an overturned stagecoach. Six passengers stood by, all hurt in various degrees. Carol wanted to stop and help.

"What can we do?" Mulholland growled. "We have enough trouble helping ourselves."

Carol pouted, as I'd sometimes seen her do with Teddy. But she said nothing and we went on at a determined plod.

A postman in a mail buggy came at us going the opposite way and we had to move to the side of the road to let him pass. I wondered if I had any mail from James waiting for me at home. I wondered if he was still alive. Then I pondered if I should write to Major McCoy when I got home and tell him about my adventures.

Of course I will, I decided. *Why not?* I felt so much older now than when I had left home. I felt old enough to correspond with a twenty-three-year-old man, if Teddy would let me.

And then I realized that it was the first time in a long time that I found myself wondering if Teddy would allow me to do something. For how long now had I had to make my own decisions, with no Teddy to advise me, to guide me?

We passed some thickets of plums and I begged Mulholland to let us stop and pick some. Old Bad Face glumly agreed, and I got down off my horse and gathered a goodly amount and gave some to Carol. Oh, they were warm and luscious.

We continued on and soon we went by acres of cornfields. At some point here, without saying a word, Mulholland brought his horse to a halt, jumped down from his gray gelding, turned his back, and peed into the tall grasses at the edge of the road.

Carol and I just looked at each other in disgust. *Clod-pate*, I thought. *The man is disgusting. He simply has no dignity.*

We went on. From a thicket of corn a little way up ahead stepped out a young, likely-looking negro girl. Her apron, which she wore over a washed-out calico dress, was raised into a bundle, holding something. Her feet were bare.

Mulholland stopped and raised his hand. "Hello there," he said in his most cultivated voice.

"Hello." But she would not look at him. She lowered her head.

What she apparently held in her apron was a pot. And the fragrance of whatever she had in it drove us all mad.

"What you got there?" Mulholland asked.

"Soup," she said softly, "made of Indian corn, with salt and some bacon and some other things. Would you like a taste?"

Mulholland would indeed like a taste.

From somewhere in her apron she pulled out a wooden spoon, dipped it in the soup, and offered it to Mulholland. He got off his horse and went over to her. She spooned it into his mouth.

"Ummm," he said.

She gave him another spoonful. Then another.

It was like some kind of a religious ritual. Carol and I looked at each other, embarrassed. She was enticing him into the thicket of corn.

With each spoonful she backed up a little more and he stepped farther and farther into the thicket. Then he turned to us and said he must go and help her pick more corn so she could replace the mixture that he had eaten. And we should wait for him.

We waited for him in the sun for at least three-quarters of an hour.

When he reappeared he was almost apologetic, guilty for making us wait so long. They had to pick a lot of corn, he said. "Tell you what. About two miles up the road apiece, there's an inn. They serve decent vittles. We'll stop there for supper. My treat."

It was called Diamond's. They allowed us to come in with Buster, if he was good, which he was the whole time.

The place was crowded and Mulholland was extra nice to us, looking around all the while to see who was watching. *He's looking for those spies the doctor-captain told him he has about,* I told myself.

For supper we had some kind of fowl, red potatoes, eggs, fish, grits, corn bread, and coffee. Mulholland paid the bill and we were about to leave when our waitress told him that up the road apiece they were about to whip two negroes for killing a white man.

"Likely give 'em a hundred lashes each," she said. "Whip 'em to death. I wouldn't think you'd want the young lady and the little boy to see such."

So Mulholland got two rooms for the night and feed and shelter for our horses.

I shared Carol's room. The cots were tolerable clean. The only bad part was that Mulholland got us up at five in the morning. We did have breakfast at the inn. Fish and hominy and Indian bread and fresh butter and more coffee. I gave Buster some Indian bread and a saucer of coffee.

Two miles up the road we saw the whipping posts where they had given the negroes a hundred lashes each. They had then burned the bodies, and the burned carcasses still remained. As did the smell.

We went on solemnly and I thought of Cannice and Primus and Careen and the war we were fighting. Were we in the South fighting so we could keep the right to whip to death and burn negroes if we wanted to? What was it Louis had said?

The only problem I have is that I don't know which I'm going off to do, to kill the myth or to save it.

Nobody said anything for a while as we went on.

CHAPTER THIRTY-EIGHT

I COULD SEE church spires in the distance, so I knew we were about two miles from town. I waved my hand to attract Carol's attention and pointed. She saw the spires and smiled.

At this juncture, Mulholland drew his gelding to a halt, held up his hand for us to stop, and looked up and all about him.

I thought he was going to remark on the breathlessly beautiful blue sky, which reminded me of the color of one of my Sunday dresses at home. Good Lord, how long had it been since I'd worn petticoats and a dress! Two weeks? Like Dr. Ashton had said, in wartime a week seemed like six months.

Or was he looking at the jackdaws congregated on the telegraph wires overhead, probably deciding which field of corn they were going to destroy this morning?

No, he was looking at the telegraph wires.

And, while looking, he was taking a large pair of shears out of his saddlebags. He was going to cut them. Then he looked at me.

No, he was going to ask me to go up there and cut them.

He smiled his Bad Face smile. "One more thing you can do for me before you get home, Sam," he said. "I've been ordered to cut the telegraph wires when I got close to Roswell. But I thought it fitting that you should do it."

"Me?"

"Sure. Why not? You walked on the mill roof, didn't you? What's a little telegraph pole to a girl like you?"

"Please, Sergeant Mulholland," Carol said.

"You stay out of this. None of your business," he told her.

"Suppose she falls and gets hurt?" Carol reminded him. "What are you going to tell her brother? You think he'll negotiate with you if you hurt or kill his sister? You know how devoted he is to her."

Mulholland chewed on that for a moment. Then he scowled, made an annoyed sound in his throat, and spoke. "He don't negotiate, I just take you back with me."

"I don't think so, Sergeant," Carol said, not losing a bit of her poise. "What I think is that if Leigh Ann is killed in a fall, or hurt, my husband will never let you off the place alive. As a matter of fact, I know it. Don't be a fool." She said it as if she were disappointed in him.

Angrily, knowing she was right, he got off his horse and, shears in hand, climbed the metal hinges of the pole until he got up to the wires.

I felt a pang of disheartenment as I thought, *Here I am sitting, doing nothing, while the people of my town are being denied wire service again. But what can I do? The insuffer-able brute.*

I watched him reach out with the shears and cut the insulated wire. It swung out in two directions, and then back at him.

Teddy would say I was getting mean and nasty, but in my heart I hoped it would hit him in the head and knock him off the pole.

It did not. He ducked his head, avoiding it. Then he climbed down and mounted his horse, and we continued on.

As we approached the town, I still felt disheartened, and now scared, too. What would the town look like? Would it be destroyed?

On the road as we approached, we passed several people whom we did not know driving wagons filled with large pieces of iron, leaving Roswell.

"That iron must be from the mill," Carol said. "And since we don't know those men, they must be coming from other places to salvage it."

We also saw wagons filled with bricks, stacks of them, also likely from the mill. Then we sighted a whole herd of hogs being driven out of town by some Confederate soldiers.

Carol stopped one of them. "Tell me, what condition is the town in?" she asked. "Is there anything left?"

"A lot of the houses have been ransacked, ma'am, but not destroyed. The mansions and churches are in need of repair, but they still stand."

"Do you know"— Carol's voice broke, then she recommenced speaking —"do you know the Conners plantation?"

"Sure 'nuf, ma'am."

"Is it still standing?"

"Yes, ma'am."

"Have they ransacked it?"

The soldier smiled. "Need the whole Yankee army to do that, ma'am. That Conners fellow, he's a regiment all on his own, not to mention his negroes."

"Thank you," Carol said.

The soldier tipped his hat. "My pleasure, ma'am. Why, that Conners fellow, he'd just as soon blow your head off as look at you, you come too close 'round his place. Good day, ma'am."

He went on, catching up with his friends and his hogs.

Carol threw a superior glance at Mulholland, but he quickly looked on ahead.

꙰

WE CAME UPON the long drive, which was still the same as I had left it, though for some reason I did not expect it to be. And there were the trees lining each side. How could they not have withered, or fallen, or aged? Changed somehow, after all I had been through?

Hadn't it been a hundred years, at least?

At the end of the drive was the house, as always, where I'd been a child, where I'd run and played and done mischief, when running and playing and doing mischief was all that had mattered to me.

No one was about. Was it empty? Had it all been a dream, after all?

Was there no Teddy to ask, *Where have you been? You've missed dinner and you know I won't tolerate that.*

No Louis to say, *Look, I won't have you talking that way about our mother. No matter what she does, she's still our mother.*

We rode at a slow canter, and then we heard the barking of a dog.

It was the dog who did it.

Cicero.

He came running from around back of the house, onto the verandah. For a moment he stood there barking in his best tone. Then my Buster started in, and though I tried to keep him by me he went running down the long drive toward the house, and then Cicero came charging toward him and they met halfway and started circling each other and oh, I hoped they wouldn't fight. But soon tails were wagging.

The front door of the house opened and a figure appeared and whistled. Cicero went bounding back, Buster with him.

I suppose my brother Teddy saw the blue uniform on Mulholland, for he went back into the house and came out quickly with a rifle and stood there, legs spread, waiting.

We were only about a third down the drive when Mulholland halted and stopped us. "No farther," he ordered. "You stop right here, little girl."

For I had started on. I had even yelled, "Teddy, Teddy, we're home!"

He heard me. I know he did. But he didn't move. Just stood there with that rifle at the ready.

"What now?" I asked Mulholland.

He was studying on the matter. "You go on," he directed. "Up to the house. Carol stays here with me. You have a little consultation with that famous brother of yours. No fooling around. No hysterics. We've got no time for that. I'm giving you half an hour for this consultation. You're not back in that time, I leave with Carol. You tell him that. You hear?"

"Yes, but —"

"No buts. You tell him why I'm here, what I want. How much for his woman. And if I don't get it, I leave with his woman. He comes after me, I'll kill her right off. He kills me, it's no matter, 'cause she'll be dead already. You got that?"

"Yes."

"He says yes, he's got the money, you come right away and tell me. He gets his woman when you bring the money, not before. You got that?"

"Yes."

"Now go on. Get. Half an hour."

I got.

CHAPTER THIRTY-NINE

I RODE MY tea-colored filly swiftly up to the front verandah to where Teddy was standing, drew the horse to a
halt, got off, and handed her over to Primus, who had
appeared out of nowhere.

"Hello, Teddy."

"Hello, sweetie."

It seemed so trite. But there were no other words made
to say. I reached into my saddlebag, fetched out the letter
from the doctor-captain, and stuffed it in my trouser pocket.
Then I leaped up the stairs, and for a moment Teddy and I
just stood looking at each other.

He took my measure. "You all right?"

"Yes."

"What's that bruise on your face? Who did that to you?"

"Can we talk inside, Teddy? We don't have much
time. Only half an hour to settle things or Mulholland is
going to leave with Carol."

He peered over my head down the drive. "He is, is he?
Not while I live and breathe."

"Teddy, *please,* listen to me." Tears came into my eyes
as I looked up at him. I took his free hand, the one that
wasn't holding the gun. I gripped it in my own. And I used
the only thing I had.

"Don't let him even try to go without listening to me," I told him. "We must do this for Carol. You want her back, don't you? She's having your baby!"

Disbelief, a mask that Teddy never wore, sat on his face. "That isn't funny," he said sternly.

Now I took his hand in both my own and pulled him to the door. "Oh, please believe me. I would never lie to you. Come into the house. There isn't time, dear Teddy. Oh, if I'm lying, you can beat me. But darling Teddy, do come."

❧

WE STOOD a few feet apart, like adversaries, which I suppose at that moment we were, in his study. The two dogs settled down near us.

"Sergeant Mulholland — he's the head of the bummers — he said he wants ransom money to give Carol back to you."

"He the one who gave you that bruise on your face?"

"Oh, Teddy, does it matter now?"

"Damned right it matters. What else did he do to you?"

I could see there was no going forward until we got around this. "He beat me. Twice."

He cussed in his best manner. "When I get my hands on him, he'll be sorry he ever drew breath."

"No, Teddy, you mustn't get your hands on him. You approach him in any way and he'll shoot Carol first. He told me to warn you of this."

"You telling me how to run my affairs now?"

I raised my chin and met his eyes. "I'm only telling you what I know, Teddy."

He nodded. *Approval?* I could not worry about that now.

"Did he touch Carol?" he asked.

"No."

"Viola? Where the hell is she, anyway?"

Another thing we had to get around. "Back in Marietta. She's married by now. To a very nice man. A doctor-captain surgeon by the name of Ashton. He's taking care of her." I took the letter out of my trouser pocket, walked over to his desk, and set it down. "This is from him," I said. "He's really a good man, Teddy."

"You approve," he said sardonically.

I said yes, I did.

He nodded slowly. "How much money does this SOB Yankee want for my wife?"

I told him. "Five thousand dollars."

His eyes went wide. "What? He's crazier than a loony bird! I don't have that kind of cash on hand! You tell him I did?"

"I didn't tell him anything, Teddy."

"Why not? Did you lead him to think we had it?"

"I just wanted us to get home, Teddy, is all." Now I was truly frightened. Because I knew we had it. And more. Only either Teddy did not know how much we possessed, or he had forgotten about it.

So I must say it. It was imperative that I put my head on the block.

"We do have it, Teddy."

He scowled. He took a step toward me in a threatening manner and I backed away. But he kept on coming until he grabbed my shoulder and peered into my face intently. He felt my forehead for fever. "You sure that Mulholland brute didn't fracture your skull?" he asked.

I'd never thought about that.

"I don't know," I said. "I did have a lot of headaches on the ride home. The doctor gave me some powders and told me to watch out for feeling lethargic. But I'm thinking clearly, Teddy. We have it."

"So tell me then. Where?"

"Louis's silver that he and I buried that day so long ago now. It's worth more than twenty-five thousand. And he told me to use it, if it was needed. To save the family."

I saw my brother's square jaw tighten. I saw the tears come into his eyes. "Is this the only way out, then?" he asked. "I can't just go out there and blast his head off and get my wife?"

"Teddy," I told him, "he said that before you even got close, he'd shoot her. And if you shot him dead, it wouldn't matter, 'cause you'd never get her back again."

He took a deep breath. No, he heaved. And then my strong, beautiful brother started to cry. I went to him and he held me. And that was our hello hug. We held each other for less than a minute. And then it was over. His tears stopped, and what was surprising to me is that he was not ashamed of crying. He made no apology. It was just one of those moments that happened. Rarely, but a man accepted them in his life.

It only made me admire him more.

In an instant he was his old self, in command.

"I'll find Primus to come dig up the silver. You go tell that slithering noxious snake that I agree to his terms and he'll have his money in about twenty minutes. Then come back and show Primus and me where the silver is."

EPILOGUE

TEDDY LOST the war that day.

He lost the battle of First Manassas.

But he found himself for the first time in a long time. He forgave himself, which some men never get to do, I suppose. He looked at Carol and she looked at him as if they had just met.

I tried to stay out of their way, though both attempted to pay attention to me.

I let them have supper alone in the candlelit dining room. I did this by saying I did not feel very well. I went to my room, to bed. Because, in truth, I did not feel well at all.

Careen came to me. My friend. She brought me some soup she had made and she stayed with me while I sat up in bed and ate it.

She told me things. All the things I needed to know.

The house had not been ransacked as other mansions had been, because Teddy had given the house and field servants guns, as other owners had not. And Teddy and our house and field servants had always been at their stations, at the ready. Whereas many other owners had been away and left their places vacant.

"We take turns." Careen grinned. "Massa Teddy, he call it shifts. Even me. I have a gun."

"Did any of the servants run off when the Yankees left?" I asked her.

"Yes," she told me. And she named the several who did. "Teddy let them go," she said. "He know the day be comin' when they all go and he can't stop them."

And then, in naming them she told me, casually, "Your mama run off, too. With that Garrard fella."

My mouth fell open.

"Your mama, one day she come 'round and tell Teddy she wuz leavin' with Garrard. He tells her go. But she wants some of her things first."

"What things?"

"Old dresses. 'Cause you can't get dresses no more. Says she can't exist without them. She such a humbug, that woman! Massa Teddy, he told me to go with her to get the baggage. So I went to the garret with her. And I had to lug down an old gilt-edged mirror she just had to have. And some cut-glass champagne glasses. And some other stuff that was as worthless as a skunk in daylight."

"Teddy let her have it all?"

"Not before he make her sign a paper saying she would make no more claim on the plantation, or the mill, ever again."

"Pa?" I asked. "What about Pa? Why haven't I seen him?"

"You scarce seen anything, Leigh Ann. Your pa, he abed. He don't get outta bed no more. Massa Teddy, he don't say, but I think your pa, he dying."

She told me about the churches, how our church, Roswell Presbyterian, and Mount Carmel Methodist had been stripped of their pews and had their hymnals and pipe organs destroyed. How cavalry troops had desecrated graves in some of the cemeteries.

"They done ruined Factory Hill," she said. "Tore it apart. And you know Reverend Pratt's house?"

"They ruined that, too?"

"No, but tore up some thirty acres of his corn and wheat and sorghum. I rode up with Massa Teddy and saw it. Massa Teddy, he madder than a wet porcupine, he sure 'nuff is, 'bout that. And you know what all else?"

I didn't know if I wanted to know what all else, but I indicated to her that I did.

"Massa Teddy, he gots a telegram from way up there in Philly-delphia, from your grandmother. She tell him that you all never got there, that her man near gets arrested and gets hisself sent back. Massa Teddy, he worry it to the bone. He gets in touch with that nice Major McCoy some way and that nice Major McCoy tell him you all still in Marietta and that all he knows. I tell you, Leigh Ann, Massa Teddy going crazier by the day and talkin' 'bout takin' off and goin' to Marietta himself. He tells Primus, 'Can you all take care of the place? Can you all keep it safe if I go?' And Primus says, 'Yes, boss, we all can.'

"So Massa Teddy thinking serious-like about goin' just before you all come home."

TEDDY HAD GONE to bed early with Carol, though I saw the candlelight shining from under their door.

I could not sleep. I got up and went downstairs and out on the verandah in my robe and slippers and sat there with Buster and Cicero and looked at the stars in the heavens. My head was going round and round with all I'd been through. I could not quiet it. Likely I would never sleep again.

The night did not wait for me. I heard an owl hooting and I thought, *I wonder if that is Louis's owl come to keep me company.* There was a God-ordained cool breeze and my head hurt. I wondered if I *had* a fractured skull. What was a fractured skull anyway? Did it ever get better?

For no reason in the world I started to cry. Quietly. I did not want anyone to hear me. There was so much to cry about, and I knew I would never be able to cry enough to cover all the reasons.

I must have dozed then, because I did not hear the footsteps approach.

"Leigh Ann, what are you doing out here?"

I thought I was dreaming.

"Leigh Ann, wake up. This is no place to sleep."

He knelt next to my chair and put his hand on my head. "Child, you must come to bed now."

I'm not a child anymore, I thought. *How can I be? Doesn't he know that?*

Of course not. How could he? He doesn't know what all I've been through.

But I want *to be a child. Can you go back to being one again if you want to? And he wants me to be one. He* needs *me to be one.*

For heaven's sake, I'm still only fourteen years old!

"Teddy," I said.

"Yes. I didn't even get to talk to you tonight since you came home."

I smiled. "You had your wife to attend to," I teased. "Did you attend to her?"

"Don't be sassy."

There, I was a child again. "Is Pa dying?"

"I'm afraid so."

"How soon?"

"Soon. You visit him tomorrow."

"When is Louis coming home?"

"Soon on that, too."

"My head hurts."

"I'm going to get the doctor tomorrow. Going without sleep won't help. Come on — I'll give you a powder. Do you want me to carry you up?"

I wasn't that much of a child. I said no. But I was a little unsteady on my feet, and he held my arm and saw me to bed. When I was safely there and he'd given me a powder, he stood at the foot of my bed for a moment. "Thank you for all you did for Carol," he said.

As I'd felt before, there were no words for this. I nodded. He bit his lower lip to keep his feelings from showing, turned, and left the room.

Dr. Widmar, who was too old to go off to war but not too old to still attend to his people in Roswell, said I did not have a fractured skull, but I did indeed have a concussion. And that meant rest, plenty of it. And so Teddy and Carol saw to it. I was allowed to see Pa the next day, but after that I was consigned to the couch in the back parlor with my books and my dogs and I was fed and spoiled and I was a little girl again.

Pa was wraithlike. He had lost weight, the skin on his face was colorless, his hands scarce had any flesh on them, and his nightshirt looked as if it had been made for a man twice his size. I wanted to cry when I saw him.

Especially because he did not know me.

Teddy had warned me of this, but still it was horrifying to me. Teddy stood with me when I visited him. "I've brought Leigh Ann to see you, Pa," he said.

"Told you," Pa scolded, "no strangers. What do I want with strangers?"

Tears came down my face, and I tried to talk him into knowing me, but Teddy made me leave. I was only making him excited, he said. I felt slapped. Like I was being punished for all my sins. So I left, and I did not go to see him again before he died.

I returned to my couch in the back parlor.

I stayed there, obediently, for two days. Then I began to wonder why there were no letters lying about the house for me from James.

Teddy was seldom around the house. He was always out and about the plantation on his horse, inspecting things, giving orders, arranging things, sometimes getting down from his horse and pitching in to help the negroes with an especially knotty situation.

Without saying anything to anyone I sneaked out to the barn, took my horse, and without asking went to see Mrs. Stapleton, but she was not there. Her house was boarded up, empty. I felt terror seize me and rode swiftly home.

I found my brother out in the cornfields. The jackdaws had done their mischief here the night before, and had I known he was in a rage I would have turned my horse around and gone back to the barn.

He turned, saw me. "What the hell are you doing here? You're supposed to be on the couch. You heard the doctor."

"Where is Mrs. Stapleton? Why is her house boarded up? Why are there no letters for me from James?"

He cursed, using the Lord's name in vain.

"Not now. Can't you see I have trouble here? Primus, I thought I told you to stuff old coats and hats on sticks like they do up north to scare the crows. Why wasn't it done?"

"Ole Beetle who was 'posed to do it run off yesterday, boss," Primus said.

Teddy said nothing. I was just deciding that this was not the kind of news he needed, that I'd best go back to the house, when he spoke to me without looking, while separating the ruined stalks of corn from the other.

"James was killed," he said. "At Hagerstown, Maryland, on July sixth." He went on with his business with the corn, still not looking at me. He pulled some more ruined stalks and threw them aside. "I'm sorry," he said.

It was quiet for a moment. James! My own James. *Killed.* I just sat there on my horse for a few moments, looking across the cornfield and the wheat field beyond and trying to reason it out.

Why James? What did it matter to anyone if he came home or not? Why did he have to die to prove anything? I closed my eyes, feeling a dizziness overtake me. I saw his face in front of me, remembered the evening I'd kissed his cheek.

Then something else came to me. "Why didn't you tell me?" I asked my brother.

Now he looked at me. "Damn, Leigh Ann, I haven't even had time to talk to you yet!"

"It would have been better." I started to cry. I could scarce talk. "It would have been better if you had told me. It was your job to tell me."

He took off his hat. He scratched his head and watched me as I turned my horse and went back to the house.

He came to me later, when I was on the couch again, and stood over me.

"Don't ever tell me again," he said severely, "in front of the servants, what is or what isn't my job. You hear me?"

I said, "Yes, Teddy, I hear you."

Then he said, "I'm sorry I didn't tell you right off about James. I didn't know how in hell to do it. I had to find the right moment. It just didn't come."

Then he said, "Are you going to be all right?"

"I have to be," I said. "What else is there to be?"

He leaned down and kissed my forehead. His hand lingered on the top of my head. "You're my sweet girl," he said. Then he left the room.

WHEN LOUIS CAME home two weeks later, I hugged him and told him thank you for letting his owl take care of me in Marietta. He said, "I don't know what you're talking about."

Yet he knew. I could tell by the twinkle in his eyes that he knew. But this was a part of him that Louis would not let himself talk about.

After all, I reminded myself, *remember. He knows nothing whatsoever about my even being sent to Marietta. Carol and I spent hours telling him and Camille tales about it.*

So how, I pondered, *did he know enough to have his owl help me?*

Something in him, I decided, just knew I was in trouble.

I also decided I would never fully understand my brother Louis. And that I should just be grateful I had him.

In Roswell they made him continue his term as mayor. Lord knows, with the destruction, the organization needed to raise money to restore the churches and houses, the families of the mill workers already wanting to know what happened to their women, and those wanting to salvage iron from the mill having to be kept out of town, Louis had his hands full.

I healed from my concussion.

I wish I could say I healed from my heartbreak over James. Nobody knew where Mrs. Stapleton went, and her house stayed boarded up for a long time.

Pa died right after Louis and Camille came home. It was as if he were waiting for Louis to come. Because he knew Louis. He recognized him, spoke with him, while he never knew me.

We had services for him in our churchyard and buried him there. I never go to his grave.

Teddy said I could write to Major McCoy, and so I did. I told him the why and the how of our return to Roswell. I sent the letter on to Ohio, as he suggested. He wrote back, saying how happy he was for me, and proud.

He wrote another letter to Teddy, asking permission to correspond with me.

"Do you want to?" Teddy asked me.

"I don't know."

"He likes you. But he's twenty-three years old."

I remained silent, then said, "We can be friends, can't we?"

"There's no such thing, sweetie. Not between a man and a woman. Not the way he looked at you. You should know that from the get-go."

"I'm too young to marry."

"Damned right, sweetie. I'll be waiting on the verandah for him with a rifle, if that's what he wants."

"Why don't you write to him and tell him I'm too young, but we can still write. That would work, wouldn't it?"

He smiled. "Sure. I can do that. Big brother says give it time. You need a few years yet. But he can write. Even visit if he fancies. But the war will keep him busy, don't worry."

So Major McCoy and I wrote back and forth for the rest of the war. And he was kind and respectful and dear. And even when he got leave at Christmas and came to visit, he was respectful and dear, though everyone was talking already about negotiations between the North and the South. Being a Yankee, he did not lord it over us.

Viola had her baby in January, and in March she and the doctor-captain came to visit. It was a darling boy and they stayed two weeks.

The end of the war was coming and everybody knew it, and the only question was how and when. On the fourth of March, Abraham Lincoln had been inaugurated for a second term. There were still skirmishes all around, of course, but the South did not have much left. Just spirit, Teddy said.

Teddy and Carol had a baby boy in February and again it was, between them, as if they had just met. Teddy had moments with that baby when he was as I'd never seen him before, and I thought, *That is why God gives us children. They are our second chance.*

In April the war ended and we wondered why we had done it at all.

Teddy freed his people. Many left, but not all. The rest he paid, and they stayed on with us.

Cannice and Careen and Primus stayed, and the other house servants and most of the field servants.

Something they called Reconstruction came to Georgia, and to Roswell, and it was as terrible as it sounded. For one thing, Louis could not be mayor anymore, because he had been a Confederate and now he and Teddy could not vote. There were all kinds of new rules, and we were under military occupation.

In July, Teddy and Louis and some other men who wanted to put in money had a meeting because they wanted to rebuild the mill. Then Teddy and Louis said there was certainly enough cotton on hand, and they had enough money to build the mill themselves, without asking for a dollar from others.

They mulled the matter over for a while. They were having other thoughts, too.

The idea had come to them from something Major McCoy had written to me in one of his letters.

So they telegrammed the doctor and Viola, and asked them to come from where they were at the moment, at the doctor's home in Washington City.

When all were present and accounted for, we had a family dinner, for it was a year now since Carol and I and Viola had been shipped off to Marietta.

In that year, Major McCoy had gotten a leave and gone west, he had written. As far as Kansas, and he was thinking of staying in the army and fighting the Indian wars. Unless he had any reason to establish a cattle ranch.

Louis, of course, did not like the idea of Indian wars, but there were lively discussions, plans, talk of selling the plantation and the mill site at that dinner.

Nothing was decided. They would think on it, my brothers agreed.

"But we all must go together," Teddy told us. "It has to be a family decision."

Then he was silent for a moment. "If we go west, we won't build a ranch," he said. "We'll build a homestead."

AUTHOR'S NOTE

THE BURNING of the mill in Roswell, Georgia, in 1864, and the arrest and forced relocation of hundreds of women and children who worked in the mill is a true story.

These women and children had committed no crime, other than working hard in the mill on a daily basis or being connected with it in some way. But the order came down from the Union general William T. Sherman to burn the mill and transport the workers far away to places north, as he and his army made their way across the South, looking for a way to cut the South in two.

Roswell, Georgia, was in the way of that maelstrom of pillaging, unnecessary destruction, heart-rending ruination, and unremitting desolation that became known as Sherman's March to the Sea.

The women and children were charged with treason simply for making cloth for the Southern army. No one was excused. Not even those who were "with child."

Likewise, the same sentence was pronounced on women and men at the New Manchester Cotton Mill in Sweetwater Creek, a village some thirty miles away. Along with the Roswell workers, they were taken to Marietta, the county seat, where they were detained until they could be put on trains and taken north.

Theophile Roche and Olney Eldredge were freed in Nashville. In mid-July, trains carrying the women and children began arriving in Louisville, Kentucky, which was, by nineteenth-century standards, considered a metropolis, but by our standards was a crowded, filthy river town.

Sherman had ordered them sent north of the Ohio River.

The women possessed nothing. In Louisville they were confined to a refugee house without food or water, and many were in need of medical attention. Some were hired out as servants, taking the places of freed slaves. Finally they were sent farther north to places such as Evansville and New Albany, Indiana, towns where they were not welcome because those towns were already overrun with refugees, runaways, and the like, and because there was no place for them to live or work.

Newspapers, North and South, protested the arrests and deportation of these women and children. From Richmond, Virginia, to Cincinnati, Ohio, and beyond, there were stories and editorials holding similar views of the harsh treatment and hopeless futures allotted to these unfortunate creatures.

While many of the leading families of Roswell eventually returned to the town, only a handful of the mill workers did, some years later, by foot. Some returned with children. Others married and settled in Indiana or Ohio, where they worked in cotton mills.

ALTHOUGH THE STORY of the Roswell, Georgia, cotton mill being burned is true, my book is a fictionalized account. In July 1864, General William T. Sherman, in his March to the Sea, did order the arrest and deportation of anyone who had to do with the Roswell cotton mill.

The Conners family did not own the mill. It was owned by the King family. Its patriarch, Roswell, founded the village and had the vision to see the possibilities of the land that lay on the north side of the Chattahoochee River.

In researching this story, what led me to write it was that this same land, before King came along, once belonged to the Cherokee Indians, the most intellectually advanced tribe at the time, who had an alphabet, a newspaper, established schools, and written laws. Indeed, this was the place where the famous and tragic Trail of Tears began, when the white men, motivated by the discovery of gold on this very land, drove the Cherokee out of their six-thousand-acre area.

This was too good a story not to write. Here I could have my family be descended from a Cherokee, own the mill, have sons in the Civil War, and a mother who was a Yankee. I was halfway through the book when my protagonist decided she would be the one to plant the French flag of neutrality on the roof of the mill and get herself arrested when the Yankees came, and sent off with the mill women. A pivotal point in the novel, but it only came halfway through the book.

My characters took over and I followed them. Of course the research was endless and difficult. I found myself making mistake after mistake in the writing and had to go back and rewrite many times. I ran into roadblocks and mental blocks as I always do when writing fiction. I wrote the prologue sixteen times, then when the book was finished found the prologue all wrong and wrote it again.

My characters eluded me and did things that at first I did not understand. There is Louis suddenly, for instance, with an owl on his shoulder. Then I find that same owl coming back in the last part of the book in a fanciful way to help Leigh Ann when she is in dire straits. I did not plan that. There is the "doctor-captain" coming around a corner of the women's quarters in Marietta and bumping into Leigh Ann and knocking her over. I never intended him to be a character in the book. But not only is he instrumental in giving Carol and Viola jobs as nurses, thus saving them from the terrible plight of the women who get shipped north, but he *marries* Viola!

And, when Major J. C. McCoy of the Yankee army rides up to the Conners plantation and dismounts his horse, I did not know he was going to have such a presence, be so polite yet so in command at the same time, and, on first seeing Leigh Ann, be so taken with her. McCoy was actually a real person.

What to do with him now? He is twenty-three, she is fourteen. I did not know what to do. I left the situation unresolved at the end of the book, as I left unresolved the business of whether the family would or would not end up going west. Perhaps they will, I thought.

Perhaps they will establish a "homestead," as Teddy likes to call their plantation in Roswell. Which means, simply, "a place for a family's home."

I have not decided yet. But what is the sense in my deciding? My characters make their own minds up, don't they?

❦

I HAVE LOOSELY based my character Louis on Captain Tom King of Roswell, who was wounded at First Manassas, came home, and was elected mayor of the town. Here is a good place to mention that the North had one name for every battle (First Manassas was Bull Run to the North). Second Manassas was fought on August 29–30, 1862, so by the time Major J. C. McCoy came to see Teddy Conners when the mill was being burned in 1864, the battle that Teddy and Louis had fought was already being called First Manassas.

I have taken a few liberties for the sake of story. Train travel was closed to civilians on April 6, 1864, as a result of General Order #6 issued by General Sherman. I have train travel being closed to civilians in May instead.

For the sake of story I have my character Leigh Ann planting the French flag on the roof of the mill. Historically, there is no mention of who did it. Marietta, the county seat, was a four-hour horseback ride to the west. I have the trip taking two days by wagon.

I calculated that it would, what with all the stops with the women aboard, for meals, for hunting, for all the other incidents that happened and for sleeping. Likewise, I figured about a day and a half for the trip home that Leigh Ann and Carol and Mulholland made.

As far as my research could tell me, the first Confederate flag was seen by a young woman in May 1861. (Cornelia Peake McDonald, in her diary, *A Woman's Civil War*.) See my bibliography.

As with the abovementioned Confederate flag, all the rest of the facts in my story are carefully researched. Special thanks should go here to *The Women Will Howl*, the wonderful book by Mary Deborah Petite about Roswell and the burning of the mill, the fate of the mill workers, and the town.

❧

HISTORICALLY, THE ROSWELL mill was rebuilt and back in operation by 1867. It continued to operate until a flood put it out of business in 1881. In 1882, a new mill was constructed on a hill above the old factory complex. The old mill was struck by lightning in 1926, and the mill, picker house, and warehouse were destroyed. Instead of putting more money into that complex, the directors expanded the 1882 arrangement on the hill.

In the Great Depression, the Roswell Mill operated only occasionally. In the 1940s it made laundry netting and carpet backing, some cotton yard, and cotton cloth.

In 1975, it ended its operations and sold its machinery for scrap iron.

One wonders what Teddy would think about all that.

❧

TODAY ROSWELL, Georgia, is a beautiful town, retaining all the hints of pre–Civil War Georgia. The lovely old homes have been restored and most are within the Roswell Historic District, which was added to the National Register of Historic Places in 1973.

Many of the mill workers' cottages still stand on Factory Hill. In Old Mill Park there is a monument to the Roswell mill workers.

There is a ten-foot-tall granite Corinthian column that was unveiled in July 2000 in a small park in the mill village that honors the men, women, and children who were taken from Roswell and sent on a long journey north by decree of General William T. Sherman, most of whom would never return again.

The song of the rushing water flowing into the creek below and finding its way to the Chattahoochee River is the continual hymn of mourning just for them.

BIBLIOGRAPHY

Burke, Emily. *Pleasure and Pain: Reminiscences of Georgia in the 1840s.* Savannah, Ga.: Beehive Press, 1991.

Faust, Patricia L., editor. *Historical Times Illustrated Encyclopedia of the Civil War.* New York: Harper and Row, 1986.

Foner, Eric. *Reconstruction: America's Unfinished Revolution, 1863–1877.* New York: HarperCollins, 1988.

Golay, Michael. *A Ruined Land: The End of the Civil War.* New York: John Wiley & Sons, 1999.

Hennessy, John. *The First Battle of Manassas: An End to Innocence, July 18–21, 1861.* Lynchburg, Va.: H. E. Howard, 1989.

Kemble, Frances Anne. *Journal of a Residence on a Georgian Plantation.* Savannah, Ga.: Beehive Foundation, 1992.

Lane, Mills, editor. *The Rambler in Georgia.* Savannah, Ga.: Beehive Foundation, 1990.

Long, E. B., with Barbara Long. *The Civil War Day by Day: An Almanac 1861–1865.* Garden City, N.Y.: Doubleday, 1971.

Massey, Mary Elizabeth. *Ersatz in the Confederacy: Shortages and Substitutes on the Southern Homefront.* Columbia: University of South Carolina Press, 1952.

McDonald, Cornelia Peake. *A Woman's Civil War: A Diary, with Reminiscences of the War, from March 1862*. Madison: University of Wisconsin Press, 1992.

Petite, Mary Deborah. *"The Women Will Howl": The Union Army Capture of Roswell and New Manchester, Georgia, and the Forced Relocation of Mill Workers*. Jefferson, N.C.: McFarland & Company, 2008.

Varhola, Michael J. *Everyday Life During the Civil War: A Guide for Writers, Students and Historians*. Cincinnati, Ohio: Writer's Digest Books, 1999.